PRAISE FOR R.J. PATT~~....~~

"R.J. Patterson does a fantastic job at keeping you engaged and interested. I look forward to more from this talented author."

— **Aaron Patterson**, *bestselling author of SWEET DREAMS*

"Patterson has a mean streak about a mile wide and puts his two main characters through quite a horrible ride, which makes for good reading. "

— **Richard D.**, *reader*

"Like a John Grisham novel, from the very start I was pulled right into the story and couldn't put the book down. It was as if I personally knew and cared about what happened to each of the main characters. Every chapter ended with so much excitement and suspense I had to continue to read until I learned how it ended, even though it kept me up until 3:00 A.M.

— **Ray F.**, *reader*

DEAD SHOT

"Small town life in southern Idaho might seem quaint and idyllic to some. But when local newspaper reporter Cal Murphy begins to uncover a series of strange deaths that are linked to a sticky spider web of deception, the lid on the peaceful town is blown wide open. Told with all the energy and bravado of an old pro, first-timer R.J. Patterson hits one out of the park his first time at bat with *Dead Shot*. It's that good. "

-Vincent Zandri, bestselling author of THE REMAINS

"You can tell R.J. knows what it's like to live in the newspaper world, but with *Dead Shot*, he's proven that he also can write one heck of a murder mystery."

— **Josh Katzowitz**, *NFL writer for CBSSports.com & author of* Sid Gillman: Father of the Passing Game

DEAD LINE

"This book kept me on the edge of my seat the whole time. I didn't really want to put it down. R.J. Patterson has hooked me. I'll be back for more."

— **Bob Behler**, *3-time Idaho broadcaster of the year and play-by-play voice for Boise State football*

DEAD IN THE WATER

"In Dead in the Water, R.J. Patterson accurately captures the action-packed saga of a what could be a real-life college football scandal. The sordid details will leave readers flipping through the pages as fast as a hurry-up offense."

— **Mark Schlabach**, *ESPN college sports columnist and co-author of* Called to Coach Heisman: The Man Behind the Trophy

ALSO BY R.J. PATTERSON

Fury

State of Play

Seige

Seek and Destroy

Into the Shadows

Hard Target

No Way Out

Two Minutes to Midnight

Against All Odds

Any Means Necessary

Vengeance

Code Red

A Deadly Force

Divide and Conquer

Extreme Measures

Final Strike

Cal Murphy Thriller series

Dead Shot

Dead Line

Better off Dead

Dead in the Water

Dead Man's Curve

Dead and Gone

Dead Wrong

Dead Man's Land

Dead Drop

Dead to Rights

The Sleeper

© Copyright 2023 R.J. Patterson

First print edition 2024

Published in the United States of America

Green E-Books

PO Box 140654

Boise, ID 83714

THE SLEEPER

THE PHOENIX CHRONICLES
BOOK 10

R.J. PATTERSON

For Drew Hanna

A blessed soul who left this earth way too soon. May we all strive to "live like Drew"

CHAPTER ONE

PRAGUE, CZECH REPUBLIC

THE COLD STEEL pressing against Brady Hawk's temple made him uncomfortable in every way imaginable, chief among them the realization that he was only a trigger pull away from dying. He drew in a deep breath, the scent of sweat mixed with rotting street garbage wafting up through the cracked window at the end of the hallway from five stories below. He took a second to steady his nerves before considering his options. With the asset he'd been tasked with extracting on the other side of the wall, Hawk had come too far to blow the mission. He refused to be undone by a guard he hadn't account for. But that wasn't the only obstacle remaining for Hawk.

His most important looming task just might be convincing the deep cover CIA officer to abandon his work and leave with him.

"*Kdo jsi*?" asked the sweaty man, his scruffy face pressing painfully against Hawk's, almost as disagreeable as the gun.

Hawk never considered himself fluent in Czech, but he knew enough to understand what the man wanted to know.

"Who are you?"

If ever Hawk had been asked a loaded question, this was one. And there was no real truthful way to answer it. Or was there?

Hawk accessed the far recesses of his brain for the Czech words he wanted to hurl back at the man who'd stumbled upon him in the hallway and stealthily drawn his weapon.

"Tvá nejhorší noční můra," Hawk said with a growl and all the conviction of a judge banging his gavel and sending away an unrepentant murderer.

Your worst nightmare.

Hawk, his nose flattened against the wall, punctuated his answer by jabbing his elbow into the man's sternum. Before the attacker could react, Hawk spun and grabbed the man's hand, pinning it against the far wall. A knee to the stomach, and the man dropped his gun like it was a fresh loaf of bread straight from the oven. As he instinctively bent over to pick it up, Hawk drove his knee into the man's nose. Hawk had never before found the crunch of cartilage so satisfying.

The assailant crumpled to the ground, muttering a few curse words, while Hawk kicked the gun down the hallway. He knocked the man unconscious with a kick to his head.

But before Hawk could celebrate, he heard the cock of a pistol from just behind him. The move was bold, yet measured—aggressive, but not rushing to judgment.

"We're on your side, Kyle," Hawk said in a gravelly voice barely louder than a whisper.

"We?" the man asked before glancing in both directions down the hallway. "I only see you. And who the hell are you anyway?"

"He's definitely not alone," came a strong Southern voice down the hallway.

The man looked away again, which gave Hawk the opening he needed. He forced the man's hands upward while driving him back against the wall. The gun clattered out of his hands and onto the floor.

The interloper—Hawk's new young partner, Dallas Ryder—rushed over to secure the asset, one undercover CIA officer named Kyle Lundt. He struggled, kicking at them in an attempt to get free.

"Would you just stop," Hawk said. "We're on the same team."

"I still don't know who the hell you are," Lundt growled.

"Your cover's been blown," Hawk said as he rolled Lundt over onto his back.

"How is that even possible?" Lundt asked with a scowl. "I haven't had contact with Langley in two years other than a couple of dead drops. And that last one was six months ago."

"We had a breach," Hawk explained as he helped Lundt to his feet. "It's not your fault. But your name appeared on a site on the dark web that's selling details about undercover CIA officers. The first two were dead before anybody figured out what was going on. You'll be next if you don't leave with us."

Hawk scanned the hallway, ever aware of the clock ticking in his head.

"We really need to go," he said.

Lundt offered his hands and gave a sympathetic tilt of his head. Ryder understood the gesture and yanked his K-bar knife out of its sheath and sliced through the bindings. Lundt rubbed his wrists, mumbled a "thank you," and then eyed Hawk.

"I hope you've got a plan for getting us out of here," Lundt said. "The Grosniaks aren't exactly the kind of crime family to let you just walk out the front door."

Hawk's ears perked up when he heard footsteps thundering up the stairwell at the other end of the corridor.

"Gotta move," he said.

Hawk darted into an empty room with an open door and lifted the window. He stuck his head out and surveyed the landing area about fifty feet below.

"Hope you ain't afraid of heights, cowboy," Ryder said as he slapped Lundt on the back.

"Terrified, actually," Lundt said as he joined Hawk at the window.

Lundt took a quick peek and drew back, shaking his head.

"You gonna be okay?" Ryder asked. "You look as white as the porcelain commode in my mama's guest bathroom."

Lundt squinted as he turned slowly and glowered at Ryder.

"He's got a special way with words," Hawk said, patting Ryder on the shoulder and then handing him a harness.

"Are we really doing this?" Lundt asked.

"Beats the hell outta fighting our way out," Hawk said as he scrambled into his harness.

Lundt and Ryder followed suit, and in a matter of seconds, they were all ready to be hooked and rappel to the ground. Hawk affixed the grappling hook to the ledge and threaded the rope through a belay device.

"Have you done this before?" Hawk asked.

"Not willingly," Lundt said.

"Well, this is your brake," Hawk said before giving Lundt a brief explanation on how to operate the equipment.

Ryder poked his head out the doorway.

"Better hurry," he said. "These guys are climbing faster than a squirrel with his tail on fire."

Lundt stared slack-jawed at Ryder.

"How do you—never mind," Lundt said before he climbed out the window and began his descent.

Hawk and Ryder wasted no time following their asset on separate ropes secured to the ledge. When they were about halfway down, they heard shouting coming from the open window. Hawk cursed under his breath as he heard a shot fired.

Instinctively, Hawk released the brake on his belay and zoomed downward, before braking and grinding to a halt mere inches off the ground. He unhooked the carabiner from his harness and fell flat on his back. He rolled over and jumped to his feet as gunshots echoed off the surrounding buildings and bullets peppered the cobblestone street.

Hawk sprinted toward their SUV parked in the alley thirty meters away, shouting instructions to Ryder and Lundt.

"Get in and keep your heads down," Hawk said.

Within a few seconds the trio was loaded into the vehicle and zooming toward the main street. More shots whizzed past them before one tore through the back window and shattered it. Ryder turned around and fired from the front passenger seat.

"I said stay down," Hawk said as he reached over and forced Ryder's head down.

As Hawk neared the end of the alley, a black sedan skidded to a halt and blocked the exit to the street. Three gunmen scrambled out of the car and opened fire on them. Hawk had the presence of mind to drop lower in his seat as bullets sprayed the windshield. The glass spidered then exploded into thousands of shards, raining down on Hawk and Ryder.

With no room to turn around and gunmen firing at them from both directions, Hawk realized he only had one option remaining.

"Hold on," he shouted.

Hawk jammed his foot onto the accelerator, the engine responding with a lurch and then a high-pitched whine. Just before Hawk collided with the sedan, the gunmen dove aside and Hawk slightly angled the SUV to hit the back end of the car. The force of the impact spun the car out of the way and Hawk hurtled onto the main street. He took a wide turn, tires screeching as he maneuvered his vehicle onto the right side of the road.

"Good thing the roads are empty," Ryder said.

Hawk sat up, his hands still clutching the steering wheel. He checked his mirror and saw a pair of headlights turn as another car raced toward them.

"That's about the only thing that's gone right tonight," Hawk said. "Check your six."

Ryder whipped around and trained his weapon in the direction of the oncoming car. Hawk saw muzzle flashes from a gunman hanging halfway out the side. A moment later, bullets pinged off the back of the SUV.

Hawk took the next corner hard, tires squealing. As he fishtailed, his back end tagged the side of a car parked along the narrow street, setting off an alarm and flashing lights. More bullets pelted the SUV, enough to make Hawk wonder how much longer before one of them punctured a tire. He slammed on the brakes again, drifting into a roundabout and then straightening out and bearing down on Prague's iconic Legion Bridge. He zipped over it, headlights illuminating late-night pedestrians struggling to find cover.

Hawk looked down at the fuel gauge and realized he'd forgotten to check for a full tank. Despite his deft driving skills, he wouldn't be able to last much longer based on the remaining amount of fuel.

"Who's up for a game of chicken?" Hawk asked as he spun the SUV around and headed straight toward the car firing at them.

"What are you doing?" Ryder asked. "Are you trying to get us killed?"

"I'm trying to give us a chance," Hawk said as he crouched low in his seat.

As the pursuing vehicle rumbled toward them, Hawk could feel his heart pounding in his chest, his hands sweaty as the color left his knuckles gripping the steering wheel. Images of Alex and little J.D. flashed in his mind. He looked over at Ryder, who was bracing for impact in the fetal position. Hawk glanced over his shoulder at Lundt.

"I hope you're buckled up," Hawk said.

Seconds later, Hawk averted a head-on collision, darting to the side before redirecting his SUV into the back end of the car. It was only a nudge, but that was more than enough to knock the car off kilter. As Hawk skidded to a stop, he turned and watched as the driver frantically tried to regain control. The car fishtailed, jutting left and then right and then left again before hitting the sidewalk curb and going airborne.

The car hit the stone railing before plunging nose-first into the icy Vltava River. Hawk jumped out of the vehicle and watched with satisfaction as the headlights and taillights dimmed, the car sinking into the murky depths. A few seconds later, a head bobbed in the middle of the river, a man gasping for breath. Hawk considered taking a shot and popping open the man's head. But that'd only make the Sediak crime family more determined to find out who he was and exact revenge. Besides, these men didn't know Lundt was being extracted. They likely thought he was being abducted, a pawn in their fight in a lingering turf war with a rival crime family. Hawk figured if they'd known the truth, the Sediaks would've sent an army after Lundt and captured him alive to torture him for his betrayal. Death would've been an easy way out.

Hawk continued the ruse, rushing over to Lundt and shouting at him to get back inside. Lundt retreated to the SUV and Hawk drove off, the sound of screeching tires echoing through the crisp night air.

"I was so close to securing their trust," Lundt said as Hawk slowed to the speed limit.

"It wouldn't have done you any good," Hawk said. "They were about to find out. And this time tomorrow night, you would've had a bullet lodged in your brain, your work completely wasted."

"It's wasted now," Lundt said.

"But at least you're alive," Hawk said. "And that was the goal of this operation."

Lundt sighed.

"How could this happen?" he asked.

Hawk grunted and shrugged.

"It's the world of espionage," he said. "Anything can happen. You almost need to count on it."

A bullet ripped through Lundt's arm, resulting in a primal

scream from him. Ryder turned around to tend to Lundt before another shot tore through the dashboard.

Hawk darted down a side street before re-emerging onto the main road three blocks away.

"You gonna be all right?" Hawk asked.

"Hurts like hell," Lundt said through gritted teeth.

"Like I said, *anything* can happen."

CHAPTER
TWO

WASHINGTON, D.C.

CIA DIRECTOR ROBERT BESSERMAN tweaked the American flag lapel pin affixed to his jacket and gave his appearance one final look in the mirror before leaving the restroom down the hall from the conference room in the West Wing of the White House. He nodded at the Secret Service agent positioned by the door and found a seat near the far end of the table. Though the Presidential Intelligence Advisory Board consisted only of five people including the president, the room was abuzz with conversation. The meeting hadn't begun in any official capacity, but the discussion about how to handle the CIA breach wasn't one that could wait.

President Charles Bullock cleared his throat, ending their pre-meeting conversation. He turned and looked at Besserman, giving him a knowing look. Besserman surveyed the rest of the meeting's attendees—Secretary of State Barbara Wheeler, NSA Director John Wicker, and U.S. senator and head of the Senate Intelligence Committee Paul Ashton—and then directed his gaze back toward Besserman.

The meeting agenda was simple: determine how to address the obvious leak in the CIA that was slowly exposing agency officers embedded in various terrorist organization and crime syndicates the world over. Besserman had suspected a leak with the death of Terry Turner, a highly-decorated agent who had infiltrated the Taliban in Afghanistan and had provided top-tier intel on the group. Though Besserman initially hesitated to rule out that Turner had been compromised another way, he was convinced there was a mole somewhere in the agency. The death of officer Christopher Edwards a week later all but confirmed it in his mind. However, none of his suspicions became official until Mallory Kauffman unearthed the site on the dark web that announced it was releasing one new name of an agency operative each week. Besserman realized what a disaster this would be for the world's preeminent intelligence organization. Every officer would become more paranoid, always wondering if each person they met was someone assigned to kill them. That level of paranoia would unravel the CIA's best efforts, never mind how it would stunt its recruitment. Even with just a handful of confirmed identities, the person behind the leak could hamper the agency through just the mere threat of another release.

Bullock locked eyes with Besserman.

"I only have one question for you, Bobby," Bullock said. "Can you make it stop?"

Besserman pursed his lips.

"The better question would be how do I plan to make it stop being disseminated because it seems that this information is already out there in the hands of someone intent on disrupting what we're trying to do."

Bullock loosened his tie and then interlaced his fingers before resting them on the table in front of him. He leaned forward as he closely eyed Besserman.

"I really don't care about the semantics of my question," Bullock said. "I just want to know if this is going to be a lingering issue, starting with do we know how anyone managed to hack into the CIA and extract such sensitive info?"

"That's the real head scratcher," Besserman said. "According to our cybersecurity team, no hacker has successfully penetrated our firewall for five years running."

"So, what are you saying?" Wicker asked, his gravelly voice sounding as if it might crack. "This is information that someone's just been sitting on for five years?"

Besserman shook his head.

"Certainly seems unlikely given that Edwards wasn't even with the agency five years ago."

"So, it's a recent job?" Bullock asked.

Besserman nodded.

"And, apparently, an inside one too."

"Can you see who's accessed their files internally?" Wheeler asked.

"Of course," Besserman said. "But no one has looked at the files of all three officers before this started. We can't find any common link, not even among multiple people in the same department who could've been working together. That's why I said it's a real head scratcher."

Senator Ashton cleared his throat before jumping into the inquisition.

"So, what's the prevailing theory?" he asked. "There has to be a paper trail of some sort, right?"

"Key word there is *paper*," Besserman said, pointing at Ashton. "At this point, the only plausible explanation is that someone accessed the paper files we have."

"Is that an easy thing to do?" Wicker asked.

"Not really," Besserman said. "We have cameras around and in our archives where that kind of paperwork is kept. It's guarded, even when the building is closed for regular business hours."

Bullock stroked his chin.

"Did you look into that?" he asked.

"We've looked into everything," Besserman said. "And nothing unusual jumped out at us. There wasn't anything we saw that gave any indication someone had gained access to those files and stolen them."

"What about your server backup that mirrors all your files elsewhere?" Wheeler suggested.

"That's also something we've looked at. Nothing suspicious and no record of any breach."

"Is there anyone affiliated with all three of those officers?" Ashton asked. "Maybe someone who could just expose them?"

Besserman shook his head.

"We thought of that too. We came up empty there as well."

Bullock sighed and then massaged his forehead before responding.

"So, someone is getting access to all this information—or already obtained it—and we can't figure out how they did it?"

"I'm afraid so," Besserman said.

"Then that makes it pretty damn hard to prevent this from happening again, doesn't it?"

"You're correct in that assessment, sir," Besserman said. "We're doing our best to tamp this down, but we first have to figure out where the leak is coming from."

Bullock closed his eyes and slowly shook his head, making his disappointment obvious to the rest of the advisory board.

"Anyone else have any ideas on how to handle this?" he asked. "Or are we all out of ideas?"

"We're still pursuing every possible lead," Besserman said. "My team is working around the clock to fix this and figure out what's going on. The very existence of the intelligence community feels threatened at the moment—and there isn't anything anyone on my team won't do to put a stop to this."

"As reassuring as that might sound," Bullock began, "that doesn't change the fact that we've got two dead agents and hundreds and hundreds of embedded officers around the globe who could be next on the list. Your commitment to hard work is hardly the answer we need right now. We need a name and we need it yesterday."

Bullock pounded the table for emphasis.

"You're going to make me look like a fool," he continued. "Hell, you're going to make us all look like fools. Now figure it out."

As frustrated as Bullock appeared, Besserman felt ten times more upset over the situation. Based on what he saw, the simplest explanation was that someone internally had collected that intel on his operatives and was spreading it around with the clear purpose of being disruptive. There was no clear pattern regarding the officers who'd been exposed, no obvious connections. To Besserman, the whole scenario felt like a disruptive event, a different kind of terror attack, one designed to make CIA officers uncomfortable and more paranoid than ever.

And it was working.

In the last three days, Besserman had seen more than a dozen embedded officers request extraction, claiming a variety of excuses. But he knew the truth—they all thought they were next. He couldn't really blame them either. If they had all the officers' names and residences, who's to say his wasn't buried on that list somewhere? Or maybe his would be next.

"Let's stay connected over this," Bullock said. "And if anyone has any ideas, please don't hesitate to share them with me or Bobby."

Bullock nodded at everyone, signaling the end of the meeting.

"And Bobby?"

"Yes?" Besserman asked as he rose.

"If you can't figure out what's going on and put a stop to it soon, I'm going to find someone who can."

Besserman fought the urge to scowl. He responded without a word, instead just giving the president a knowing nod. Not that Besserman needed to be told such things. But now that it was said out loud, he knew his time to uncover the mole was short.

"Hang in there," Wheeler said as she patted Besserman on the back. "We'll find out who it is—and I can promise you they're going to regret their actions until their last breath."

"Thanks, Emma," he said. "I appreciate the support."

Besserman shuffled off down the hall, wondering what else he could do that he hadn't already done.

CHAPTER
THREE

BEIJING, CHINA

JUN FANG TWIRLED his cane as he entered the press room of JF Dynamics. Sporting a pair of dark sunglasses and a white suit and white shirt with a pink bow tie, Fang strutted as he made his way onto the stage in front of reporters shoehorned into the tight space. A pair of flat-screen monitors flanked the stage, which contained a winnowing glass lectern. The room dimmed, lit only by a couple of bright stage lights overhead narrowing the focus on Fang. He inserted his cane into a small hole at the base of the lectern and rotated the handle. LEDs positioned on the outside flickered to life, turning the lectern pink.

Fang smiled and he scanned the room, unable to view the sea of journalists on hand for his presentation. He clasped his hands together and rested them on the lectern, which also displayed his speech for the event. Rapidly clicking his tongue as he often did when nervous, he took a deep breath and glanced down at his speech before looking up and starting.

"I want to wish you a sincere welcome here today," Fang said in flawless English, placing his right hand over his heart. "Every time we host these events at JF Dynamics, I often wonder if it's going to be the last time my incredible team dreams up something else to better society. As you may well know by now, the purpose of this incredible organization is 'turning imaginative ideas into practical products,' a phrase you've no doubt seen painted on the walls as you entered our facility today. It's truly the heartbeat of our mission. Unlike many others in my profession, my chief goal isn't to engorge my bank account. No, I want to leave a mark on the world like Thomas Edison or Nikola Tesla or Alexander Graham Bell. Long after I'm gone, I want what we create at JF Dynamics to be life-changing."

Images of some of JF Dynamics' previous inventions flashed on the screens on both sides of him, all with people smiling broadly as they used the devices. In the tech world, Fang had ascended to the rank of God-like status, maintaining a very public presence online but a very private personal life behind closed doors. All his publicity was tightly controlled, every article written about him constricted in its scope. He would grant credible reporters one-one-one interviews, each one hoping to score a big scoop about Fang's past or a little nugget about how he came up with a particular invention. But they'd all failed. Nobody had been able to pry much more than a nominal story out of him. In some ways, he seemed cold and robotic. But his personality was warm and engaging whenever he talked about the world around him.

Fang introduced his latest item, a refrigerator that tracked what you consumed and alerted you when certain items were in danger of spoiling or were nearly gone. It also created a weekly shopping list for perishable items based off regular usage rates of the dwindling products.

"In many first-world nations, households throw out on average up to forty percent of the food they purchase," Fang said. "Meanwhile, there are millions of starving people all over the world. This new refrigerator from JF Dynamics will not only save you money but allow you to see the difference on your grocery bill each month as well as donate to non-profit organizations doing the necessary work to get food to places desperate for it. As always, we seek to do good with our products, all while empowering and encouraging you to do good as well. We better your lives so you can better the world with us."

Fang delivered the lines smoothly and with conviction, so much so that the journalists broke into applause. He knew that everyone in that room who could afford one would have his new refrigerator in their kitchens by the end of the year.

As the lights in the room came up, he could see the energy in the room as well as feel it. He hated the American game of baseball, but he appreciated the way batters who smashed the ball over the fence stood and admired their blasts. Mimicking that movement had become a trademark for him, growing to the point that everyone waited for him to do it so they could capture pictures and videos of him.

Fang flicked up his cane out of its holder next to the lectern and then caught it with one hand. He wrapped his hands around the top of the cane and drew it back like he was batting before uncoiling with a wild swing. As the cane cut through the air, it made a whooshing sound. Seconds later, more applause.

Fang twirled the stick again as he sauntered off the stage and disappeared through a back doorway. Even as the door slammed shut behind him, he could hear the buzz still humming throughout the press room.

"You did it again, sir," said Li Huang, the media relations chief for JF Dynamics. "Your swing is getting better. Maybe the New York Yankees will call soon."

Fang grunted.

"The only way I take their call is if they want to buy my refrigerators for all their fans."

"Like Oprah?" Huang asked.

Fang furrowed his brow, signaling that he didn't understand the comment.

"You remember, right?" Huang said. "You get a refrigerator. And you get a refrigerator. And you get a refrigerator. No?"

Fang shrugged.

"Didn't see it. You know how much I hate television," he said, poking Huang in the chest with the cane, "unless I'm on it."

He smiled as he tossed his cane into the air and caught it again with one hand. Lowering his sunglasses, he gave a coy wink before strolling out through the back entrance and climbing into his black Bugatti La Voiture Noire. The engine purred as he pushed the ignition button. He double tapped the accelerator pedal before shifting into gear and speeding off the property.

When he arrived at his palatial mansion, he slowed just long enough to offer a weak two-fingered salute to the guard at the front gate. The tires barked as he stopped in the driveway near the front porch steps. He hustled up the stairs and nonchalantly tossed the keys to one of his employees coming out to greet him.

"Put it in the garage, sir?" the man asked.

"Always," Fang said, his tie and jacket already removed.

He hustled into his room and pulled on a swimsuit and a Hawaiian shirt, leaving it unbuttoned to show off the results of his daily regimen in the weight room. With his sunglasses still on, he exited through the French doors leading out of his room and onto the veranda. Gliding down the marble staircase, he made his way to the pool where he found four women sunbathing. His arrival interrupted their peaceful afternoon. They peppered him with questions about his presentation, while one of the women bragged that she'd watched the event live streamed on her phone.

They all pretended to fight over him, though he knew it was likely staged and discussed before his arrival. His security cameras had captured several such discussions. And even though Fang knew it was all for show, he still enjoyed the attention. He also enjoyed pretending like he didn't want it.

One of the women came up to Fang and gave him a kiss, making him wonder if he should change his plans for the afternoon. But then his phone rang.

"Sorry, baby," he said, pointing at his cell. "I need to take this."

Fang rushed up the staircase, skipping every other step, until he reached the veranda and was out of earshot of his groupies.

"Another name has been released," the man on the other end of the line said.

"Just now?" Fang asked.

"A half-hour ago."

"And I'm just now finding out about this?" Fang asked, irritation evident in his voice.

"Sorry, but I had to confirm a few things first before I told you. I needed to verify that it was legit. I know how you don't like false alarms."

"This release was faster than the previous three," Fang said. "Is something going on that I need to know about?"

"Not that I can tell. Want me to handle this one?"

"Of course," Fang said. "That's what I pay you for, isn't it?"

Fang didn't wait for the man to respond before continuing.

"And make it flashier this time. I'll double your fee if you do."

"As you wish."

Fang ended the call and then stared at the blank screen on his phone. Something was off—and he didn't like it.

Better not fail this time.

CHAPTER
FOUR

WASHINGTON, D.C.

MORGAN MAY SIPPED HER COFFEE, her face souring upon
tasting it. Still unfamiliar with the area of the Magnum Group's
new offices in downtown, she purchased a latte at the coffee shop
nearest to her townhome. She just hadn't counted on the soul-
sucking gridlock on the Beltway delaying her commute so much
that her once piping hot treat devolved into a tepid disappointment.

As she hit the brakes and joined the cascading sea of red tail
lights, she searched for a station on her radio. The reporter on the
news talk radio station discussed a heightened terror alert for
several large cities along the eastern seaboard, the first such warnings in nearly a decade. While there had been a handful of attacks,
the reporter explained how federal agencies had teamed up to
thwart the threats, oftentimes without the public even realizing
the potential danger.

Morgan laughed quietly and shook her head.

"Federal agencies?" she scoffed. "What a crock. Uncle J.D. was
the one making sure Americans were safe."

She paused and continued talking aloud to herself.

"And now I am—with some of the same help he had."

Now she was doing it in the same city that he had, too. After the last mission, President Bullock had said that he wanted the Magnum Group closer to him, more accessible to discuss sensitive information in person. He claimed it was a way he could mitigate leaks, but Morgan suspected he wanted to exert a little more control over the covert group. While she wasn't a fan of Washington and preferred L.A.'s weather and warm beaches, she couldn't complain about the new office building that he secured for her and her team.

An anchor woman followed up the report by delivering more bad news as it related to the economy, job market, and education, all of it projected to negatively affect the country's future.

During the commercial break, a soft-spoken woman shared about how her adoption service was changing lives.

"Who would want to bring a child into a world as dark as this?" she asked herself.

Morgan knew she certainly didn't at the moment, though she knew that had more to do with the fact that she hadn't found the right man than simply viewing the bleak future as less than ideal conditions for raising children. She also knew that she had the power to change that direction.

After parking her car in an underground deck, Morgan strode up to the sparkling new office on K Street and tossed the paper coffee cup in a trash can. She made a note to find the nearest coffee bar when she had a break. With the exterior constructed almost entirely of glass, the structure appeared futuristic in its design complete with impressive overhangs and architectural features that shone like a jewel in the midst of a dusty bone field. At night, the lighting turned the building into a beacon on a street littered with drab Federal buildings from a bygone era when the U.S. government handled its citizens' money more frugally.

Several federal agencies occupied about half the building, while the rest was leased out to various businesses. A handful of the private enterprises were major partners with government enti-

ties, while others were simply looking for space. For all anyone else
in the building knew, the Magnum Group was one of the latter.
Housed on the fifth floor next to an upstart law firm, Morgan's
organization advertised itself as a think tank on issues of national
security. The boring description was by design, almost guaranteed
to end any follow-up questions.

The building's doorman wore a sharp blue wool suit with a
cap, the only amenity of the facility that didn't flex its high-tech
muscles. Ocular scanners gave employees access to their particular
floors, state-of-the-art server rooms for each business, a world-
class chef and restaurant housed on the balcony, and a surfing
pool in the massive gym that occupied half of the first floor. The
latter feature was a concession Bullock made for taking her away
from the southern California surfing scene. But she still intended
to maintain an office in Los Angeles despite shifting the headquarters across the country.

"Good morning, Miss May," said Arnie, the doorman.

"Good morning," she said. "Say, Arnie, you wouldn't happen
to know where I could get a good cup of coffee around here, do
you?"

Arnie shook his head.

"Unfortunately not, since I don't drink caffeine," he said, his
voice slightly wheezing. "It makes my heart act up."

"I understand."

"But I'll ask around for you," he said with a wink.

She thanked him and then entered the building. At the security checkpoint, she flashed her access badge and then went to the
elevator designated for the fifth floor. She entered and then waited
until the door shut before approaching the ocular scanner. A light
turned green and the motor hummed as she ascended to her
office.

After reading several reports that had been sent to her inbox,
Morgan compiled some of the more important details for the
briefing with the rest of her team. Satisfied that she had everything
she needed, she grabbed her documents and headed down the hall

to the conference room, which sat in the corner of the building. She waved her security card over an access panel and entered a number on a keypad. Moments later, the room slightly darkened. From the outside, no one would be able to make out who or even how many people were inside, rendering even the best infrared devices useless with the new technology Dr. Z had designed for their floor.

She entered the conference room and found everyone seated and waiting for her. Brady Hawk, Dallas Ryder, and Big Earv sat at the far end across from Mia. Dr. Z sat to her left, while Hawk's wife Alex was on a large flat-screen on the interior wall, piped in via video conferencing. A couple of analysts were also on hand for the first official meeting in the new facility.

"If I could get a good cup of coffee around here, I think this place would be perfect," she said with a faint smile.

Mia held up her cup.

"Talk with me afterward," she said. "I know just the place."

"Great," Morgan said. "At least I'll get one thing knocked off my to-do list today."

She clapped her hands and took a deep breath.

"But we've got much bigger things to tend to," she said. "I appreciate you all being here so early. I don't typically like to call 7 a.m. meetings, but this is important. And as much as I'd love for us all to get acclimated to our beautiful new surroundings, we've got what qualifies as an emergency. However, I'd be remiss if I didn't mention the incredible job Hawk and Ryder did bringing home Kyle Lundt, which really was a team effort. Let's keep up the good work."

Morgan stood and paced the floor before indicating toward the flat-screen on the opposite wall of the monitor depicting Alex, who was clutching a cup of coffee and her hair swirled up into a messy bun.

"While we were able to save a valuable operative, the source of the leak internally remains a big mystery," Morgan said. "However, Mia was able to work some of her magic through some cyber sleuthing and find out that the ultimate source for the names of the CIA officers is coming from a black hat hacker that goes by Mayhem. We've never been able to uncover Mayhem's actual identity, but this has given us a way to monitor more closely who's being outed. This method of dripping one agency officer each week has everyone on edge."

Hawk shifted in his seat.

"So, did Mayhem hack the CIA?" he asked.

Morgan looked toward Mia and nodded knowingly.

"I'll take that one," Mia said. "When there's a data breach of some sort, there's always a trail of bread crumbs, so to speak. We can see what was accessed from an outside entity. But in this case, we haven't been able to find evidence of any hacker downloading a tranche of information, let alone even hacking into the agency's system."

"So, we've got someone stealing information internally and passing it along to Mayhem?" Ryder asked.

"That seems like the most likely scenario at this point, which is an even more unsettling scenario," Morgan said. "It's going to take some old fashioned detective work to solve this. But in the meantime, we've got another officer to extract."

"Already?" Alex asked. "Weren't the other names all released a week apart from one another?"

Morgan nodded.

"Not sure if they're just trying to keep us on our toes or if they're upset about us saving Lundt. Either way, Simon Lee's name and information was put out onto the dark web about an hour ago."

"What do we know about Lee?" Hawk asked.

"He's on a deep cover assignment for a prominent London businessman named Nigel Ackerman, who's been suspected of being the mastermind behind an underground human trafficking ring. Someone at the agency already put together a full workup on him with suggestions on how to best reach Lee for a successful extraction. Since Alex is still just helping us out remotely, I want Hawk and Ryder to team up again for this operation."

"When do we leave?" Ryder asked.

"Wheels up in one hour," Morgan said. "Good luck, gentlemen. And Big Earv?"

Big Earv sat upright, his eyes locked on hers.

"I've got a special assignment for you," she said. "We've got a State Department official I want you to look into. I think he might have some connection to Beijing."

She dismissed the meeting as everyone returned to work. Dr. Z caught Hawk in the hallway before he left.

"Can I grab you for a second?" Dr. Z asked.

Hawk stopped.

"You know I've gotta hurry, but I'll always make time for you," he said.

"Thank you," Dr. Z said. "Now, I've been thinking about Alex out on the ranch all by herself with little John Daniel—"

"He's going by J.D. now," Hawk said with a smile.

"Okay, she's out there with little J.D. all alone and—"

"She's more than capable of taking care of herself," Hawk said. "I wouldn't worry too much."

"I know, I know. But do you think she'd mind if I sent her something? It's a little thing I cooked up in the lab that I thought she might find helpful."

"Knock yourself out, big man," Hawk said. "You know she adores all your creations, right?"

"Excellent. I also have something for you."

Dr. Z held out his hand, revealing a small device about the size of a thumb drive.

"You know flash drives have already been invented, right?" Hawk said with a wink.

Dr. Z pushed a button and a blue light emanated from the gadget.

"It's a smart ass detector," he said. "And look. It's going off right now. Wonder what could've caused that."

"Okay, okay," Hawk said. "What's this thing do?"

"It's a discreet jammer," he said. "You want to disrupt cell phone calls or security cameras in about a hundred meter radius, just press this button. Almost anything electric will start having trouble."

A couple of people shouted into the hallway about having problems with their computer monitors before Dr. Z smiled and pressed the button again, turning off the device.

"I thought this might come in handy for you since Alex isn't around to handle the technical side of your missions," he said.

Hawk took the device and pocketed it.

"That's most thoughtful of you, Dr. Z. I'm sure I'll find a way to use it. Now, if you'll excuse me, I have to get going."

"Of course," Dr. Z said as he and Hawk pumped hands. "Good luck."

Hawk looked at Ryder, who was patiently waiting against the wall.

"Let's go, rookie," Hawk said. "Simon Lee awaits."

CHAPTER
FIVE

BRIDGER, MONTANA

ALEX HOISTED a saddle onto the back of Dusty and then slipped a bit into his mouth. The horse whinnied and stamped, expressing his mild displeasure at being forced to ride.

"Come on, Dusty," she said. "You love going on rides, especially when we leave Buckaroo behind."

Alex glanced over at Buckaroo frolicking in the meadow just outside the barn.

"Okay, so maybe you'd rather be running with him," she said. "But I'm taking you somewhere that Buckaroo has never been."

Little J.D. raced into the barn before skidding to a stop and stirring up a dust cloud. He wore a broad grin on his face, his cheeks already dirty from playing outside.

"You ready?" she asked.

"Born ready," J.D. said.

She laughed.

"You are your daddy's son," she said. "No doubt about it."

Before she could help him, J.D. jammed his foot into the stirrup hanging from Tucker's saddle and pulled himself up. He leaned forward and rubbed the top of Tucker's head.

"Where we going today, big fella?" he asked.

Alex climbed onto Dusty's back and maneuvered him next to J.D. and Tucker.

"I haven't told him yet," Alex said with a wink. "He doesn't know anything."

"Mom, I know he knows," J.D. said with an eye roll. "I've heard him talk before."

Just when Alex thought J.D. had grown out of her playful ventriloquist act with the horses, he wanted her to do it again.

"Okay, okay," she said, playing along. "Maybe he does know where we're going."

"Tucker, where are we headed today?" J.D. asked again.

Alex cleared her throat.

"I was thinking maybe we could go explore the middle fork of Five Mile Creek up near West Pryor Mountain," Alex said in a gruff voice with a slow southern drawl. "How's that sound, J.D.?"

"Sounds great," J.D. said. "Let's go."

He gave Tucker a little kick in his sides and the horse started moving forward. While Tucker could be obstinate at times, he was a safe horse for the young boy. Tucker had never thrown any rider and rarely reared back without a rider and never with one. It gave Alex the peace of mind she needed after experiencing first-hand the dangers of horses. She'd just spent the last six weeks recovering from a hairline fracture she got on her arm when Buckaroo decided to throw her. Now, she was ready to ride again and enjoy the reason she and Hawk moved to this remote area of the country—and she couldn't wait to go with J.D.

While Hawk was preparing for another harrowing mission, she was riding horses. And as much as she wanted to be with him, the lure of spending time with her son overrode any sense of duty she felt. She ignored the twinge of guilt gnawing at her after getting off the conference call. Everyone else on the Magnum Group team was risking their lives to help protect the country, while she was galloping over Montana mountains with her son. But she also understood that there were other duties she had as well, ones that couldn't be mitigated or reasoned away. Alex had managed to strike a balance between serving the country she loved and serving the son she had. With the cluck of her tongue and a quick jab into the side of Dusty with her heel, she forgot about the guilt conjured up by a culture that celebrated achievement over responsibility and family.

Alex and J.D. drank in the mild weather as they rode along a path that meandered along Five Mile Creek. They managed to reach a ridge just below the peak of West Pryor Mountain before turning back.

"What'd you think?" Alex asked J.D. "Did you like it?"

J.D. didn't say anything, pretending like he didn't hear her.

Alex smiled and then modulated her voice, reverting back to the gruff version with the slow Southern drawl.

"What'd you think, J.D.?" she asked. "Was it fun?"

"It was amazing!" he said with a big smile. "Let's do it again tomorrow."

Alex beamed as she put up the saddles in the tack room.

But her smile faded as she approached their house. She noticed a note pinned to the front door with a knife. Carefully removing the note, she pocketed the knife and stared at the message. It appeared to be written in some sort of code, which made it even more puzzling.

Why not just tell me what you want to tell me?

She scanned the property and saw J.D. running alongside Buckaroo while telling him all about their adventures. But there weren't any other vehicles or interlopers in plain sight.

"Weird," she said to herself.

Then she fished her phone out of her pocket and sat down in a rocking chair on the front porch. She dialed Hawk's number.

"Where are you?" she asked.

"We're about halfway over the Atlantic on our way to London," he said. "Will you be ready to go when we land?"

"I'll have the system up and ready to go. I'll be your eyes and ears whenever you need me."

"Good," he said. "How's the rest of your day been?"

"It was going pretty good until I just got back from a ride with J.D.," she said. "That's why I was calling."

"Did anything happen? Is he all right?"

"He's fine," she said. "But after I put up the horses, I found a note on the front door."

She told Hawk what she'd found and waited for his response.

"That's odd," he said. "Just be extra careful until you can figure out what's going on. I know you can handle yourself."

"Sure, but that doesn't make this any less nerve-wracking."

"See if Mia can help you," he said. "But tell little J.D. I love him."

Alex ended the call and then stared down at the note in her hand. She wasn't sure if she needed to be concerned.

After calling in J.D. to wash up and help her fix lunch, she hustled over to the security cameras to see if she could determine who her visitor was. But it didn't take her long to realize she was dealing with a professional. The cameras all went dark for about five minutes, giving whoever the intruder was time to get in and out without being recorded.

She cursed under her breath.

Alex was officially worried.

CHAPTER
SIX

LONDON

HAWK HUNCHED over the wheel of the BMW 725i creeping along Hillshire Street in the Tower Hamlets borough, while Ryder studied the changing scenery. As Hawk rounded a corner, the headlights swept across a brick wall serving as a meager barrier between the traffic and whatever was on the inside. He adjusted the rearview mirror, wary of the car he noticed that had been following them for the past mile and a half. But Hawk kept driving, eyeing rundown townhomes peeking over the walls, dilapidated rooftops and rusted iron fencing on balconies still visible at dusk. Graffiti decorated the neat red brick, making Hawk wonder if the walls were really there to keep others out or to keep the residents in.

A man waved his hands at Hawk, urging him to stop and help his friend, who was lying on his back, his leg tucked awkwardly beneath him. The man shook, his eyes wide open as he stared skyward vacantly.

"Should we stop?" Ryder asked.

Hawk eased onto the accelerator.

"If there's one thing that you need to learn about this job," he began. "You need to have a singular focus if you expect to live, let alone complete each mission."

"Yeah, but did you see that guy?"

Hawk nodded.

"I saw a guy who's made a series of poor life decisions and can't be helped until he decides that he wants to help himself."

Ryder smiled and shook his head.

"What's so amusing?" Hawk asked.

"I've heard that Bible verse that says, 'God helps those who help themselves'."

"That's not in the Bible," Hawk said flatly. "But there's still some merit to it."

"You think that guy cares about merit? He looks like he was stroking out."

"You think he cares if we help him or not? He doesn't even know what planet he's on. Nor would our good Samaritan detour benefit him."

"Maybe not, but if we help him, it might give someone else a chance to help him in the future."

"He could also be a psychopath killer," Hawk said.

"What are the chances of there being three psychopaths in the car at once?" Ryder asked with a wry grin.

Hawk glanced in his rearview mirror and noticed the car still behind them.

"On second thought, maybe you're right," Hawk said. "What would it hurt to help that man?"

Hawk wheeled the car around, dropping Ryder's jaw. He placed both hands on the dashboard to brace himself as the vehicle whipped into the opposite direction. He rolled to a stop near the man and hustled out to help him with Ryder joining in.

"Does anyone know this man?" Hawk asked as he looked up and down the street.

The few pedestrians within earshot either ignored him or shook their heads and kept walking. Hawk glanced down the road to see if the car had followed him. He spotted it before it rolled past them and kept going.

Hawk and Ryder hoisted the man in the backseat and drove toward the nearest hospital a half-mile away.

"I'm glad to see you had a change of heart," Ryder said. "I feel like compassion is what keeps us different from the people we're fighting."

Hawk nodded subtly, not wanting to break his young partner's innocence. If a car hadn't been trailing them, Hawk would've continued on. But at the moment, the junkie served a purpose, helping them shake their tail. Hawk decided it'd be a more in-depth discussion to have at some other time.

After they delivered the addict to the hospital, they resumed their search for Lee.

"See," Ryder said, "was that so bad?"

Hawk forced a smile and gritted his teeth.

"It could've been worse," he said, hoping to end the conversation and focus on their mission again.

"I know we can't save everybody, but even in the middle of a mission, we need to remain human," Ryder said. "We can still save someone who needs help."

Someone needs to save me.

Hawk's phone rang with a call from Alex.

Perfect timing.

Hawk answered the call.

"Why aren't your coms on?" she asked. "And is something wrong with your phone? I tried calling you twice but went straight to voicemail."

"Maybe we were in a spot with poor cell service. I don't know."

"Well, I wanted to let you know that it looked like a car was following you."

"Already figured it out."

"Yeah," she said. "You stopped and then he drove past. What were you doing?"

"I'll tell you about it later," he said. "And I'll turn on our coms now. I was waiting until we found Lee before I tried to get your help. I thought you might be busy with little J.D. and didn't want to bother you until we really needed you."

"Okay," she said. "I'm monitoring you right now. You're only about two blocks from Lee's house after that detour."

"Copy that."

Hawk parked along the side of the road outside of the flat belonging to Lee. A cursory glance of the area didn't find Lee's car. It was nearly midnight, so Hawk wasn't surprised that Lee was taking so long to come to the door. Hawk banged again. He ran the risk of waking up neighbors and angering them, but it wouldn't matter. If Lee answered, his neighbors would never see him again.

Hawk turned around and looked up and down the street. Everything still appeared quiet.

"Watch for any lights coming on," Hawk said to Ryder. "I'm going to go around the back."

Hawk hopped a fence and found a narrow alley separating the two buildings facing opposite directions on the small block. Counting off the apartments until he found Lee's, Hawk hopped a short wooden fence and knocked on the back door. The drapes were open in a large bedroom on the bottom floor, the bed still made. Hawk tried the handle but it didn't budge. Moving along the back of the house, he placed his hands against the glass and peered into the kitchen. All the dishes and food were neatly stowed, making Hawk wonder if Lee had even been living here. It looked more like a model house than one that someone lived in.

"You see anything?" Hawk asked Ryder over the coms.

"All's quiet out front."

"He's not here," Hawk said.

"The briefing listed one other place we might find him, just off Mile End Road. It says use extra caution in this area."

"What kind of place is this?"

"According to this, authorities believe an illegal gambling

enterprise exists here and Nigel Ackerman has been rumored to have his fingers in that pie. Lee's previous mission had him in Johannesburg where he infiltrated the inner circle of an illegal arms dealer who also had a gambling business on the side. It was his way in. They suspect he might be using that angle again to engender trust with Ackerman based off the last report they received from him six months ago."

"Six months ago?" Hawk asked.

"Yeah, he's been quiet for a while now."

"That means he's either wormed his way into the leadership circle and is being careful—or he's already dead."

"Likely the former, which means he's going to really be upset about getting pulled out."

"I'm sure he'll get over it when he finds out why," Hawk said. "What's the safe phrase?"

"Ohio State Buckeyes," Ryder said. "Doubt he'll hear much of that over here. If he's in the gambling world in London, it'll be Manchester United and Liverpool and Chelsea."

"And his cover?"

"Goes by James Arthur."

Hawk found a parking spot along the street and climbed out. He scanned the area before giving Ryder a knowing look and then heading down an alley where the gambling allegedly took place. After hustling past several shuttered businesses with rolled-up doors, he found a couple of men leaning against the wall of a pub and smoking. Hawk and Ryder ducked inside and wove through the establishment until they reached the back. A tall burly man stood with his arms crossed, his back to a door. They stopped in front of him, eyeing him carefully.

"What d'ya blokes want?" the man asked in a thick Cockney accent with a sneer.

"We're here to see James Arthur," Hawk said.

"I ain't never seen ya here before," the man said.

"We're new clients of his," Hawk said.

"Well, he ain't here t'night. Called in sick."

"Is there anyone else we can talk to?" Hawk asked. "I'd like to place a few—"

The man put a finger to his lips and cocked his head to one side while glaring at Hawk.

"Mind your tongue, man. Besides, I already told ya he ain't here. And I'm beginnin' to wonder if you didn't have something to do with him being gone."

The man raised his wrist near his mouth and started speaking into a coms unit hidden in his sleeve.

"I've got two gentlemen who need to be escorted out," he said.

Hawk raised his hands in a gesture of surrender.

"We're leaving," he said.

The two Magnum agents turned and headed toward the door. However, when they were halfway across the pub, Hawk noticed a pair of men hustling around patrons and heading straight toward them. He reached back and tugged on Ryder's shirt.

"We gotta move," Hawk said.

He navigated his way around the pub's revelers, bumping a few arms along the way and spilling some drinks, resulting in some nasty looks and derisive comments. But Hawk didn't have time to apologize.

Once he hit the exit, he broke into a sprint with Ryder right behind him. However, Hawk stopped abruptly when he saw three men marching toward him, one of the men smacking a wooden stick against his hand.

"Come on," Hawk said, switching directions.

There were only two men coming at them from the direction of the pub. Hawk fancied his odds better against them. Rushing back toward the establishment, Hawk grabbed an aluminum outdoor chair with his right hand and urged Ryder to do the same. They both hurled the chairs at the men, knocking them over as they scrambled to get out of the way.

Hawk pumped his arms, his legs powering him forward. He darted down a side street in hopes of making the block. After a few seconds, he noticed the pursuing footsteps faded in the distance.

"I think we lost them," Ryder said.

"Don't be so sure," Hawk said.

As they made the block, Hawk stopped and slammed his hand hard against Ryder's chest, forcing him to halt. Hawk peered around the edge and saw the men stalking the sidewalk, shouting and yelling threats.

Hawk scanned the area and then activated his coms.

"Alex, you still watching us?" he asked.

"I've just been standing by waiting to see if you need any help."

"Well, we need some help right now," Hawk said. "We're being pursued. Do you see a way out of here?"

"There's an alley about fifty meters away from you on the opposite side of the street. See it?"

"Yeah," Hawk said.

"That's your way out."

Hawk and Ryder sprinted down another narrow passageway before reaching a major street. Hawk flagged down a taxi and gave him an address about ten miles away. Ryder sat in silence, understanding that they couldn't talk.

Once the taxi came to a stop, Hawk paid the fare and got out with Ryder. They walked several blocks without speaking.

"You mind telling me what the hell we're doing out here?" Ryder asked.

"The agency has a safe house about a block from here," Hawk said. "It's the only other place I can imagine he might be right now."

"You think he got wind of the leak?"

"It's possible. This has to be big news in the crime world."

A few minutes later, Hawk approached the safe house and entered a code into the security keypad. The door clicked open and the two agents eased inside.

"Who is that?" a man called from the back of the room.

"Simon Lee?" Hawk asked.

"Yes," the man said.

"This is Brady Hawk with Dallas Ryder, two agents assigned to extract you."

Lee stepped into the hallway, his face dimly lit by a street lamp pouring into an open window.

"They know about me," Lee said. "My name was leaked. They came to my apartment to kill me tonight. I just ran. I didn't know where else to go."

"We didn't know if you knew or not," Hawk said, offering his hand.

The two men shook and Lee let out a sigh of a relief.

"I was starting to wonder if the agency forgot about me," Lee said.

Alex's voice chirped in Hawk's ear.

"Save the celebration for later," she said. "You've got five hostiles approaching the safe house right now."

Hawk cursed as he pointed to the com unit in his ear.

"Alex just told me we've got company."

CHAPTER
SEVEN

WASHINGTON, D.C.

PRESIDENT BULLOCK LEANED against a wall in the West Wing and reviewed the notes in the folder given to him by his communications director Leslie Giles. An unusually cheerful person, Leslie's forehead creased as she sifted through some of the documents she was reading.

"What is it?" Bullock asked.

"Nothing major," she began. "It's just that—"

She paused, squinting as her eyes shifted back and forth across the page.

"What is it, Leslie?" Bullock asked again, his voice edgier and bordering on impatience. "And don't sugarcoat it for me."

She bit her thumbnail, hesitating to answer him.

"For God's sake, Leslie, spit it out. I'm a big boy. I can take it."

After another few seconds, she looked up at him, her gaze meeting his.

"This isn't going to be a pleasant press conference, sir," she said. "Someone on my team handed me a printout from a website that's gaining a lot of traction on social media right now. And I don't think you're going to like it."

"What is it? Poll numbers? A foreign diplomat shoveling dirt on me?"

"You'll wish it was that," she said. "It's actually about the topic at hand and the rumors that there's a cyber leak within the agency."

"That won't be an issue," he said. "I can handle the media when it comes to a crisis. Unfortunately, I've had plenty of practice with it."

"Just be careful you don't walk into a trap," she said. "And whatever you do, don't call on Hugh McMillan. He's the one reporting the story and is like a dog with a bone when it comes to stories like these. You might recall how he pushed out the man who held my job during the last administration. McMillan kept pushing until the man snapped. He's quite skilled at luring you into a trap, which he will then leverage his influential social media accounts to make you look bad, mostly by taking what you say out of context. And he doesn't care either. It's all about the clicks, the likes, the eyeballs on his content."

"Don't worry," Bullock said. "I'll chew him up and spit him out."

"Look, I'm warning you not to press your luck," she said while tucking her long blonde locks behind her ears. "The best way to handle him is not to call on him."

She handed him an index card that contained a picture of Hugh McMillan as well as some notes about him.

"He usually wears a solid red tie, communist little bastard," Bullock said, muttering the latter half of his comment under his breath. "Has curly brown hair, thick glasses, and a nasally voice. Shouldn't be too hard to avoid him."

But Bullock didn't intend to avoid him at all. If anyone attempted to embarrass his administration and denigrate the intelligence community, he was going to go on the attack.

"Sir, you are going to avoid him, right?" Leslie asked.

"You know me all too well, don't you?" Bullock said with a grin.

"Don't tease me like this," she said. "You know if you call on him, I'm immediately going into cardiac arrest."

"And someone will revive you," he said with a wink. "Don't worry. I'm not about to call on McMillan."

Bullock collected all his notes, stacking them neatly against his knee before patting Leslie on the shoulder and meandering down the hall. A few minutes later, one of his staffers signaled for him to enter the press room. While some presidents would've taken a more humble posture given the situation, Bullock was very intentional about the way he walked in, head held high, eyes scanning those there to share his words with the rest of the world. He wasn't about to concede even an inch of ground, even to someone who had managed to gather the truth. At the moment, Bullock couldn't plug the leak, but he could disparage anyone who dared to report such rumors without proof.

Bullock strode across the podium to the cacophony of clicking cameras and the heels of his dress shoes striking hard against the floor. He stopped in front of the lectern, rested his papers on it, and licked his lips before beginning his address.

"It's come to my attention that rumors are being reported as fact among members of the press regarding a story about a pair of dead U.S. intelligence officers that the CIA has been the victim of a disastrous cyberattack," Bullock said. "But I'm here today to tell you that these stories being pushed by rogue and irresponsible journalists are little more than fanciful fairy tales designed to make our incredible intelligence community appear weak. When I assumed office, one of my priorities, in light of my predecessor's issues, was to shore up our intelligence agencies. And we've done just that in a number of ways."

Bullock glanced down at his papers, shifting his weight from one foot to the other.

"Now, I could go into how we did it, but I'm sure everyone listening would rather me focus on the reality of where the intelligence community is rather than talking points that are best delivered in a debate or on the campaign trail next year."

He offered a weak smile before looking down at his paper and continuing. And while he claimed that his speech was going to avoid talking points, he did just that. One by one, he enumerated how his office had strengthened its position globally, ultimately keeping Americans safe at home and abroad. He delivered the speech with both conviction and empathy, assuring citizens that they had nothing to worry about.

But Bullock's real strength was in fielding questions from journalists and handling them with such aplomb that they became snippets that flooded social media. Any negative attention would be swallowed whole by his sharp wit and feisty tongue.

"I'll be happy to answer any questions you might have," Bullock said.

His confidence in delivering such barbs was why he called on Hugh McMillan first. Bullock pointed at the controversial journalist and smiled.

"I believe I saw your hand go up first, Mr. McMillan," Bullock said.

He was almost certain he heard Leslie huff behind him.

"Mr. President, what proof can you give the American people that these deaths weren't the result of a cyberattack?" McMillan asked.

"To be most candid with you, Mr. McMillan, the burden of proof is on the claimant. I'm telling you that we've had no such security breach. But you seem intent on believing some *source*, if you will. You are the one, not me, that has to prove that this happened. It didn't happen and I have no way of proving otherwise."

"But, sir, when there's smoke, there's fire," McMillan said. "I believe we can at least agree upon that fact, can't we?"

Bullock pursed his lips and cocked his head to the side, all orchestrated for the cameras. He knew the subtle movements would be caught by those watching on social media, especially the growing throngs of people who mistrusted sensationalist journalists like McMillan.

"That's not a far-fetched idea, though not a hundred percent assured," Bullock said. "The problem is we don't have any smoke."

"You wouldn't consider two dead CIA officers cause for smoke?"

"No, Mr. McMillan, I would consider them sad casualties in a war waged by a handful of dedicated men and women who are all willing to lay down their lives to keep you and all the other millions of Americans safe."

"But, sir, two dead officers?" McMillan said, holding his arms out in a gesture of pleading.

Bullock went for the jugular.

"Do you think these are the first two CIA officers who've died a week apart?" Bullock asked. "You're presuming something based on what you want the story to be. Do I need to school you on how real journalists seek the truth instead of searching for support of a narrative?"

The room fell silent, breathlessly waiting the quick-witted McMillan to respond.

"With all due respect, Mr. President, I have well-placed sources within the agency that say there was a leak. Now, perhaps my source is wrong about it being a cyber leak. But there is one—and I'm going to find out all about it."

"If you're so confident there's a leak, Mr. McMillan, perhaps we should talk afterward."

"I'd like that," McMillan said.

Bullock contained his anger and answered a few more questions before ending the press conference and exiting the podium, Leslie in tow. He waited to explode until he was deep in the recesses of the West Wing and out of earshot of any lingering journalists.

"What the hell was that out there?" he asked, gesturing toward the direction of the press briefing room.

"It's like he set me up with a little bait and switch," Bullock said. "Wrote about a cyberattack and then tried to trap me with a story about an ambiguous leak."

"You could've refused to comment—or stopped sparring with him," she said. "You can't say I didn't warn you."

"I'll handle it my way," Bullock said. "I'm not gonna let him get away with this."

"Seems like the real issue is the actual source of the leak, not McMillan," she said. "And not to mention whoever his well-placed source is within the agency."

"But the fact that there's an analog leak is the kind of information we can't allow to escape into the public. It'd create a lot of suspicion among our people. And that's definitely something we can't afford."

Bullock dismissed her before retreating to his desk. He picked up the phone and called General George Hix, a trusted friend and retired general who worked at the Pentagon.

"Did you just see the press conference?" Bullock asked.

"Yeah," Hix said. "Didn't look good."

"What? Me or the story about a leak at the CIA?"

"I'd say you were fine, sir, but that story McMillan is pushing isn't far off from the truth. Isn't that right?"

Bullock sighed.

"Unfortunately, all indications are that we do have a leak, just not a cyber one."

"That's interesting," Hix said.

"But the real trouble is that we've got someone within the agency feeding that obnoxious hack precious information."

"Agreed," Hix said. "Sounds like your biggest problem right now from an optics standpoint is the agency itself. And where does the blame fall there?"

"On the man who's running it," Bullock said. "Damn that Besserman."

"What do you want to do about it?"

"Right now? Nothing. But I do want you to put together a

short list of potential replacements for Besserman. Think you can do that for me?"

"I'd be honored, sir," Hix said. "And I'd kick myself if I didn't tell you that one of the best potential candidates for the job is almost right in front of you."

"And who is that?"

"NSA Director John Wicker," Hix said. "I'll be surprised if I can find someone more capable and perfect for that position."

"Keep me informed about what you find," Bullock said. "If Besserman doesn't get this cleaned up, I might be forced to make a change."

CHAPTER
EIGHT

WASHINGTON, D.C.

BIG EARV FIDDLED with the radio dial, trying to find some good tunes as he drove across town for his appointment. A little jazz would've been fine or even his guilty pleasure—classic country music. But his search was cut short when he heard a panel of pundits discussing President Bullock's latest press conference and his adamant denial that there was a cyber leak.

"While Bullock is more genuine than most politicians, he's still a politician," said Hal Castleton, host of Beltway Bedlam, one of the most compelling and equally maddening radio talk show programs on the Washington airwaves.

"That's right," added Felicia Stonehouse, a regular on the show and former White House press secretary. "Now, I want to replay this one little snippet of the president's response to reporter Hugh McMillan's claim that he has a source with knowledge that there's a confirmed leak at the CIA."

Big Earv flicked on his blinker as he stopped at an intersection and waited for the light to turn green.

A recording of the press conference began to play with McMillan's opening question after Bullock's statement:

McMillan: "Mr. President, what proof can you give the American people that these deaths weren't the result of a cyberattack?"

Bullock: "To be most candid with you, Mr. McMillan, the burden of proof is on the claimant. I'm telling you that we've had no such security breach. But you seem intent on believing some *source*, if you will. You are the one, not me, that has to prove that this happened. It didn't happen, and I have no way of proving otherwise."

Felicia's voice immediately returned.

"Now did you catch that, Hal?" she said, not waiting for a reply. "McMillan inquired about a cyber leak, implying that this information that's been fatal for two CIA officers so far came from someone hacking the CIA. And if you listen to the president, he's picking his words very carefully in his response. He said they've had 'no such security breach,' meaning that McMillan's initial question is surgically answered."

"What are you suggesting exactly?" Castleton asked.

"Isn't it obvious?" Felicia replied. "Bullock didn't say there wasn't a leak. He just said that there wasn't a cyber leak. He was picking his words very carefully so that if anyone called him out on it in the future, he can claim that he never lied to the American people."

"But it's disingenuous, if anything."

"Of course," Felicia said. "He wants to be able to take the moral high ground in future election debates and say that he's been honest with the country. When the reality is, he's merely behaved like every other politician in this godforsaken city, more concerned about their style than their substance. Mark my word, there's definitely a leak at the CIA, but not one that occurred at the hands of some black hat hackers. No, there's a mole inside the agency that's feeding this information to someone who's sharing it with the world."

"That's quite a bold analysis," Castleton said.

"It's a Stonehouse Stone Cold analysis," she said emphatically.

The show's producer played a stinger followed by a voiceover of a man with a deep brooding voice saying, "And that's our Stone Cold take of the day."

Big Earv raised an eyebrow, intrigued by the perceptive analysis, as the light turned green and he resumed his trek across town. Entrenched in the middle of the investigation regarding the identity of the leaker, he knew they were still a long way from confirming Felicia Stonehouse's hunches. But she was on the right track—and he hoped to prove her right.

Maybe I'll do it in the next hour.

Big Earv's special assignment had been to interview Andrew Singletary, a U.S. State Department official who'd made two trips to Beijing and another one to London in the past six months. Agency assets had photographed Singletary at official government functions where both Jun Fang and Nigel Ackerman were in attendance. According to those reports, neither man held a lengthy conversation with Singletary, but it warranted a closer look. And one where Big Earv wanted to catch him off guard.

Big Earv went through the drive-through of a coffee shop and snagged a couple of cups, presenting one as a peace offering for surprising Singletary at home so early before work.

When Singletary answered the door, his hair was disheveled and he still wore a pair of sweatpants and slippers.

"What the hell, man," Singletary said as he stared slack-jawed at Big Earv. "It's a little early to be canvassing the neighborhood."

Big Earv smiled and held out one of the coffee cups.

"Not canvassing, but I was wondering if I could have a few minutes of your time," he said.

Singletary took the cup and cautiously eyed Big Earv.

"About what?" he said, his eyes narrowing.

"I'm assisting with the CIA investigation into the possible leak, and I wanted to ask you a few questions," Big Earv said.

Singletary furrowed his brow.

"Who are you again?"

"Malik Earvin," he said. "I'm working with the CIA to help determine the source of a breach that's left two officers dead."

"I thought there wasn't a cyber breach," Singletary said. "At least, isn't that what the president said?"

Big Earv looked around before gesturing inside the house.

"Can we talk about this inside?" he asked. "I'm not comfortable having this discussion on your doorstep."

Singletary sighed before turning and indicating inside his house.

"You did bring me a cup of coffee," he mumbled. "I guess I can give you five minutes."

Big Earv thanked Singletary as the two men settled into opposing couches in the living room just inside Singletary's townhome.

"I'm not sure how you think I can help," Singletary said. "I hardly know anyone at the agency, and I'm gone more often than not. You happened to catch me on a rare week when I'm home. But you could've waited and we could've done this just as easily at my office."

"I know," Big Earv said. "I'm sorry. I've just got a lot of these interviews to conduct and I was in the area. Just thought I'd pop over and see if you could chat. I promise it won't take long."

"Fire away," Singletary said.

"On your recent trip to Beijing, we have credible reports that you spoke with Jun Fang at a state sponsored event," Big Earv said. "Can you tell me about your conversation with Fang?"

Singletary scowled.

"Fang? You want to know about Fang? I thought you said this was an investigation into the agency leak."

"I did," Big Earv said. "Now, can you please answer my question?"

Singletary took a sip of his coffee and glowered at Big Earv.

"You weren't being upfront with me. I don't like this."

"Look," Big Earv said, scooting forward on the couch, "I'm not going to beat around the bush with you. There are two people of interest in our investigation that you've had contact with recently. And it's raised a few eyebrows. Now, I'm here to give you an opportunity to explain yourself."

"Explain what exactly?"

"Your conversation with Jun Fang, for starters."

Singletary shook his head and sighed.

"I knew this was a mistake."

"If it's not a big deal, it should be easy to explain."

"I never spoke with Fang," Singletary said. "I barely know who the guy is, never mind have a conversation with him."

Big Earv pulled his phone out of his pocket and swiped to a photo of Singletary chatting with Fang alone at an event.

"Maybe this will help refresh your memory," Big Earv said.

Lines creased Singletary's forehead as he studied the image.

"Okay, I guess maybe I did speak with him because that's definitely me and that looks like Fang, but I don't remember it. Maybe that was after I'd had one too many trips to the bar."

"The time stamp for the photo was seven-fifteen," Big Earv said. "According to our records, the event started at seven."

"You know how those timestamps can be off," Singletary said with a dismissive wave. "Honestly, I don't remember what I said to the man. Probably nothing more than small talk."

"Then you had another conversation with him about two months later on another trip to Beijing," Big Earv said as he swiped to another photo and showed it to Singletary.

"Sorry," he said, shaking his head. "Don't remember that one either."

"Then what about this one?" Big Earv asked as he drew the phone back, found the photo of Singletary with Nigel Ackerman, and held out the device again.

Singletary squinted as he studied the photo.

"Am I supposed to know who that is?" he asked. "You are aware that as part of this job, I'm shaking hands and talking with dozens of people each day. I can't possibly keep them all straight."

"Nigel Ackerman isn't the kind of person you'd forget. He's a strapping man with a business interest in dozens of companies that work directly with the State Department. So, you, of all people, would more than likely not only know exactly who Ackerman is, but probably be working with him. Now, if you'd like for me to pull up some correspondence between the two of you, I'll be happy to do so."

"That's not necessary," Singletary said. "Now that you mention it, I do remember speaking with him. But what we talked about wasn't all that interesting as it pertained to your investigation. We spoke for about five minutes, discussing the new pro soccer franchise he purchased in the U.S."

"That sounds rather benign."

"Like I said, it wasn't a big deal. Now, is there something else going on with these two men that I need to know about? Do you suspect them of something?"

"That's classified," Big Earv said, forcing a smile as he stood.

"Oh, so I just tell you about my conversations with them and then you leave me in the dark?"

"That's how this works," Big Earv said. "Thank you for your time and enjoy the coffee."

"That's it? I mean, if these guys are under some sort of suspicion, maybe I should know about it so I can avoid them."

"You do what you need to do," Big Earv said as he walked past the counter. But a letter sitting on top of a small package caught his eye. It had an international stamp on it and had a label from one of the subsidiaries owned by Fang. Big Earv committed the details to memory before easing toward the front door.

"Next time, Mr. Earvin, just schedule a meeting with my office, okay?"

"Of course," Big Earv said. "Have a good day."

He shuffled to his car and sighed as he settled into the driver's seat.

"What are you hiding, Mr. Singletary?" he said to himself.

CHAPTER
NINE

LONDON

HAWK EASED BACK the drapes and peered through a sliver of the window. Gathering on the front steps were five men just as Alex had reported. They were all armed, creating a new challenge in regards to getting Simon Lee out of London alive. If Ackerman had sent five men to take care of Lee, even if Hawk and Ryder managed to kill them all, more would likely be sent. Hawk had nowhere else to hide, and he certainly didn't know the Towers Hamlet area well enough to run from Ackerman's men who practically owned the borough.

"We've got a major problem," Hawk said.

"We can take these guys," Ryder said.

Hawk looked at Lee, who was biting his lip and shaking his head.

"I don't know," Lee said. "No offense to your abilities, but these guys fight dirty and have no code whatsoever. They want me dead—and won't stop until I am."

Hawk looked down the hall and then back at the front door.

"What if we beat them to the punch?" Hawk said.

Lee's eyes widened.

"You might want to clarify what you're suggesting," he said.

"We shoot you first," Hawk said flatly. "And before you freak out, I don't mean literally. What if we stage your death, have you lying dead in the hallway and let them see you?"

"And then what? Invite them in to view you and then one of their homicidal maniacs shoots me just to be sure? No thanks."

"I know it's risky, but it might be our only way of getting out of this situation," Hawk said.

Lee scowled.

"If you hadn't let them follow you—"

"You can point fingers later, but we need to act on this if we're going to get out of this alive. You with me?"

Lee huffed before nodding.

"You haven't left me much of a choice."

"You've got five more at the backdoor now," Alex said.

Hawk cursed under his breath before laying out the plan. Lee laid face down in the hallway in a spot clearly visible once the front door opened. Ryder peeked through a small opening in the drapes, watching for the reaction of the men out front.

"Everyone ready?" Hawk asked in a hushed voice.

Lee, still face down, held up a thumb, while Ryder nodded.

Hawk fired his gun twice then looked at Ryder.

"They're panicked," he said. "All of them have their guns drawn and look like they're deciding how to get inside."

"Why don't we make things a little easier for them," Hawk said.

He flipped on the porch light and opened the front door.

"We took care of him," Hawk said.

One of the men stepped forward, his weapon drawn.

"Who are you?" the man asked.

"Does it really matter?" Hawk replied. "We just made your night a whole lot easier. You were under orders to kill Lee, weren't you?"

The man nodded as Hawk eased open the door so they could see Lee lying on the floor in the dark.

"So were we, except we were contracted to kill him," Hawk said. "This is a CIA safe house and they will be going over every square inch of this place once they discover his body here. I doubt you're willing to leave any clues behind or even have the CCTV cameras across the street capturing you entering this house. You don't want that kind of headache do you, but you can just snap a photo of him and send it to your boss and be done for the night. Maybe wait until after you've been to the pub for a few pints, make him think you had to work a little extra hard to capture him. Nobody else has to die tonight. What do you say?"

The man turned around and looked at his colleagues before pulling out his phone and taking a picture of Lee, motionless in the hallway.

"Thanks, mate," the man said before patting Hawk on his shoulder.

Then he whistled, drawing the men from around the back. They separated into four groups and piled into their cars before driving away.

"All right," Hawk said. "You can get up."

Lee rolled over and sat up, remaining on the floor and leaning against the wall.

"How the hell did this happen?" Lee asked.

"The leak?" Hawk asked.

Lee nodded.

"I was so close to gaining the trust of the inner circle and finding out all the illegal activity that Nigel Ackerman was involved with," he said. "Now it's gone—*poof*—up in smoke."

He paused for a moment, shaking his head.

"Two years of my life—*two years*. And all that work was about to pay off."

"Don't shoot the messengers," Hawk said as he crouched in the hall near Lee. "We just came to help get you out of here so that you didn't have to pay the ultimate price for someone else's mistake."

"You think this is some mistake?" Lee asked. "No way. Not a

chance. The information about us didn't just grow legs and walk out the door. Someone sought out our information and purposefully leaked it."

"But why?" Ryder asked. "I mean, isn't that the real question we're all wondering? Why would someone target you? What were *you* involved in that made you the target of a leak?"

"Isn't it obvious?" Lee asked as he stood. "I was working for Nigel Ackerman. He's about as crooked as they come, but he's a genius at hiding it."

"Why? Because you couldn't figure out what he was into?" Ryder asked.

Lee looked at Hawk and then pointed at Ryder.

"Who is this smart ass?" Lee asked.

"He's still wet behind the ears," Hawk said. "Give him some time."

"Well, anyway," Lee continued, "I think we've all heard the rumors that he runs an illegal underground gambling ring, a venture I was privy to early on and eventually involved in once I'd been vetted. But that wasn't Ackerman's biggest revenue generator."

Hawk's eyes widened.

"There was something else?"

"A *big* something else. But *what* exactly is why I was still with Ackerman. If I wanted to bust him for gambling, I could've done that over a year ago. But I wanted to destroy his other business."

"Any idea what it had to do with? Illegal arms dealing? Trafficking in government secrets? A financial scheme?"

"No," Lee said. "Worse. Much much worse."

"What then?"

"There was another division of Ackerman's enterprises that was closely guarded. I'd only heard whispers from some of the other guards, a handful of which said they could never work in it if asked."

"What was it?"

"Human trafficking," Lee said. "And I'll be honest, that

would be a tough one for me, too. The only way I could endure something like that is if I knew I'd be able to eventually shut it down and ensure Ackerman spent the rest of his pathetic life behind bars."

"I'm sure you'll figure out another way to bring him down," Hawk said.

"Yeah, but who knows how many more lives are going to be ruined during that time? I was so close to finding out everything and developing a plan to expose Ackerman. I'm just getting angrier talking about it."

Ryder walked over toward the window and peered outside again.

"Let's get out of here in case they decide to come back," he said.

"Agreed," Hawk said. "I don't want to have to carry you out in a bag. That'll only create more suspicion with the local authorities and make a big mess."

"We should still call the cops, tell them there's a disturbance, if anything for optics," Ryder said.

"Then you make the call once we're in the car," Hawk said. "Let's go."

The trio left the house and walked down the street toward Hawk's car. However, as they were walking, he caught a glint of something down the street.

"Take him to the car," Hawk said to Ryder. "I need to pay a visit to a little snoop."

Hawk strode past his car and kept walking, while Ryder and Lee got inside. After going another twenty meters, Hawk crossed the road and slipped up behind the car where he'd seen the flash of reflected light. As he drew nearer to the vehicle, he hustled up behind it and then rushed up to the driver's side window where a man was taking pictures with a zoom lens camera. Hawk smashed his fist through the window, shattering it and surprising the man.

The man scrambled to get away, fumbling for his weapon. But Hawk jammed his gun against the side of the man's head.

"Put your hands where I can see them," Hawk said, "or this is going to be over real quick."

Without a word, the man complied.

"Who are you working for?" Hawk asked.

"No one," the man said.

Hawk pressed the barrel farther into the man's head, forcing him to tilt it as he groaned in pain.

"I don't believe you," Hawk said with a growl.

"I swear, I'm telling the truth."

The cell phone on the dashboard vibrated and a message appeared on the screen.

> Okay. We'll be right over to finish the job this time.

"You have men coming over to help you finish the job?" Hawk asked. "What job?"

"Uh, it's the, uh—I'm a private investigator and I was following another man—and, I—uh—"

"Let me see your pictures," Hawk said, nodding toward the camera lying on the passenger seat.

As the man moved toward it, Hawk added more pressure with the gun barrel.

"Slowly," Hawk said. "Don't think I won't pull this trigger if I feel you might be making a move."

"Okay, okay," the man said as he took hold of the device.

"Slowly," Hawk said. "Now, show me the photos you just took."

The man fiddled with the controls for a moment. At first, Hawk conceded that perhaps the man was nervous before realizing he was stalling.

Before Hawk could address the man's shenanigans, he swung the thick lens toward Hawk's head, knocking the gun aside. As the man went for his weapon, Hawk rammed his gun barrel into the side of the man's head and pulled the trigger.

Immediately, the man fell limp, the passenger side window suddenly awash in his blood.

Hawk picked up the man's phone, using his face to gain access to the device.

No worries. I went ahead and took care of it.

Then Hawk placed it back in the dead man's hand and raced back to his car. He climbed inside to find two puzzled passengers.

"What was that all about?" Ryder asked.

"That guy was watching us, waiting to see if we came out with Lee," Hawk said. "He had pictures of all three of us and had already called for support to deal with us again."

"Then let's get out of here," Lee said. "If more are coming back, we won't be able to fight our way out."

Hawk jammed the car into drive and peeled away from curb.

"You don't have to tell me twice," he said.

CHAPTER
TEN

LANGLEY, VIRGINIA

Robert Besserman checked the time on his watch before meandering over to the window. He surveyed the courtyard and closely observed agency officers and analysts shuffling across it, some toting files while others stared at tablets. Then there were those who simply walked with purpose.

What are they thinking about? What's for dinner? Why my marriage is in trouble? How I can stop the next terror attack?

Besserman had found his job with the CIA to be a demanding one, so much so that it consumed almost all his thoughts. He'd tried to make time for hobbies, for relationships, for relaxation. But he didn't need long at the agency to realize everything had to take a backseat to the job. Ensuring that the country's enemies and all their threats would be squelched required an enormous amount of mental energy. As exhausted as he was, he couldn't afford to be tired.

But even those most dedicated to their job took the opportunity to relax, to unwind, to not think about work for an hour. He couldn't make—or even expect—others to maintain the same level of commitment that he had to the agency. However, the level of loyalty to their country CIA officers and analysts were required to maintain wasn't negotiable. Pride in protecting your country and fellow Americans was foundational to the agency's mission. If you didn't care deeply about your country, why were you even doing the job?

Besserman knew there were agency employees who enjoyed the work and took great pride in it, just as there were those who were simply there to pick up a paycheck. And the latter was the group that concerned him the most. They could be turned and enticed. They were the type of people who'd grown tired of the rigorous demands placed on them by the job and searched for a way out with a soft landing, a landing padded by a massive payout. And if anyone knew how to hide financial accounts so the government couldn't find them, it was Besserman's analysts.

As he continued to observe the people scurrying across the courtyard, he wondered if one of them was responsible for the leak that had put the U.S. intelligence community on edge. Someone had committed an act of treason, and Besserman was determined to learn the identity of that person and make them pay. Two of his officers were already dead, and he refused to let there be a third, mostly out of a sense of pride but also because he knew his job—the one that had consumed him—depended on it.

The real problem Besserman had was figuring out who to trust. He had plenty of people who he'd worked with that he felt were more than competent when it came to the task of sussing out a mole. But given the nature of this leak—so mysterious and apparently so analog —selecting someone with this task would be fraught with challenges. He didn't even trust himself to make such a decision. It could be almost anyone and an open investigation could put the entire agency on edge, even more so than it already was. The last thing he wanted was the search to devolve into a witch hunt. However he decided to handle the problem, it needed to be done discreetly.

His intercom beeped with a message from his assistant.

"Miss Kauffman is here to see you, sir," she said.

"Send her in."

Besserman reached underneath his desk and activated a device that jammed all radio signals. While he had the room swept every morning for listening devices, he didn't want to take any chances that he'd either missed something or someone else had slipped into his office and activated a bug. The routine was tiresome but necessary under the circumstances.

Mallory lugged a stack of papers under her arm as she entered the room.

"Did you bring me a present?" he asked, rubbing his hands together.

"A stick in your eye would be better than what I'm about to give you."

She dropped the documents down on his desk with a solid thud.

"What's this?" he asked.

"I went through digital logs, trying to find a common user who'd accessed all four agents' records."

"And?"

Mallory sat down in the chair and crossed her arms over her chest.

"Nothing," she said. "Then I checked all the paper logs too down in the archives."

"Anything there?"

"Struck out again," she said. "I've never seen anything like this. Then I started to wonder if it was someone who already had knowledge of the four agents' assignments."

"That would be unusual," he said. "I wouldn't even know where they were unless I asked. And to be honest, I wasn't even aware of Simon Lee before this whole ordeal began."

"Makes sense because I didn't find anyone who would've been affiliated in any way with all four of those assignments, past or present."

"So, nobody knew or even appeared to intentionally seek out

their information? And there was no breach either, internally or externally? Am I understanding this correctly?"

"That's right," she said. "My only other guess was that it was planned years in advance, but the information divulged about each of the agents was current. If someone found out five years ago about where these agents were, it'd be inaccurate. Some of the information released was very current. I'm stumped on how this could happen."

"Either someone has developed a way to hack our server and crawl through it without being detected—which is scary as hell— or someone used old school spy craft methods to extract the information from our archives."

"So, what do you want me to do?" she asked.

Besserman sighed as he glanced down at the folders on his desk before leaning back in his chair.

"There's nothing we can do about new technology since we have no way of even detecting it if it's that good. But we can begin reviewing footage of the archives. Find out who was gaining access to it and seeing if anyone could've lied about what files they were retrieving."

"That would be a huge net to cast," she said. "Someone could've gathered information on all the officers in one trip. And who knows when they would've done it."

"I know it's a laborious task, but that's our only viable option to figuring out who did it. And it's a slim one at that. However, we need to let the president know that we've left no stone unturned in our quest to find out who's behind the breach."

"Okay," she said, "if that's what you want, I'll do it."

Mallory's phone buzzed and a text message appeared on her screen. She growled and shook her head.

"What is it?" Besserman asked.

"They're teasing the release of a fifth officer."

"Teasing?"

"Yeah, just an image," she said. "It's how they're creating a buzz around the actual release. The image was a little pixelated but someone on my team sharpened it and then ran it through facial recognition. It's Brock Hanson, sir."

"You know him?"

She nodded.

"He's working with an underground crime syndicate located in Prague," she said. "I worked with him three years ago when he infiltrated a terrorist group in Oman. He's one of our finest. We've got to get him out of there before they tell everyone about him."

"Get a workup on Hanson and send everything ASAP to Morgan May's team," Besserman said. "I want Hanson extracted. And then I want you to turn your full attention to cultivating a list of people who've accessed the archives and had the opportunity to gather all these names."

Mallory stood and scooped up all the files.

"You got it, sir."

Once she left, Besserman deactivated the scrambling device and let out a long breath. This breach made him feel like he was adrift in the ocean and being battered by a relentless storm with no land in sight.

When is this going to end?

Besserman stood and paced the floor. He needed answers yesterday, but he also needed a way to put an end to the leaker. It wasn't a permanent solution, but it could buy him some much needed time, something that was in short supply.

CHAPTER
ELEVEN

PRAGUE, CZECH REPUBLIC

BRADY HAWK SLUNG his pack over his back and trudged through the concourse. Ryder meandered twenty meters behind as the duo avoided appearing as if they were together. After they got Simon Lee safely to a plane headed for the U.S., they were given orders to hold tight given the increased frequency with which Mayhem was releasing the names of CIA officers. The black hat hacker had yet to reveal the latest one but the agency had figured out that Brock Hanson was next, requiring Hawk and Ryder to be re-routed there.

Hawk's phone buzzed with a call from Alex.

"I was just thinking about you," he said. "Is everything all right?"

"All right is such a relative term," she said. "Relative to dying in the hospital of a rare disease, I'm wonderful. Relative to sitting on a beach in Cozumel reading a novel, I'm terrible."

"So, what's going on?"

"Little J.D. is sick. I think he caught some stomach bug at school that's going around, but it's required my full attention since you extracted Lee. Not exactly conducive to me solving this note from my mystery interloper."

"I'm sorry to hear that, honey. But why do I have the feeling that you're going to tell me you solved it anyway?"

She laughed.

"Because you know me too well, I guess."

"So, what'd the note say?" he asked.

"Let me just preface this by saying I *think* I figured it out, because the note doesn't make a lot of sense to me."

"I'm sure you're dead on. Let's hear it."

"The note said, 'Safety is an illusion'."

"That's it?"

"Yeah," she said. "Strange, huh?"

"Do you feel like it was a threat?"

"I don't know how else to take it."

Hawk followed the signs to customs and immigration, winding his way down a desolate hallway. Fluorescent lights flickered overhead as he continued walking, while he heard the faint sound of an old Michael Jackson hit piped in through the airport's sound system.

"Well, I don't know if I can be of much help to you solving that mystery," he said. "But it certainly sounds a little ominous, especially the way the note was delivered, almost like that alone was intended to scare you."

"They had to know I'd figure it out."

"I doubt they wanted to keep it a secret," Hawk said. "They intended for you to know, but maybe they wanted to do it in such a way that you would be distracted while trying to solve it. I don't really know."

"That's what I think, but I want to know who this is to satisfy my curiosity."

"If it is someone who knows you, they won't actually mess with you. Remember what happened the last time someone tried to attack you at the ranch?"

"There are a few dead Russians buried out on the ranch who serve as a constant reminder," she said with a laugh. "But I'm more worried about J.D. than anything."

"Keep digging into it," he said. "I'll try to help when I get a minute. Do you think you'll be able to help with this operation, even with J.D. being sick?"

"I'll make it work."

"You always do," he said.

"But I think I'm going to help from our cabin," she said. "I've got the remote unit I can use there, and I'm going to set up a few battery-powered cameras to monitor our entire property while I'm gone, just in case they return."

"You do whatever makes you feel safe," he said. "Bye, honey. Love you. And give J.D. a hug for me, okay?"

"Of course," she said. "Love you, too."

He ended the call and tried not to think about being apart from Alex and little J.D. Despite Alex's competency in handling any potential threat levied against her, Hawk didn't like leaving her to fend for herself and J.D. without any backup. They all loved the ranch, but it was isolated, which wasn't always a good thing.

Once Hawk pocketed his phone, he approached the end of the corridor and found himself in line with more than two dozen other people waiting to be processed. A family of Italians overtook Ryder on his way to customs, serving as a buffer between him and Hawk. However, when Hawk reached the kiosk with his customs agent, he gestured for Hawk to stay there before getting up.

"I'll be right back," the agent said in heavily accented English.

Hawk waited and then looked at Ryder, who scowled as if to ask why there was a delay. Hawk shrugged and turned his attention back to the kiosk as the agent promptly returned.

"Okay, Mr. Gordon," the agent said as he studied Hawk's passport. "Welcome to the Czech Republic. Can you tell me about the nature of your visit?"

"Leisure," Hawk said.

The agent sifted through the passport before finding an empty page and stamping it. But he lingered for a moment. As he did, Hawk peered through the glass separating him from the agent and noticed a bulletin that had a black-and-white photo of him on it with a series of his legends listed on it. Fortunately, "Jack Gordon" didn't make the list. But Hawk noticed Ryder's new legend and photo was just below his.

Hawk glanced over at the adjacent kiosk where the Italian family had been standing to be processed. They shuffled off toward baggage claim, while Ryder approached the counter. A young man with a tight-fitting cap and a thin mustache held out his hand to take Ryder's passport.

"Stay cool," Hawk said in a hushed tone as he walked by Ryder.

Such a situation wouldn't normally be concerning, but Ryder's green eyes and blond hair made him stand out. Between the two Magnum Group agents, Ryder was likelier to get flagged. How he handled it would determine what kind of agent he was.

Before Hawk could ponder the situation any more, he felt his shoulder nudged from behind as someone sprinted past. Hawk stumbled and he spun around to see what had hit him. But he already knew.

Ryder!

The young agent's hulking frame nimbly wove in and out of the passengers heading toward baggage claim. The customs agent hustled after him, speaking into his handheld radio unit. With no one else responding and the corridor leading to baggage claim almost deserted, Hawk raced after the man, catching him from behind and tripping him. The customs agent fell face first across the sterile tile floor, skidding several feet before coming to a stop. Hawk kicked the man in the head, knocking him out and then taking his radio. Hawk also snagged his cap and handed it to Ryder.

"Here," Hawk said. "Put this on."

"Thanks," Ryder said, his face pale.

"And just be casual. No need to draw unwanted attention to yourself. And take off your jacket and shove it into your bag."

Ryder quickly complied as they both hustled. They rounded a corner and Hawk noticed two police officers racing toward them.

"Hurry," Hawk said, jerking a thumb over his shoulder. "A customs agent is lying on the floor back that way."

The officers thanked Hawk and rushed in the direction of the agent.

"We've gotta move," Hawk said.

They were herded into another line where newcomers to the country scanned their bags before being released. Hawk glanced behind them and knew they didn't have much time. The moment police officers raced around the corner and spotted Ryder, they were going to be trapped.

"You ready to run?" Hawk asked.

"What are you thinking?" Ryder asked as they continued to work their way toward the scanners.

"We can't stick around and wait for the cops to come after us," he said. "If we don't get out of here immediately, Brock Hanson is as good as dead. And we'll have a helluva lot of explaining to do."

"So, what's the plan? Run like hell?"

"That and jump into the first cab we see," Hawk said.

"Works for me," Ryder said.

"And then we're going to have a serious conversation about what you just did back there. On my mark. Three, two, one, go."

Hawk and Ryder rushed toward the front of the line, creating a commotion. By the time the customs officers overseeing the scanning noticed what was going on, Hawk and Ryder were nearly past them. However, one portly passenger noticed what was happening and decided to get involved. Just as Hawk tried to maneuver around him, the man swung his hip out, catching Hawk in between steps and knocking him to the ground.

A police officer drew his weapon and rushed toward Hawk, the gun trained on him.

"Don't make another move," the officer said.

CHAPTER
TWELVE

WASHINGTON, D.C.

BIG EARV DOUBLE-CHECKED his notes to make sure he was watching the correct car. For the past hour, he'd been hunkered down in the parking garage utilized by U.S. State Department employees waiting for Andrew Singletary to leave work. While Big Earv had interviewed more than a dozen suspects, nobody raised more red flags than Singletary. His contact with two men on the Magnum Group's Alliance watch list made him more than just a person of interest. If there was one thing Big Earv had learned while conducting investigations, it was that coincidences rarely happened, if ever. Whenever something appeared suspicious, it more than likely was. And Singletary didn't just appear suspicious —he appeared like a compliant pawn in Fang's operation or Ackerman's—or both.

Big Earv looked at his watch and then surveyed the quiet garage that had thinned out over the past hour. Most of the State Department employees had trudged to their vehicles and driven away, but there hadn't been any signs of Singletary.

Big Earv called Mia.

"Are you still monitoring Singletary's position?" he asked.

"I'm tracking his cell phone movements right now, if that's what you mean," she said.

"Is he still in the building?"

"Yes, though he hasn't moved in the past hour. If he leaves his phone, I can't tell where he's gone."

"Any chance he could've already left?"

"He'd have to leave without his security card, which registers when he comes in and when he goes out," she said. "I could see him leaving without his phone, but not his security card."

"Surely he knows that these things can track him and record his movements, right?"

"Probably. But he could be in a meeting or just left his phone at his desk as he went to some other part of the building."

"I couldn't sit still that long," Big Earv said.

"Did you stand for hours on end while guarding the president?" Mia asked.

"He rarely remained anywhere for more than an hour. We were always on the go, either scouting out the next location or securing it for him. But at least we were always standing. Just sitting in this car for the past couple of hours waiting for Singletary is driving me insane."

"I'm not fond of stakeouts either, but I can definitely sit in front of my computer monitor for hours on end," she said. "It's weird, I know."

"You were a hacker."

"Still am a hacker," she corrected. "I just changed teams."

"Well, can you hack the State Department security cameras and find out if Singletary is still inside?"

"That's a little over the top for this mission, don't you think?"

Big Earv's breath hitched as he watched the door to the third floor open and Singletary stride through it.

"Never mind," he said. "Singletary finally appeared."

"And he did so by leaving his phone *and* security card at his desk."

"Then this ought to be interesting," Big Earv said. "I'm going to see where he's going before I confront him. He's obviously doing something he doesn't want anyone knowing about."

Big Earv put his foot on the brake of his Tesla, which quietly came to life. He bought one after learning just how quiet the machine was, perfect for surveillance. The make had become so popular that he could blend in with one as opposed to standing out. But it was the near silent engine that sold him on its usefulness if he didn't want anyone to detect him.

Singletary, however, revved his Porsche 911 Carrera before backing out of his space and leaving the garage. Big Earv would've found owning such an expensive car suspicious had he not done his due diligence. While Singletary's position at the State Department earned him a comfortable salary, he had received a substantial inheritance when he turned twenty-five. His father had been a prominent investment banker who drowned in a boating accident while fishing alone. Singletary was supposed to have gone with his father but backed out at the last minute, according to police accident reports. Had Big Earv been on the case, he would've investigated a little more deeply given the money at stake. There had also been reports that Singletary's father and mother had a rocky marriage and she had visited a divorce lawyer a few weeks before the accident. Maybe it was a coincidence, but Big Earv struggled to believe that was the case. He was more inclined to believe mother and son conspired to kill the old man and split the loot. There was too much smoke around Singletary for this to be shrugged off. But that was five years ago and everyone had apparently moved on, especially Singletary, who embraced his new life awash in riches.

Big Earv followed Singletary west across the Theodore Roosevelt Bridge and north onto George Washington Parkway.

Where are you going, Mr. Singletary?

As Big Earv continued tailing his suspect north, he realized the most likely destination, one that was confirmed when he veered onto Dolly Madison Boulevard.

He's going to Langley.

Big Earv dialed Mia's number.

"You won't believe this," he said after she answered. "Singletary is headed to CIA headquarters."

"That is interesting," she said. "But maybe not entirely odd. I don't know how thoroughly you read that briefing on him, but Singletary's got clearance there. Apparently, he works with some sensitive information."

"You think maybe he's part of another operation with Fang and Ackerman, one we don't know about?"

"If that was the case, it's hard to imagine that Besserman wouldn't know about it and immediately eliminate him as a suspect," Mia said. "And why would he try to be so secretive about it? He left his cell phone and his security guard, at least giving off the impression that he's still in the State Department building."

"Maybe I'll just ask him myself," Big Earv said.

"Just be careful," she said. "At least wait until he comes out before you confront him, if you still feel like that's necessary."

"Of course," Big Earv said. "But I'm going to follow him and see where he's going. We could totally be wrong about all this, but I tend to agree with your line of thinking. He's acting too secretive for this not to be something suspicious."

Big Earv slowed down and allowed a couple of cars to get in front of him, creating a small buffer between him and Singletary. When Big Earv approached the gate, he held out his credentials before the guard swiped them and then waved him inside. Big Earv parked in a spot at the garage about thirty meters away from Singletary. He was walking away from his Porsche, checking over both shoulders before scurrying toward the CIA's front entrance.

Big Earv followed him toward the entrance, ambling inside far enough behind Singletary to see him dart into a stairwell at the end of the long hallway. After going through security, Big Earv attempted to find out where he was headed. He meandered around the next two floors and didn't see him anywhere. Thinking his search was futile, he remembered Mallory

Kauffman, who was a friend of the Magnum Group and one of the agency's top analysts. She worked closely with Director Besserman and might be able to help.

Big Earv found her office a few minutes later and asked her to help him.

"Of course," she said, gesturing to the chair opposite her desk. "I just got back to my desk a few minutes ago after running some papers up to Besserman. What is it that you need?"

"As you know, we're working in identifying who else might be involved with the leak, and I've got someone I've been tracking, a State Department employee named Andrew Singletary. And he's here in this building now. Ever heard of him?"

"The name isn't ringing a bell," she said. "Sorry."

Big Earv dug his phone out of his pocket and swiped to a photo of Singletary.

"Here he is," Big Earv said. "I know this is a big place and was wondering if maybe you've seen him around."

"Wait a minute," she said, reaching for his phone and taking it.

She squinted as she studied the image.

"Well—" Big Earv said.

"I think I just saw him a few minutes ago," she said. "I was dropping something off in HR and saw a guy who looked just like the man in this photo go into Catherine O'Donnell's office."

"Catherine O'Donnell," Big Earv said, shaking his head. "I'm not sure I'm familiar with who she is."

"She's the head of HR."

"Interesting," Big Earv said. "Wouldn't she have access to everyone's records?"

"Of course, but they're closely guarded. She couldn't just waltz in there and start picking through everyone's files. All the hard copies we keep are meticulously logged."

"What if you said you were going to get something else but then decided to look for another file?"

"I guess you could," she said, "but even the filing cabinets are access protected, so we have record of which drawers were opened."

"Wouldn't someone like her be able to open a drawer and say they were looking for some other files, all while knowing that what she was really looking for was like two files behind?"

"Yeah, but we ran a search for that too. No common denominators there either."

"Maybe I should just go in there and ask them what's going on," Big Earv said.

"Have you spoken to Singletary yet?"

Big Earv nodded.

"He wasn't real enthusiastic about talking with me."

"Did he seem suspicious of you?"

"Very much so," Big Earv said. "If I confront him now, he'll definitely know I'm all over him. But that also might explain why he left his phone and security card at the State Department building. He'll need an alibi."

"Except we'll have him on our security cameras here," Mallory said. "He won't be able to easily explain that."

"Can you get me footage of that?"

"Sure," she said. "I'll do it right now. Just give me a second. I've got access to our security footage, something Besserman gave me when we opened a soft investigation before handing it over to Magnum."

Mallory punched up a program on her keyboard, and moments later her monitor was filled with small squares with different video feeds. She sifted through several pages of these screens until she clicked on one.

"This is the camera outside Catherine O'Donnell's office," she said. "When did you say he entered the building?"

"About twenty minutes ago."

"So, let's scan for the last twenty minutes outside her office. I should be able to see myself and then find him."

Mallory moved the timeline forward, speeding up the footage to four times the real rate.

"Huh," she said as she furrowed her brow.

"What is it?"

"I know I was on this hallway a few minutes ago, but I can't find any footage of me," she said. "It's so weird too because there's hardly anyone left at this time of day. Other than the real hardcore analysts who have no life—that was me once upon a time—and the department heads. I know I walked down this hallway around the timestamp on this security feed."

"Then where'd you go?" Big Earv asked.

"And where'd he go?" she asked. "I mean, I see you walking in the front entrance. But no Singletary. It's like he doesn't exist."

Big Earv cursed under his breath.

"I'm going to O'Donnell's office right now to figure out what the hell is going on."

"Next floor up and to the right," she said before giving him the office number. "Good luck. And be careful. Something's not right about all this."

Big Earv followed Mallory's directions, hustling up one flight of stairs before reaching the floor and hallway where O'Donnell's office was. Big Earv knocked on the door, but no one answered. He tried several times before a young woman rounded the corner and eyed him closely.

"Can I help you?" she asked.

"I was trying to get in to see Catherine O'Donnell in HR," Big Earv said.

"Oh, she's already gone home for the day," the woman said. "Just left about five minutes ago."

Big Earv thanked her before darting down the stairwell. He exited the building and sprinted back to the parking deck. Once he arrived there, he looked around and noticed Singletary's Porsche was gone.

He dialed Mallory's cell number.

"You find them?" she asked.

"They're both gone," he said. "The door was locked and someone told me they'd left five minutes earlier."

"Well, this has gone from odd to highly suspicious in a hurry," Mallory said.

"What kind of car does O'Donnell drive?"

"I'm not sure, but she's got a designated spot on the ground floor of the parking deck. It's one of the ones closest to the walkway."

Big Earv rushed over to a section with a couple dozen reserved parking spots. He found O'Donnell's name on a placard in front of an empty space.

"She's gone too," he said.

"And all the footage of her leaving CIA headquarters is gone as well," Mallory said. "It's like she didn't want anyone to know who paid her a visit—or that she ever left."

Big Earv sighed and thanked Mallory for her help.

At least he knew who his prime suspect was. And to shut it down, all he had to do was prove it.

CHAPTER
THIRTEEN

PRAGUE, CZECH REPUBLIC

HAWK LOOKED up at the gun barrel aimed at his chest. The customs inspection area that had been relatively quiet just a few moments earlier was buzzing. Many of the people who'd been patiently waiting in line were scrambling to grab their cell phones to document the confrontation. Hawk looked away, hoping to avoid having his image captured. As he did, he felt a weight drop onto him. He glanced at his midsection to see the officer collapsed, knocked out from a solid hit to the head. Then with his hand offered stood Ryder.

"Like you said, we gotta move," Ryder said as he yanked Hawk to his feet.

They spun and sprinted toward the door, eluding several officers who'd just arrived at customs. Within a half-minute, they emerged outside and didn't see an available cab in sight. But Hawk eyed a man getting out of his car and waving at a woman in the opposite direction along the sidewalk. He rushed over to greet her, leaving his car unattended and the driver's side door wide open.

"This is our ride," Hawk said, pointing at the vehicle.

He slid across the hood and scrambled behind the wheel, slamming the door shut behind him. Ryder piled in, sliding into the passenger seat. The engine was already running. Hawk jammed the car into drive and stomped on the accelerator. The car lurched forward and they sped through the airport terminal section before peeling out onto the main highway leading toward the city center.

Hawk's eyes bounced between the road in front of him and the rearview mirror. He only went two miles before exiting onto a surface street and choosing to navigate on a less obvious route. Once he figured out how he wanted to proceed and felt like he'd avoided detection by law enforcement, he turned his attention to Ryder.

"We need to talk," Hawk said. "What the hell were you thinking back there?"

"I can explain," Ryder said.

"I hope so because you almost assured failure for this mission."

"But I did save you from being arrested."

"Something that never would've happened in the first place if you'd just stayed calm."

"You don't understand," Ryder said.

Hawk held out an open palm.

"By all means, explain yourself. The floor is yours."

"I saw a customs agent there who I recognized," Ryder said.

"And that's part of this business," Hawk said. "We sometimes run into people we've seen on other missions. But the chances of that happening are incredibly low—and the way you avoid making a scene like you just did back there is to carry on like you don't recognize the person. You make them think they're the crazy ones for thinking you're the same person as someone else."

"What if they don't believe in coincidences?"

"Most people don't, but if you don't act like you recognize them, they'll start to question if their mind is just playing tricks on them. Most of the time you can get out of it."

"But what about the time when you can't get out of it? What about those times where the person is just dead set on the fact that you're that guy?"

"Those are tough," Hawk said. "Running for your life is almost always a last resort."

"Well, it worked, didn't it?"

"It did, but again, you could've gotten me thrown in jail or worse. And Brock Hanson wouldn't have a chance to survive. Such a decision would almost single-handedly result in his eventual death, one way or another."

"I'm sorry, but you probably would've run too if you'd seen the kinds of things that guy does to people he doesn't like. And I can promise you that he doesn't like me."

"What'd you do to engender such hatred?"

"I shot his little brother."

Hawk winced.

"That is serious."

"Yeah," Ryder said. "And one time, I saw him collapse a man's wind pipe by simply squeezing his neck. It was brutal."

"And where did you meet this guy?" Hawk asked.

Ryder shook his head, biting his lip.

"There's still a lot you don't know about me," Ryder said. "A lot that's not in my files—nor will it ever be."

Hawk returned his attention to the road, wondering if he really wanted to know the truth about his partner.

"You want to share?" Hawk said as he made a sharp turn.

"Maybe some other time," Ryder said. "I just want to make sure Brock Hanson gets home safely."

Hawk glanced at the address that had been forwarded to him by Alex. According to the GPS app on Hawk's phone, he was only three blocks away from Hanson's location. But the surface streets were littered with blockades and detours, construction equipment crowding into the roadway and making maneuvering quickly almost impossible.

A siren wailed in the distance, putting Hawk on edge.

"It's a big city," Ryder said. "I doubt they know where we are."

"Unless this car has a tracking device on it."

Ryder ran his hand across the dashboard, the leather cracking in several spots and revealing a yellow foam cushion behind it.

"There's not even a display screen in this car," he said. "I doubt there's a GPS in here. And the man had his phone with him. I doubt they're going to be able to hunt us down before we get to Hanson."

"We're going to have to think about an alternative route out of the country. We certainly can't just walk back into that airport, especially after what just happened."

Ryder shrugged.

"Why not? Who would think anyone who'd just been chased out of customs would have the gall to go right back to where they started?"

"They'll have our passports flagged," Hawk said. "We'd be arrested within minutes, and most likely Hanson with us. And it'd take us at least a day to get new passports."

"So, what do you recommend?"

"We drive to Germany and fly out of Dresden."

"And you don't think they won't try to set up some blockades along the border?"

"I doubt it," Hawk said. "It's not like we murdered anyone and we're on some crazy killing spree. They'll hunt for us for a few more hours before they throw in the towel. We just need to avoid any law enforcement for a few more hours."

"So, don't make any more scenes?" Ryder asked.

Hawk glared at his young protégé.

"I hope you're enjoying pushing my buttons."

Ryder chuckled and shook his head.

"It was an honest question," he said. "You never know what we might need to do to escape. I just want to know what options we have."

"Well, anything that attracts attention is off limits. Clear enough for you?"

"Crystal," Ryder said with the hint of a faint smile.

"You better not be messing with me," Hawk said, shaking a stern finger.

"Of course not," Ryder said. "I'd never do that to you."

Hawk arched an eyebrow.

"Never?"

"Okay, maybe *almost* never."

Hawk continued to navigate the labyrinth created by construction until they reached the townhome where Hanson lived. They parked on the street and hurried up to the front porch.

Hawk rapped on the door several times before he heard the faint sound of footsteps coming from the other side. A few seconds later, the door opened just a crack, but it was wide enough for Hawk to identify Brock Hanson as the man standing behind the door.

"Can I help you, gentlemen?" Hanson asked in Czech.

"We're actually here to help you," Hawk responded in English.

Hanson scowled.

"Here to help me? What on earth for?" he asked.

"Let me back up," Hawk said before introducing himself and Ryder.

"And I'm just supposed to believe you?" Hanson asked.

Hawk reviewed a few details of Hanson's life that only someone with access to his CIA file would know. Hanson paused for a moment, still unsure if he trusted Hawk.

"Look, I know this might be difficult to swallow, especially given the fact that you've been working undercover for three years, but there's been a breach at the CIA and your name has just been released," Hawk said. "Someone will kill you very soon."

"I don't care," Hanson said. "I'm not going anywhere with you. I've worked far too long to bring down these bastards."

Hawk glanced over his shoulder before looking back at Hanson.

"Can we come in and talk about this?" Hawk asked.

"Is someone following you?" Hanson asked.

"Not a chance," Ryder said. "But the old man here is a little skittish."

"You mean he's wise and experienced," Hanson corrected.

"I mean, if you want to put it like that—"

"I do," Hanson said, gesturing for them to come inside. "Just be quick about it."

Hawk and Ryder hustled inside before Hanson shut the door behind him.

"I hope you understand that I can't do anything to jeopardize my mission," Hanson said. "I've been cultivating plenty of evidence on Victor Pacheco, the kind that's going to end his little illegal arms ring."

"Pacheco? Little?" Ryder asked.

"You're right," Hanson said. "It's anything but that. I can potentially bring this massive organization to its knees and expose a number of the partners working with him. There's a large gathering in Prague in a few days that's going to help me expose many of those people hiding in the shadows."

"If you stick around," Hawk began, "you won't be around to see it. This isn't worth it. You're too valuable to the agency. You can go on other missions, work as an analyst, transfer to the FBI—but staying here is suicide."

Hanson pursed his lips before drawing in a deep breath.

"I'd rather take my chances," he said.

"Did you know they got to Terry Turner?" Hawk asked, knowing that Hanson and Turner had been long-time friends.

Hanson muttered, cursing to himself.

"Are you sure?" he asked. "Terry was so good about making sure nobody knew where he was. He was a master at that. It took me forever to find him one year just to wish him a happy birthday."

"Well, he didn't realize he was being targeted by these people until it was too late," Hawk said. "You, on the other hand, have a chance to get out now, a chance to avoid the same kind of fate Terry suffered. But you need to come with us right now."

Hanson grimaced.

"They really got to Terry?"

Ryder nodded.

"It was gruesome, too," he said.

"What'd they do?" Hanson asked, his sorrow mingling with rage.

"We'll tell you all about it on the way," Hawk said.

"You're not going to tell me anything then, because I'm not going anywhere with you. You don't understand. I'm so close."

"I do understand," Hawk said. "I would've hated to leave any of the undercover missions I was on, especially if I was as close as you were to exposing some of the worst illegal arms dealers in the world."

"Thank you," Hanson said. "I'm glad you understand."

"But you're likely to be dead before sunrise if you don't leave with us," Hawk said. "A hacker named Mayhem is releasing names and information to the underworld—and you can bet that everyone is watching. They're going to come straight here and kill you."

"Okay," Hanson said. "Let's say I decide to go with you. If I do, these people will spend an enormous amount of resources to kill me, sparing no expense. And I'll still be dead."

"The agency can protect you."

"Bullshit," Hanson said. "The only way I can protect anyone is to protect myself, make it look like someone got to me first."

"I'm open to whatever ideas you have to make that happen," Hawk said.

Hanson held up an index finger.

"Hold that thought."

He disappeared to the back bedroom and re-emerged from the hallway with a body wrapped in a blue tarp.

"Who's this?" Hawk asked.

"I'll tell you all about it on the way," Hanson said with a wink. "Now, if I'm going to leave with you, I need to leave with you without anyone else knowing I really left. So, we're going to make it look like you killed me. They won't keep looking for me if I'm dead."

Within a few minutes, the house was drenched in gasoline. Hanson lugged a bag over his shoulder, proclaiming that everything he needed was inside it.

Hawk and Ryder walked toward the front stoop and then gestured for Hanson to get in their freshly stolen car.

"Here goes nothing," Hawk said before he struck a match and tossed it into the house. Immediately, flames engulfed the home, the fire lapping at the tops of the drapes before tearing around the house. Thick black smoke billowed high into the night sky.

"We better get the hell outta here," he said.

Hawk and Ryder hustled to the car and drove off without looking back.

CHAPTER
FOURTEEN

WASHINGTON, D.C.

PRESIDENT BULLOCK BOUNCED the tennis ball on the ground twice before tossing it in the air and smashing a serve just long. The ball skipped past the line and clinked against the chain-link fence. He scowled and then held his hands up, as if to ask what happened.

"That ball was out by six inches," said John McEnroe, Bullock's playing partner.

"Six inches? Are you kidding me? It was in by at least twice that," Bullock said. "You're just old and can't get to every ball anymore."

"You're an absolute joke," McEnroe said with a laugh. "I even have an app on my watch that will show you how badly you missed."

McEnroe held it up to show Bullock, but the display screen was barely visible from across the court.

"See," McEnroe said. "It's clearly out."

"You know, you haven't changed one bit," Bullock bellowed.

"I thought you said I was slow and couldn't get to anything these days."

Bullock whacked a ball across the net that nearly hit McEnroe.

"Stop being a smart ass," the president said. "You know what I mean."

"There's a security camera right there," McEnroe said, pointing to a pole with a camera perched atop it. "I'm sure you can get one of your minions to pull the feed from it and we can watch it together."

Bullock growled.

"Fine," he said. "I'll give you the point."

"And the game," McEnroe said. "It's my serve now."

Bullock hit the rest of the balls across the net to McEnroe. The tennis legend then drew his racket back and smashed a serve just off the center line. Bullock waved his racket at the ball as it whooshed past him.

"Out," Bullock called.

"What the hell," McEnroe said. "Do I need to come over there? Do we need to fight right now?"

"What's your watch say now?" Bullock asked.

"It can only tell serves on my side."

"Well, my watch says it was out."

"You don't even have the app," McEnroe said with a snarl.

"I'm the president—and that ball was out."

"Is that how things work in Washington? You just declare it so and people believe you."

"Damn straight," Bullock said with a smirk.

McEnroe looked at his watch and then shook his head.

"Well, would you look at the time?" he said. "Our time is up, Mr. President. Good game."

"Maybe next time I'll let you win two sets."

McEnroe glared at Bullock as they walked to meet at the net.

"Keep this up and I might have to vote for the other guy in the next election."

"And you think he'd let you play tennis at the White House?"

McEnroe shrugged.

"If my donation is big enough. Isn't that how this works?"

Bullock put his index finger to his lips.

"Don't let the cat out of the bag, okay?"

The two men smiled and then shook hands, acting as if there had never been a contentious second between them. Two Secret Service agents escorted McEnroe off the court and they disappeared around the corner.

While Bullock was toweling off, Emma Washburn, his chief of staff, appeared at the edge of the court.

"Sir, it's time for your next appointment," she said. "John Wicker is here."

Bullock flashed a thumbs-up sign as he grabbed the rest of his gear and hustled toward his office.

"How was the tennis?" she asked.

"Oh, you know how Mac is," Bullock said. "I think he just comes over to play so he can yell at me. Not many people can get away with yelling at me to my face."

"Don't think you're anything special, sir," she said with a wink. "John McEnroe is an equal opportunity screamer. He probably yells at his masseuse and mail carrier."

"Wouldn't surprise me one bit," Bullock said.

She handed him a folder about Wicker. As they walked, Bullock scanned the first couple of pages and then snapped the folder shut.

"I know most of this stuff already," he said.

"I figured as much, but I didn't want you to be unprepared in case there was something about his past that you wanted to ask him."

"I've got a list of questions I wrote down," he said. "I just want to see where he's at with all that's going on related to this breach at the CIA and get his opinion on how to fix it—and tell me without everyone else in the room."

"Knowing Wicker, I'm sure he'll relish the opportunity, sir. Good luck."

As they reached the door to his office, she peeled off to the right and disappeared down the hall. He put his shoulder into the door and opened it. Once inside, he scratched down a few more questions that had come to him after reviewing Wicker's file and waited for him to be brought into the room. A couple of minutes later, Wicker was escorted in by a White House staffer.

"So good to see you," Bullock said as he offered his hand to Wicker.

"Likewise."

The two men pumped hands before they sat down opposite one another on small couches in a cozy sitting area in the corner of the office.

"So, what'd you want to talk about, Mr. President?" Wicker asked. "Your note made it sound like this was a little urgent."

Bullock clasped his hands together, resting them in his lap.

"I think that was a safe assumption, though I wouldn't characterize this meeting as critical in nature," he said. "I just wanted to get your unabated opinion on the CIA leak. I feel like it can be tough to go against the grain when it comes to issues like this, and there was something in me that told me you had more to say. Was I reading you correctly there?"

"More questions, perhaps, than anything else. I just can't figure out how the CIA doesn't have a better system to preserve the integrity of its documents. At the end of the day, the truth is contained in the agency's papers, not in news reports or recollection from other employees. What's written down in those reports constitutes the heart of what happened in every agency operation. And those reports are mingled with personnel records that seem easily accessible by anyone. It just doesn't make sense to me how they couldn't already determine who was stealing the files and hold them accountable. Boggles my mind, to be honest."

"Based on what I've heard, Besserman has undergone an extensive search for whoever is responsible for the breach, and so far he hasn't been able to winnow the list down to just a couple of people. But they're getting closer."

"How close?"

"Besserman didn't say, but I have to believe they're honing the small group of suspects to a manageable list. But I know you have experience in this sort of thing as the head of Naval intelligence. So, I wanted to hear how you'd handle a situation like this."

"I'd be looking at every possible angle, including any possible linkage between the CIA officers who were being burned. And then I'd also set up a new system in place for who gets to access personnel info. From that, if the leakage stopped, I'd be able to re-examine the employees who'd visited the CIA's hard copy archives and figure out the likeliest suspects."

"Sounds like an interesting approach."

"Look, I don't want to tell Besserman how to do his job, but I feel like some gentle guidance might be necessary in this case. Conducting an investigation to pluck a mole out of the general population is far different than managing the day-to-day operations conducted by the world's best espionage organization. He's great at the latter, but the former requires perhaps more experience than he's got."

"Sounds like you're just the guy to help suss this mole out," Bullock said. "Would you mind giving Besserman a call and offering your help? I think if you two worked together, that might be something that puts an end to this sooner rather than later."

"Of course," Wicker said. "I don't mind offering my ideas or any other expertise I can pass along."

"Excellent," Bullock said, offering his hand again. "This is going to be most helpful."

The two men shook again before Wicker exited the room.

———

ONCE WICKER REACHED his car, he dialed Besserman's private cell number.

"John," Besserman said upon answering, "to what do I owe this pleasure?"

"I just left the White House after meeting with the president, and he suggested I give you a call."

"Is this about the leak?" Besserman asked.

"Don't ever let anyone tell you that your sense of premonition is dull."

"Putting two and two together isn't that hard, John. So, what's going on?"

Wicker proceeded to recount his conversation with the president and then asked Besserman if he'd like any help.

"I'll take all the help we can get at the moment," Besserman said. "Sometimes I can get so myopic while trying to solve these types of issues, so it's always good to get a fresh set of eyes on the problem."

"Outstanding," Wicker said. "I'll send over some of my thoughts and we can regroup to discuss later, if that's all right with you."

"Of course," Besserman said. "And I truly do appreciate your willingness to help."

"Any time," Wicker said through gritted teeth.

After Wicker hung up, he sighed and eased out into traffic.

I'm not sure I really want to help Bobby.

CHAPTER
FIFTEEN

LANGLEY, VIRGINIA

ROBERT BESSERMAN HAD BARELY SAT DOWN and taken the first sip of his coffee the next morning before Mallory Kauffman requested to meet with him. While he wanted to get his bearings first, she claimed the reason for their meeting was urgent and related to the leak—and he wanted to hear immediately whatever it was that she had to say. He'd welcomed help from John Wicker at the NSA, but it made Besserman uneasy, wondering if President Bullock was preparing to fire him. Or was he just being paranoid? Besserman had been in Washington long enough to know blindsides were only inevitable if he didn't expect them to be lurking around every corner of his career. And he trusted no one. Not Bullock. And especially not Wicker.

Five minutes later, Mallory strode into his office lugging a stack of documents. He groaned as he looked at the mountain of paper.

"Don't look so down," she said. "I've actually got some good news for you."

"Now that would be a welcome change."

Mallory dropped the folders onto his desk, landing with a solid thump.

"Is this related to the suggestion I gave you last night?" he asked.

"The one from Wicker?"

He sighed.

"Yes, the one from Wicker."

She chuckled and punched him playfully in the arm.

"Look, your job as director isn't to necessarily come up with all the good ideas. It's to figure out how to implement them in a way that produces results. Anybody could've recommended what Wicker said. And if you don't want him getting all the credit, just tell the president that this was already in the works before Wicker suggested it."

"You mean, lie to the president?"

"*Lie* is such a harsh word," she said. "I prefer something like *a re-telling of the truth*."

"That's saying exactly the same thing."

She cocked her head to one side.

"This is Washington. Everyone in this city is *re-telling the truth* on a daily basis. It's why the country doesn't trust anything that happens here."

"And that's also why I'm not about to contribute to this debased culture."

"Debased? This is just politics."

"Shouldn't someone stand up to it? Would you rather me perpetrate it?"

"Trying to fight it is like flying a kite in a hurricane," she said. "The idea sounds great until you try to execute it. One minute you're smiling as your kite launches; the next you're holding on for dear life as you get caught up in a funnel that will destroy anyone who dares to defy it."

"Mallory, at some point, you have to operate with some integrity. Otherwise, you're just contributing to the problem."

"Suit yourself," she said. "But when Bullock uses that against you, don't say I didn't warn you."

"I'll take my chances and let my record speak for itself."

"Well, let's make sure your record doesn't give him any excuse to let you go," she said. "Because I'm not sure I could do this job with anyone else sitting in your chair."

Besserman clapped and rubbed his hands together.

"So, let's see it."

Mallory spread open one of the folders and turned it around so Besserman could see it.

"What am I looking at?" he asked.

"After you gave me Wicker's suggestion, I started to expand my search for commonalities," she said. "And I took it much farther than anything he suggested. I found four different people who accessed the archive files that contained the personnel information related to the burned agents, each three days before the names were released."

"But what good does that do, unless you can link them all together?" he asked.

"I'm still working on that, but it seems like there's something there. However, there are also some other interesting anomalies, one in particular that I feel needs to be addressed ASAP."

Besserman took a long sip of his coffee as he gestured for her to continue.

"I've got a new suspect, one that's materialized out of the blue," she said.

"Someone who wasn't on our radar before?"

She shook her head.

"And not someone you would imagine either because this person isn't even trained in spy craft."

He raised an eyebrow.

"Who is it?"

"Catherine O'Donnell."

"Catherine O'Donnell? The head of HR, Catherine O'Donnell?"

"That's the one."

"How the hell did she become a suspect?" he asked, his eyes widening.

"The Magnum Group has been investigating a number of suspects. One of those is Andrew Singletary, a lower-level State Department employee who has some rather odd coincidences, to say the least, when it comes to working with people suspected of being a part of The Alliance."

"Like who?"

"Jun Fang and Nigel Ackerman, for starters."

"Have we looked in to who else he's spoken with?"

"Like I said, the Magnum Group is the one investigating him. They're taking the lead on this, but Big Earv brought me in on this yesterday when Singletary paid a visit to Langley. And more specifically, paid a visit to Catherine O'Donnell."

"What business could he possibly have with her?" he asked. "Is he applying for a job here?"

"That was the only plausible reason I could come up with for him to visit her. So, I did a little digging through potential personnel files."

"And?"

"Nothing," she said, slapping the desktop for emphasis. "He hasn't submitted an application, which would be a record I'd easily have access to. Catherine sends me names of potential candidates all the time for administrative-type positions so I can vet the person for her. She wants me to make sure she's not hiring someone with a hidden identity or anything like that, even though the position wouldn't have access to any sensitive material."

"And Singletary hasn't submitted anything?"

Mallory shook her head.

"Not even a shred of paperwork."

"So, that begs the question: what was he doing here?"

"Even more so when you hear the rest of the story."

Mallory proceeded to relate the story of how Singletary's visit to Langley seemingly disappeared from all the security footage along with his strange behavior leaving the State Department, all in what seemed like an effort to ensure that no one found out he'd ever left his office.

"Is O'Donnell here this morning?" Besserman asked.

"She's always the first one in after you, of course. I stopped by to see her before I even made it to my office."

"And did you confront her about this odd behavior and interaction with Singletary?"

"Not yet," she said.

"What are you waiting on?"

"For starters, I don't want to seem like a crazy lunatic. I can't prove anything even happened yesterday. At least, according to security footage. I think if I said it aloud to her, she'd think I was on something. And I certainly don't want her suggesting that I'm hallucinating, which is something she could say to get me fired or put on administrative leave. She's got to be handled by someone with a lot of experience. Anyone who underestimates her and goes in with both barrels blazing might learn just how powerful of a position she holds. I mean, if she sees a need to get you recommended for a psych eval and it comes back that you're having some problems and it's recommended that you take a leave of absence, she totally has the power to make that happen. And there's nothing you or I can do about it. See why it's a tough predicament?"

"So, we just need to gather more information about the situation before taking action?"

"Exactly," she said. "But that's not all. Before she left, she visited the archives, swiping her access card."

"Let's keep an eye out for when the next name is released by Mayhem," Besserman said. "If it's three days from now, we might be able to form a pattern."

"The interesting thing is the other four employees who all visited the archives and would've been able to access those personnel files three days earlier—none of them were at work yesterday."

"Curious, for sure."

"It could mean nothing, but given all the strange coincidences around this situation, I'm not prone to ignore anything."

Besserman shifted in his seat.

"Is that all?" he asked.

She shook her head.

"There's one more thing I found that I thought was noteworthy."

"And what's that?" Besserman asked as he stood up to stretch his legs.

"There's one other person—an outsider, actually—who visited a day before each one of those names were released. Someone who was even here yesterday."

"That seems strange, for sure. Who is it?"

"You might want to sit down first," Mallory said. "It's the Secretary of State. Madam Secretary Barbara Wheeler."

CHAPTER
SIXTEEN

WASHINGTON, D.C.

THE FOLLOWING MORNING, Morgan May tapped her pen on the conference room table as she waited for the rest of her team to file into the room. She shifted in her chair as she examined an email she'd received from President Bullock's office outlining the importance of uncovering whoever was leaking the names of some of the CIA's most vulnerable officers embedded with high value targets. While Bullock's tone in the note was softened by his cordial approach, he was direct in what he wanted to see happen as well as what he would do if they failed.

She sighed as she re-read the final line of the sentence again: "If your team can't handle the moment, I won't hesitate to rebuild the Magnum Group with a leader and operatives who can."

Based on her conversation with Besserman, Bullock had told the CIA director essentially the same thing. They both understood that in no uncertain terms their jobs were on the line. Although she thought it was unfair given all they had done, she understood. But what she found most challenging was that she and her team were facing an enemy that held the upper hand, almost as if they were cheating in a game of poker, retrieving an endless supply of aces from their sleeve.

Dr. Z shuffled in at last, closing the door behind him and then sitting down next to Morgan. She pushed her chair away from the table and stood, pacing for a few moments before starting the meeting. She clasped her hands behind her back and took a deep breath before starting.

"I'm glad everyone has made it back safely," Morgan said, "but I need everyone to understand that this search for the mole is about to intensify. We've been uniquely positioned to extract some of these officers who've been burned by Mayhem's postings. But we're trying to tackle three problems at once—the source of the leak, Mayhem's regular outing of this damaging information, and the agency operatives who've been endangered by the leaks. And so far, you've all done a good job with the extractions and following up on leads, but I believe we need to attack the one issue that could solve everything—capturing Mayhem."

Mia raised her hand and Morgan nodded at her.

"But would it really solve this problem?" she asked. "What makes you think that whoever the mole is wouldn't just find someone else to keep pushing CIA officer info out onto the dark web? And never mind the fact that Mayhem's never going to talk, even if we do manage to bring him in."

Morgan forced a smile.

"Aren't you just a ray of sunshine this morning, Mia?"

Mia shrugged.

"I just want us all to realize what a difficult task we're facing when you ask us to change course like this. I've only seen Mayhem once—and that was rather serendipitous as opposed to actually seeking him out."

Morgan stopped pacing and put her hands on the back of her chair.

"For now, you're the one who's the key to upending everything," Morgan said as she eyed Mia. "You're the only one who knows Mayhem and might have a chance at getting him to talk."

"That's crazy," she said. "He's never going to say a word. If he goes to prison and doesn't say anything, that's only going to strengthen his brand. The fact that he's so protective of his contacts is exactly why he's the one who's been chosen to out these officers. We're dealing with a mole who understands the foundational principles of operating on the dark web. The better you can keep a secret, the more valuable you are. And Mayhem sits at the top of that list."

"I know," Mia said. "I've heard the stories, like the one about how he used a mother pushing her baby in a stroller to avoid capture during a shootout."

"Except the French tactical team trying to capture Mayhem still shot, killing both the mother and baby before he managed to elude capture," Hawk said.

"That's right," Morgan said. "We're dealing with a psychopath who operates without the trappings of humanity. He does whatever benefits him and him alone. Make no mistake, I'm not under any illusion that he's going to be difficult to find. But while we catch our breath from the task of extracting burned agency officers, I want all of you poring over everything we have about Mayhem. Every little detail, every little idea. No stone unturned until we find this bastard, understand?"

Everyone at the table nodded.

Mia raised her hand again.

"What is it now, Mia?" Morgan asked.

"What do you think Mayhem's going to do once we get him?" Mia asked. "He's not going to give up his sources or tell us where to find the emails on his computer, which, coincidentally, will take days, if not months, to crack."

"Everyone will talk."

"Not Mayhem."

"*Everyone* will talk," Morgan said. "Sometimes you just have to know the right buttons to push in order get them to start talking."

"Mayhem is one of the most mysterious icons of the dark

web," Mia said. "The fact that we even know his handle is nothing short of miraculous. He used to just have a tornado icon where his name would be until someone started using the actual handle of CyberTornado, making him take the Mayhem handle in order to maintain a brand identity."

"Exactly," Morgan said. "That means he's just like everyone else. You can paint him as a monster all you want, but we can connect with him. It just requires patience and digging deep into his past."

"Which is a problem since we don't know much about him."

"But we do know something, which is where we'll start," Morgan said.

Alex, who'd joined the meeting via teleconference, piped up.

"That's my specialty," she said. "I can help with that from here."

Morgan pumped her fist.

"We're gonna do this, people. We're gonna find Mayhem, bring him down, and end the intelligence disaster."

Everyone nodded in determined agreement. Then Dr. Z eased up to the camera, putting his nose a few inches from it.

"Alex," he said in a loud voice, "are you there?"

"I can hear you just fine, Dr. Z," she said. "And see you too. You don't have to get so close to the camera."

"Oh," he said as he took a few steps back. "Did you get my little gift I sent you?"

"I did," she said. "And I appreciate it."

"Good," he said. "I hope you don't ever have to use it, but just in case you do, it's there for you."

She thanked him again before Morgan ended the meeting and spurred on the team to get to work.

CHAPTER
SEVENTEEN

BRIDGER, MONTANA

ALEX SHUFFLED down the hallway toward J.D.'s room at their cabin deeper in the woods. She'd managed to throw on a blouse for the teleconference with the Magnum Group team, but she still wore flannel pajama bottoms and moccasin slippers, her hair twisted up in a messy bun held in place by a pencil. It beat getting up two hours earlier to shower, dress, and crawl through Washington's gridlock while listening to the radio newscaster prattle on about the bad news of the day. Despite her thirst for adventure, raising J.D. was a task she wasn't willing to sacrifice. She'd do what she could to help the team from afar—and today that was digging into the mysterious Mayhem and uncovering a way to make him talk.

The door to J.D.'s room creaked as she opened it.

"Come on, little man," she said, mustering a cheerful voice. "It's time to rise and shine."

In the darkness, the lump draped with covers and bed sheets didn't move.

"J.D., we don't have time to play games this morning," she said. "I need you to get up and get going, okay?"

Nothing.

"*Okay?*" she repeated.

When he didn't move yet again, she flipped on the light and realized he wasn't in his bed. She flipped open the covers, hoping she'd been wrong. But he wasn't there.

Alex darted from room to room, calling out for him, her pulse quickening with each passing second.

"This isn't funny, J.D.," she said. "Where are you?"

She froze and strained to hear something, anything.

But nothing.

Alex cursed under her breath before she sprinted outside, stopping abruptly on the front porch. She scanned the property, the early-morning fog still blanketing the ground, the fresh mountain air tinged with the faint smell from the nearby dairy farm wafting on the gentle breeze.

"J.D." she shouted, "are you out here?"

She paused and listened for his response, praying he would call back to her. But still, not a peep.

Alex hurdled the railing and raced toward the cramped barn, wondering the whole way if her heart might burst in her chest.

Not J.D. Do whatever you want to me, but don't mess with my little boy.

She yanked back on the barn door and called J.D.'s name again, hustling to the back of the structure that opened into the sloping pasture with rolling hills. She didn't see him and collapsed to the ground, wondering if all her breath had been sucked out of her lungs. Then she felt a hand on her back, a small and gentle hand.

"Mom, are you all right?" J.D. asked.

Her breath hitched as she looked over her shoulder to see J.D. standing next to her with a fistful of hay in one hand.

"Since Dad's gone, I thought I'd help out by feeding the horses this morning," he said. "What's wrong?"

Alex turned back around and wiped the tears from the corner of her eyes, taking a deep breath before looking back at J.D. again.

"Come here," she said as she held her arms out.

He walked over to her.

"What? Did I do something? I promise I'll clean my room after I finish feeding the horses."

Alex wrapped her arms around him, pulling him down into her lap. She squeezed him tightly, nestling the side of her face against his.

"You didn't do anything wrong, sweetie," she said. "I was just worried something had happened to you after you didn't answer me. But, look at you, out here helping around with the family chores."

"You always work hard, so I thought I could help somehow."

"Well, I appreciate it," she said before kissing the top of his head and nudging him to his feet. "But once you finish this, I need you to pack a bag. You're going to stay with your Uncle Victor and Aunt Gertie for a few days."

J.D.'s shoulders dropped.

"Do I have to?" he whined. "You know I hate going over there with all those cats."

"I get it," she said. "But I need you to help me out, okay? Just like feeding the horses is helpful, so is obeying without complaining. Understand?"

"Yes, ma'am," he said before trudging back to the feeding trough.

Alex hopped to her feet, dusted the dirt off her pajama pants, and hustled back inside. Once she got to the kitchen, she sat on a stool at the bar, closed her eyes, and let out a sigh of relief. Those few minutes had been terrifying as she let her mind run rampant with the absolute worst case scenarios, something she'd been trained against doing when she was with the agency many moons ago. But when it came to being a mother, things were different. She had a much harder time falling back on her training rather than unleashing her mama bear.

An hour later after she'd successfully delivered J.D. to her aunt and uncle, Alex returned home and began delving into the scant details she had on the life of Mayhem. For years, the intelligence community had tried to unearth Mayhem's identity, pouring an inordinate amount of resources into the effort. But it had been a near fruitless endeavor—but not an entire waste.

Alex examined one detail she found of interest in Mayhem's posts. He often remarked about how cold it was, even in the summer. If he'd mentioned it was cold in the summer months and warm in the winter months, she would've assumed that he was somewhere in the southern hemisphere like southern Chile or Argentina or maybe even parts of Australia or New Zealand. But he was always talking about how cold it was.

Russia was her first guess, but given the vitriol the Russian government held for Mayhem after he aided Chechen rebels in an attack on the Kremlin five years ago, she doubted he would be bold enough to risk staying there. Mia had once met him at a rave in a nightclub in Germany, recognizing him by a catchphrase he often posted after a successful campaign: "And the party goes on and on and on ..." He'd asked her to dance, and, once she agreed, he uttered the saying and her eyes lit up. Mia managed to get him to open up just a little bit about his life, though that was before she'd been offered a position to work with the Phoenix Foundation and eventually the Magnum Group. She'd kept the conversation light and fun, mostly concerned with having a good time. But he'd let his guard down for a moment and shared with her a few things about his life, a rare glimpse into the hacker known for his reclusiveness. But Mia told Alex that she always wondered why he'd been there that night. He boasted about almost never leaving his house, conducting all his business—business that paid him millions of dollars—from the comforts of his home.

The only thing Mayhem had told Mia was that he had a mother and a twin sister. He had admitted to never knowing his father, who abandoned them not long after they were born.

But Alex leveraged those revelations as a way of helping her zero in on Mayhem's outspoken disdain for living in a cold weather climate. She believed he would remain in such a climate willingly. Something had to pull him there, more or less forcing him to stay. She understood how family could have that magnetic draw, though that wasn't something she'd felt personally in her life for very long. Orphaned as a young girl, Alex didn't have an instinctual pull to a certain area, let alone a person. At least, that was until she married Hawk and later had J.D. She was already surrendering so much of her life to be with J.D., spending any other time she had apart from her husband wishing she could be with him.

As Alex's eyes scanned the screen, something arrested her attention.

You've got to be kidding me. How did I miss this earlier?

While activity on the dark web was anonymous by design, devoid of the identifying marks like IP addresses that are easily tracked on the world wide web, it wasn't impossible—at least, not if you knew something about the person and the types of sites they visited. Alex conducted a search for Mayhem's catchphrase: "And the party goes on and on and on ..." She was able to identify all the sites he visited, including The River, which was only visible through Eve's Garden, a specific browser used only on the dark web.

Then she gasped.

Mayhem was online at that moment. Now she just needed to write something to get him to log off or upload something, anything that would help her identify him elsewhere. If she could get him to log off, she might be able to find out his login credentials on Eve's Garden, which required an email address. From there, she would be able to winnow his potential locations to a manageable number.

Alex sprang into action, keys clacking as she laid out her plan. She texted Mia and got the Magnum Group's chief hacker involved, giving her instructions on how they could catch Mayhem. Minutes later, Alex hammered out a message designed to bait Mayhem into making an identifying move online: "I see you Mayhem. The party won't go on and on and on for much longer now."

Almost immediately he logged off.

Alex pumped her fist and then texted Mia.

Did you get it?

Worked like a charm

A half-hour later, Alex had the name of the town where Mayhem had been operating, a small fishing village on the northeastern coast of Iceland. A few minutes later, Alex had the exact address, cross-referencing a list of residents with single women living with a grown daughter around the same age as Mayhem was estimated to be. There was only one that matched.

Got 'em!

Alex jumped out of her chair and performed a celebratory dance. Of course, there was no guarantee he'd still be there, but at least they had a place to start—and a name. Mayhem was anonymous no longer—Elias Korhonen, a Finnish man aged 35 who had been living in Iceland to help care for his mother Anneli and sister Sophia. A twinge of guilt shot through Alex as she considered how the Magnum Group team would be using a mother ridden with cancer against Mayhem. It felt cruel, yet so was releasing the kind of information that resulted in the murder of innocent men serving their country. But Mayhem didn't just have blood on his hands; it was three coats thick. Besides, Alex knew Hawk would never hurt Mayhem's mother, at least she hoped he wouldn't have to. The mere threat should be enough to get him to reveal who the mole was—if he even knew the person's identity.

She called Mia and told her to let the team know that she'd be sending over a briefing shortly. Moments later, Alex sat down and compiled all the information she'd gleaned from the operation and sent it to Morgan May and the rest of the Magnum Group team.

It was early afternoon when she finished and Alex was starving. She'd worked straight through lunch, forgetting to eat in her excitement. She fixed herself a sandwich and a cup of tea and prepared to eat when she heard a knock at the front door.

Alex growled as she pushed away from the table and went to answer it. But when she peered through the peep hole, she didn't see anyone. Furrowing her brow, she eased open the door and looked around.

Nothing.

Then a shot rang out and ripped off a chunk of the doorjamb. Alex scrambled inside, locked the door, and hustled downstairs into the basement. She picked up her phone and dialed Hawk's number. Within seconds, the call failed. She tried again. This time, she didn't even have service.

She cursed under her breath and leaned against the wall, closing her eyes and wishing she knew what was happening. Then she heard the stairs creaking as someone walked down them. Alex clutched her gun, her heart racing. Seconds later, the lights went out and she couldn't see anything.

Anything except the two red dots dancing on her chest.

CHAPTER
EIGHTEEN

LINCOLNIA, VIRGINIA

ROBERT BESSERMAN KICKED at a rock along the dirt path leading to Crenshaw's Shooting Range. A raven squawked from its perch atop a light pole before abandoning it after a gunshot echoed through the wooded area. As Besserman neared his designated stall, he saw a blonde woman taking aim at a distant target with a rifle. When she finished, she removed her goggles and muffs and picked up a pair of binoculars to inspect her results more closely. She pumped her fist and started reloading. Before she sighted in her next target, Besserman cleared his throat from a few feet behind her.

"If I didn't know any better, I'd think you were getting ready to assassinate the Russian president on your next trip to Moscow," Besserman said.

She turned around and winked at him.

"Who says I'm not?"

Then she refocused her attention on the target, took a deep breath, and squeezed the trigger. The bullet ripped through the center, eliciting a jubilant "yee haw" out of the woman.

"You can take the woman out of Texas, but you can't take the Texas out of the woman," she said.

"Barbara Wheeler, if people only knew about your immense talents," Besserman said, stopping short.

"Then what, Bobby?" she asked. "Would they be more afraid of me than they already are? Because I can name about six senators who will shit their pants when they see me coming."

Besserman chuckled.

"And maybe one CIA director, too."

"Now you're just patronizing me," the Secretary of State said with the cluck of her tongue. "Did I ever tell you how much I hate being patronized?"

She didn't wait for an answer before firing another shot that drilled the middle of the target.

"I'll just say it's not something I'm very fond of," she said after turning back around to face Besserman.

She held a solemn gaze for a few seconds before breaking into a broad smile.

"You know I'm just messing with you," she said before placing the rifle back in its case.

"I'm never sure with you, which is why you scare the hell outta me sometimes," he said.

"Whenever there's a fear that you might act unhinged, people tend to take you more seriously," she said. "If you're predictable, people only take you seriously when you signal that you're serious. I like to keep 'em guessing."

Besserman gestured toward the inside of her stall.

"Mind if I fire off a few rounds?" he asked.

"Be my guest," she said as she stepped back. "But only if you want to place a little wager."

Besserman scowled.

"Now, Barb, I don't want to take your money."

"Trust me, I've seen you shoot," she said. "The only way you'll be taking my money is if you turn that gun on me and put a few bullets in my head and then run off with my wallet. Fifty bucks sound good?"

"Okay, if you insist."

"Let's go for the target about thirty meters away."

"Fair enough," Besserman said before he sighted in the target and pulled the trigger.

His first shot whistled just slightly off the bullseye. His second one hit dead center. Satisfied, he eased back and indicated toward the stall.

"It's always age before beauty, so you're naturally up after me," he said.

"Oh, Bobby, always the charmer. I've gotta keep my eye on you."

"You don't have to worry about me. I don't want to end up like your first husband. I'm happy to flatter you as a friend."

Barbara rolled up her sleeves and then fired two more shots. When she was finished, she made sure the chamber was empty before inviting Besserman to join her to inspect their shooting. As they drew nearer, Besserman scowled.

"What is it?" Barb asked.

"Oh, nothing. I just—" he paused, letting his words hang.

"Just *what*?" she asked. "If you've got something to say, let it out. Once you open your mouth, commit to the thought."

"Fine. You asked for it. I just thought that you were a better shot than that."

"Than what?"

Besserman eased closer to the target.

"Than not hitting the target twice. Maybe I was making you nervous."

She drew back and grinned.

"For starters, you don't make me nervous, Bobby. But I'm starting to think we need to get your prescription checked for those contacts you're wearing if you think I missed twice."

Besserman squinted and eyed the target closely again. He still didn't see anything that made him change his mind.

"Maybe I do because all I can see are my two shots."

"Look again," she said as she knelt next to the target.

He bent over and leaned in closer. He threw his hands up in the air as he stood up and took a few steps back.

"I give up," he said. "Point them out to me."

She rested her finger just below his shot in the bullseye.

"Yes," he said. "That's my shot. I already saw that."

"And mine, too," she said.

She proceeded to show him how the hole was larger than one a single bullet would make. He turned red-faced, half from embarrassment, half from realizing she'd bested him again in a shooting competition, something she'd done more than a dozen times. Every time he knew he should resist her constant baiting, but he never could. It was almost as if she put him under a trance. But it didn't take much.

Barbara's blue eyes, golden locks, and glamorous looks had every magazine editor salivating over being the first to have Washington's most powerful woman on their front cover. She spoke openly and often about how she hated being considered a celebrity, insisting that she was simply a public servant and didn't want people to see her any other way. Her attitude toward the attention was akin to dumping kerosene on a raging fire, only leading to more attention. After a while, she just accepted the fact that people were going to adore her no matter what and went about her business.

They both marched back to the stall, waiting until they arrived before speaking.

"So, Barb, I know you didn't just call me out here to the middle of nowhere just to win fifty dollars off me," he said as he fished the bills out of his wallet.

"Keep your money," she said, shoving it back toward him. "You know I don't need it."

"Sure, but a bet's a bet."

She snatched it out of his hand and shoved it into her pocket.

"Whatever," she said. "I don't have time to stand here and listen to you moan about this. But you're right, I didn't call you out here just to take money from you. That's always a given if we're shooting. However, I did have a more important reason."

"I'm all yours."

She rolled her eyes and smiled coyly.

"You wish. Now, here's what I wanted to talk about, and it's something I didn't want to say aloud at the State Department building. And Lord knows you've got your own problems keeping secrets at Langley. So, I thought it'd best that we come out here and have our own frank discussion without anyone else around."

Besserman glanced around the range. They were alone except for one of the guards from Barbara's private detail standing atop the hill overlooking the range.

"So what is it?" Besserman asked.

"It's Andrew Singletary," she said. "I know that you've had those guys from the Magnum Group looking into him, but I want to suggest that you investigate him a little harder, maybe even bring him in for some informal questioning."

"Why all this suspicion all of a sudden?"

"I've been monitoring him for a while, but his behavior has been a little odd, to say the least," she said. "One of his co-workers reported that Singletary asked her to swipe his security card when she left for the day and drop it off at his apartment later. That didn't sit well with me, so I've been watching him. Would you believe that yesterday he left his phone and his security card before driving to Langley. Went straight to your HR director's office, Catherine O'Donnell, before they snuck out together a half-hour later."

"We had someone watching him yesterday and noted all the things you just mentioned," he said. "Anything else give you reason to suspect him?"

"He also made a large deposit into an offshore bank account

of his we've been watching as well," she said. "To me, that's enough reason to suspect him and bring him in for questioning. But this isn't my world. I just see what you guys do on TV. I love NCIS."

"Well, I'm director of the CIA," Besserman said. "So, we operate very differently than NCIS, but there are some standards that everyone adheres to during an investigation. But we've already spoken with him twice—and he's acted like we're insulting him by suggesting he might be involved in something. So, we're still trying to gather more information. But based on what you're telling us, we definitely need to make him more of a focal point of our investigation."

"Thank you," she said. "That'd make me sleep better at night, if I'm being honest."

"You're one helluva shot, Barb, but you think there's something I can do to make you sleep better at night?"

"Believe it or not, I do."

"We've already got one of our best guys on it," he said. "But I'll make sure he knows to tighten the screws."

She thanked him for coming out to see her before packing up her gun and leaving the range. Besserman utilized the rest of his time, practicing his shot, hoping he'd get another chance to beat Barb, though he knew deep down he'd never beat her.

Then he sat down and questioned himself over why he failed to ask her about why she kept going to the agency headquarters. Was she really following Singletary all those times? Or was he a convenient excuse for her? Maybe even an excuse she manufactured? How could he know if anything she was telling him was true?

Besserman didn't wait until he was back at his car to call Big Earv.

"What is it?" Big Earv asked as he answered the phone.

"I need you to stop all your other investigations," Besserman said. "We need to either prove that Singletary is our guy—or we need to find another one fast. And one more thing?"

"What is it?"

"Let me know if you see Barbara Wheeler hanging around Langley again?"

CHAPTER
NINETEEN

WASHINGTON, D.C.

HAWK PUSHED AWAY from the conference room table, announcing that he needed a break to stretch his legs. But in reality, it was more his brain that needed a break than anything else. He was more than happy to help the team sift through files to look for anomalies and clues that could help them plug the leak at the CIA, but he could only take so much desk work. The sunshine and the outdoors were calling. The Magnum Group's new Washington office was located just a block away from the Constitution Gardens, which he decided was the perfect place to get some fresh air.

Hawk stuffed his phone into his pocket and put a shoulder into the front door, exiting the Magnum Group's discreet building. There was no signage on the glass door that led to a series of second-floor suites that created comfortable yet tight quarters for the organization. What they lost in floor space, they made up for in camaraderie. However, almost everyone acknowledged that hearing something explode or catch fire in Dr. Z's lab every few minutes might not be the most conducive to fostering a productive work environment.

For the next few minutes, Hawk ambled along the sidewalk before crossing a few streets to reach the gardens. He drank in the fresh air mixed with diesel exhaust and rotting garbage from the restaurant's dumpster located on the adjacent corner. It wasn't mountain air, but he would manage as long as he was outside. The thought of home triggered his desire to talk with Alex and congratulate her on sleuthing skills. Identifying Mayhem was a big deal, but if Hawk could capture him, it'd be a big enough win to maybe even offset the loss of two stellar CIA officers. He wasn't sure the media would view it that way, but if a good journalist interviewed anyone in the intelligence community, that's the story that would be propagated. And Hawk's pride swelled, not just because it was his team that uncovered Mayhem's identity, but mostly it was because the woman who did was his wife.

Hawk fished his phone out of his pocket and dialed Alex's number. The phone rang five times before going to voicemail. He shrugged it off, thinking maybe she was out riding horses or eating lunch. After a short trip around the pond, he stopped to look at the memorial remembering all the signers of the U.S. Constitution.

What would you guys think if you were here today?

With the growth of a nation—and a couple of centuries later —the United States of America had transformed drastically. And Hawk wished he could invite the founders to the present to see if this was the country they'd dreamed of. Whether Hawk liked how it was or wished it would change, it wouldn't matter if he couldn't keep the country's innocent civilians safe from both terrorist masterminds and covert takeovers. Lately, it seemed like the latter were having their way with the U.S., adroitly navigating the cultural and political roadblocks to successfully claim positions of prominence and influence. The Alliance certainly seemed to be a big part of that, both in the shadows and in the open. For years, the organization had avoided the limelight, but Jun Fang didn't seem to care if anyone knew who he was or not. He'd become bold in speaking out about initiatives he viewed as important to his organization, even if everyone thought he was simply talking about JF Dynamics. But Hawk knew what Fang was really talking about when he talked about reshaping the way the world did business—and it wasn't some altruistic crusade he was on. Fang, with The Alliance's help, wanted to dominate the world.

After Hawk finished his walk, he marched back to the Magnum Group headquarters. And on his way, he dialed Alex's number again. This time, it went straight to voicemail. He then sent her a quick text message.

Where are you? I wanted to catch up and hear all about how you managed to find Mayhem, as well as hear about how little J.D. is doing.

Under most circumstances, she would respond right away. And if truth to be told, Hawk knew she would've called him back the first chance she had once she listened to his message. But a half-hour had passed since he placed his first call to her and still nothing. To soothe his conscience, Hawk rattled off a half-dozen ideas as to why he still hadn't heard from her. She was at the cabin, so maybe the service wasn't any good. *She was riding horses in the mountains. She was fishing at the pond at the bottom of their property. She'd gone to pick up J.D. from school.*

The list was endless. But it didn't fully explain away why she hadn't called him—especially since he didn't know what she was doing and if the excuse was a valid one. Instead, he just tried to push it out of his mind and think about their next steps, which appeared more and more likely that it would require a trip to Iceland to confront Mayhem in person. Unknown entities like a reclusive hacker certainly made Hawk feel uneasy. But he decided to dwell on that as opposed to his missing wife.

Before Hawk returned to the office, he stopped outside and

called Alex's uncle, Victor, to find out if he'd possibly contacted her.

"Hey, Brady," Victor said. "I wasn't expecting to hear from you today."

"Well, I'm just full of surprises."

"You sure are. What can I do you for?"

"I was wondering if you've heard from Alex in the past hour or so. I can't seem to reach her and I'm a little concerned."

"Oh, I'm sure she's fine. You know she's more than capable of taking care of herself."

"Of course, I just—well, I was just kind of missing her today and wanted to check in and see how she was doing."

"Everything's going swimmingly, as far as I know. She dropped off little J.D. early this morning and told me she was going back to the cabin to work. He's with me and is doing fine. Now, have you tried calling her up there?"

"I have, but you know how the reception is along that part of the mountain."

"Oh, I know," Victor said. "Getting a solid signal up there is about as easy as trying to get two Nigerian Dwarf Goats to mate."

Hawk stifled a laugh.

"I imagine that must be difficult, even though that's something I've never actually attempted," he said.

"You ought to try and keep them from foraging a hillside," Victor said. "That might be an even bigger challenge. Either way, you end up with a mess—either a mess of goats or a mess of a hillside. But hang in there. I'm sure you'll hear from Alex soon enough."

Hawk thanked Victor but warned him to be careful before ending the call. The crazy rancher's assurances that everything was going to be okay did absolutely nothing to calm Hawk's growing anxiety.

At least little J.D. is all right.

Hawk returned to the office and asked if anyone had heard from Alex. When nobody affirmed that they had, he tried calling her again. Still no response. No answer. No text. Not a thing.

Hawk entered Morgan May's office at the end of the hall, closing the door behind him.

"Is everything all right, Hawk?" she asked, lines creasing her forehead.

"Not really," he confessed. "I haven't heard from Alex since she told us all about her discovery of Mayhem's whereabouts. And it's really starting to worry me."

"I'm sure she's fine," Morgan said.

"Most of the time, I'd tend to agree with you, but she had some strange things happening to her. And she's at the cabin now, which isn't the safest place in the world if she were to get attacked. It's more where we go when we don't want to be found. But if someone did find her, it could be major trouble."

"Just calm down. Wait until you hear from her before you respond with any drastic measures, okay?"

Hawk nodded, though he didn't agree with her approach. He was tired of waiting, tired of sitting around and doing nothing while Alex might be in grave danger. Out of desperation, he called Mallory Kauffman at the CIA.

"Agent Hawk, so nice to hear from you today," she said. "I already received a message about Alex discovering the identity of Mayhem. Pass along my congrats to her."

"Well, I would if I could find her," he said.

"What do you mean?"

"This isn't a social call. I need your help."

"Sure. Anything for you. What do you need?"

"Can you find out if there are any agency satellites tasked over these coordinates near my home?" Hawk asked before reading off the numbers to her.

"Yeah, give me a second," she said. "Let me see if we've got anything over that part of Montana."

He waited anxiously, hearing nothing but the clicking of her keyboard.

"Okay," she said. "We do have one over that part of Montana."

"Great."

"What are you searching for?"

"Those coordinates I gave you are for a cabin we own in the woods about fifteen miles from our house. I want to know what's out there."

"Hmmm," she said, pausing for a while before saying anything else. "Looks like there's a white truck and then a black SUV parked out front."

"A black SUV?" he asked. "Are you sure?"

"I'll text you a screen shot," she said.

Seconds later, his phone buzzed, depicting exactly what she'd conveyed to him.

Hawk let a few choice words fly before thanking Mallory and then hustling down the hall to Morgan's office.

"Anything new?" she asked as he rushed into her office.

"There's a black SUV parked outside our house," Hawk said. "That can't be good."

"Of course not," Morgan said. "Go. Take Ryder with you, too. And report back as soon as you can."

Hawk announced he was leaving for the airport.

"I think she needs my help," Hawk said. "I'll keep you all updated."

He heard a few people mutter some comments about his paranoia, but he didn't care. It was Alex. And he'd do anything to keep her safe.

Anything.

This was one of those times where he needed to do anything, something. And in this moment, it required him to return to Montana to find her for his own peace of mind—and maybe for their future too.

CHAPTER
TWENTY

WASHINGTON, D.C.

BIG EARV SLUNK DOWN in his seat, his eyes barely able to see over the steering wheel. He was almost certain that Singletary had looked straight at him, though that didn't seem likely since he walked the opposite way after staring in Big Earv's direction. If Singletary had noticed Big Earv, he was almost certain that would've been a confrontation. Singletary would've marched over to the car, reached into the open window, and pulled Big Earv through it—if he was strong enough. And while Singletary maintained a buff physique, dragging Big Earv out of a vehicle required enormous strength. But instead of a fight, Singletary simply spun and headed into the restaurant.

Woodhaven, a new five-star Italian restaurant, had opened just a few months earlier downtown to rave reviews. Fine dining and even finer wine attracted a posh clientele that could pay the eating establishment's exorbitant prices. An eight-ounce fillet cost a couple hundred dollars, while a Caesar salad cost thirty-five. Big Earv knew because he'd tried to eat there once before, only to do an about-face the moment he read the menu prices.

"I can buy groceries for a week at the same prices it cost me to eat here for one meal," he'd mused to himself at the time.

If Singletary hadn't inherited a healthy trust fund, Big Earv would've found it unlikely that a low-level State Department would have the means to eat at a restaurant like Woodhaven. Big Earv removed his binoculars from the console and peered through them, straining to see what he could through the restaurant's large tinted glass window facing the street. Singletary paused for a moment to speak with the woman at the hostess stand, laughing with her before she led him to a back corner booth.

The tables were thick, comprised of what appeared to be dark oak, the backs of the booth soaring six feet high and creating a sense of privacy. And from Big Earv's perspective that was true. He watched Singletary slide into the booth and face the street. He smiled as he grabbed a menu off the table.

Who is he meeting with?

Big Earv was wearing appropriate attire—a long-sleeve oxford shirt with a tie and slacks—but he hadn't anticipated having to get out of his car to see who Singletary was meeting with. Based on the slender build of the hand and arms Big Earv could see, he was confident it was a woman. But was it some random woman? Was it some woman Singletary had met on a dating app? Or was it someone else? Someone he was intimate with? Whoever it was, Singletary was prepared to spare no expense in treating her to dinner.

Or was the woman treating him?

Big Earv hoped he could determine the identity of the woman without taking such drastic measures as entering Woodhaven and potentially getting exposed. But he couldn't just sit there and hope for the best. He needed to take action, chancing his cover being blown. Not that he really had that much to worry about. If Singletary wasn't certain he was being watched by now, he was either extremely naive or an idiot—or possibly both. If it was just a random date, Big Earv could rest easy, set a timer for an hour and catch a quick nap before tailing Singletary to wherever he planned on spending the rest of his evening.

Just as Big Earv decided to get out of his car, he noticed Singletary get up and shuffle over to the other side of the table, sitting adjacent to the woman in the booth.

"At least I know it's not his mom or sister," Big Earv mumbled to himself before shutting his car door.

He adjusted his tie and tugged down on his shirt, hoping the latter would remove the unsightly wrinkles gathering around his upper chest. They only vanished for as long as Big Earv held the material. He shrugged, giving up hopes of looking dapper, which he knew was imperative to getting into Woodhaven.

Once Big Earv entered the restaurant lounge, he strode up to the hostess stand and winked at the young woman clutching a tablet with a diagram of the restaurant and all its tables displayed on it. All the tables were colored red.

Not a good sign.

"How are you doing this evening, Miss?" Big Earv asked, beating the hostess to the question she was trained to ask him.

"Better than I deserve," she said with a wide smile. "What can I help you with?"

"Well, I'm just wondering if you're going to share some of that *better-than-I-deserve* love with me," he said, his eyes brightening.

She dropped her head and sighed, her finger lazily swiping up along the side of the device.

"I'm afraid I don't have any open tables," she said. "Wish I had better news for you."

"And when's your next open table?" he asked.

"I've got one three hours from now if you just have to eat at Woodhaven tonight," she said. "But I imagine if you came in here hungry, you're not gonna want to wait that long. Right?"

"True," he said, his mind whirring how he could get into the restaurant as discreetly as possible to get a peek at Singletary's table. Then an idea came to him.

He tapped the hostess stand, drumming a little beat on it.

"You know, on second thought, why not put my name on the list?" he said. "I told my date we were going to eat here tonight—and that's what we're gonna do."

The hostess looked around with a puzzled look on her face.

"Your date?" she asked.

"Oh, she's still in the car," he said, jerking a thumb over his shoulder. "I told her I'd check and then go back and get her."

"That's mighty chivalrous of you," the hostess said.

Big Earv couldn't tell if she was being sarcastic or not. But he didn't care. All he wanted to do was establish that he was a nice guy before he asked his next question.

"Do you think it'd be all right for me to use the restroom before I go back out there and deliver the disappointing news?" he asked.

"Of course," she said. "It's straight that way."

Big Earv thanked her and entered the dining area, navigating around tables situated out in the open. He glanced over his shoulder to see the hostess watching him closely. She pointed in the opposite direction, mouthing to him what he needed to do.

Big Earv feigned surprise before complying. He hustled into the restroom and found refuge in the stall at the end. He set a timer on his clock and waited three minutes before leaving. When he did, he peered down the corridor and toward the hostess stand where the young woman who'd just steered him to the facilities was engaged in a conversation with what appeared to be a disappointed couple.

Without hesitating, Big Earv seized his opportunity. He darted down the hallway back toward the dining area and started to maneuver around the tables, following a hustling server gliding through potential pitfalls with ease. As he spun around, he stopped right in front of Singletary's table and began to dole out their dishes.

Singletary and his date were positioned with their backs to the rest of the patrons that only one other table could see their faces.

And that table was empty, strangely enough. But as Big Earv moved into a place where he could see who Singletary was with, he saw who it was and seethed.

Big Earv rushed out of the restaurant, flying past the young hostess who called after him that she just had a table come open. He merely offered a dismissive wave as he veered north onto the sidewalk and marched to his car. Immediately, he fished his phone out of his pocket and dialed Morgan May's number.

After they exchanged pleasantries, he addressed the reason for his call.

"I followed Singletary tonight and found him at dinner," he said.

"And who was he with?"

"See, that's the thing. He was with the CIA's HR director Catherine O'Donnell. They were holding hands and gazing into one another's eyes."

"There still could be some impropriety going on between them regarding the agency," Morgan warned.

"Maybe," Big Earv said, "but it just looked like Singletary is having an affair with a married woman."

"Well, that's why we conduct investigations, isn't it?" she asked, not waiting for him to answer before continuing. "I'll let Besserman know so he can deal with that issue as he sees fit. In the meantime, keep following them. You never know where this might lead."

Big Earv ended the call, disappointed that it couldn't just be over and let him move on to something else. But, no, he had to babysit the trust fund kid and watch him indulge all his senses while wasting away his father's money.

There might be a million other things I'd rather be doing tonight than this.

An hour passed before Big Earv saw Singletary exit the restaurant with O'Donnell in tow. They hustled over to his car. He revved his engine and peeled out of the parking spot. Big Earv eased onto the accelerator pedal on his Tesla and didn't take long to catch up to them at a safe distance. A few minutes later, Singletary pulled up to The Hay-Adams, a five-star hotel located two blocks from the White House.

Spare no expense, trust fund kid.

Big Earv watched as they ducked into the hotel five minutes apart to avoid being seen together. But Big Earv knew.

All that was left to do was figure out a way to get into their room and find out if their meeting was about love or state secrets —or a little of both.

CHAPTER
TWENTY-ONE

UNDISCLOSED LOCATION

ALEX WASN'T sure how long she'd been unconscious after she opened her eyes. With no clock in the room and her watch missing from her wrist, she could only guess. Her pounding headache suggested it hadn't been long enough to recuperate from the blow to her head delivered by the gunmen who'd stormed into her cabin. But she couldn't be certain about anything.

The gritty wood floor beneath her shifted as she tried to sit up, her hands cuffed and tethered to the bedpost. She took a deep breath, drawing in the aroma of fresh coffee and strong pine mixed with wet earth. The restrictions placed on her movement prompted her to search for another way to regain her bearings and sit up. Then Alex laid on her back again and tried to use her feet as leverage to get the posts from the solid oak bed frame off the floor and free herself. She was able to push the legs from her side of the bed a couple of inches off the ground. But by the time she tried to slide the handcuffs out from underneath it, the thick legs crashed down again. After three failed attempts, the banging alerted the guards that she was awake. One of them rushed into her room, his weapon drawn.

"I wouldn't advise that if I were you," he said.

"So, if you were me, you'd just be fine with wallowing on the floor in this filthy place?" she asked.

"If I were you, I would've never gotten into this situation in the first place," he said smugly.

"You didn't answer the question."

The man backhanded Alex.

"Shut up," he said. "I'm in charge here, not you. And you'd be better off if you understood your place."

Alex slid her tongue to the corner of her mouth and tasted the blood she suspected was there after the guard's blow.

"You're going to regret doing that," she said as she scowled. "I'm a forgiving person, but not when it comes to beating a restrained woman. I'm going to make you pay."

The man grunted and called her a few nasty names before backhanding her again.

"Know your place," he offered as his parting shot before slamming the door behind him.

A painting rattled and then dropped to the floor due to the heavy force. He stormed back inside and looked at the damage, the frame broken and glass spread across the far corner of the room.

"Look what you did," the man said with a growl.

He marched back over to Alex and backhanded her again.

"Get your licks in now," she said, "because you're going to wish you'd never met me when this is all over with."

"How about I just shoot you now," he said with a toothy grin.

"It's not going to matter," she said. "You're still going to regret touching me. That much I can promise."

He drew back again as if to hit her and then feigned a lunge at her before breaking into a laugh.

"You're just not worth it."

Then he spit at her before exiting the room again.

Alex felt blood rushing to her face, her face throbbing from the pain. She seethed for a moment before calming down and considering her options. After being threatened the way she was, she wanted nothing more than to finish off the guard herself. But without any weapons or ideas about the layout of the house, trying to get revenge on the attack was nothing short of foolish. Based on her cramped quarters, she couldn't imagine the house being all that big. She estimated her room was about ten feet by twelve, barely big enough for her to fit between the side of the bed and the wall. The floor looked like it hadn't been swept in a few years, the 1960s era flower wallpaper faded and curled up around the seams.

A smaller house meant an easier way to make a quick exit—if she could get free of the handcuffs. It also meant having to forego revenge.

Guess you really can't have it all?

Alex studied the window across the room. A set of nearly transparent curtains covered most of it, but she could still see through a small slit that looked like they were deep in the woods. Fir trees and oaks towered over the old house, keeping it dark, even though there appeared to be ample daylight remaining.

Maybe I wasn't out that long—or I was out for over a day.

Alex's missing time remained a mystery to her. But none of it mattered if she remained imprisoned by the men who'd abducted her. However, she tried to remain positive, straining to hear their conversations. What were they planning? Why did they take her?

None of those things were yet clear to Alex, but she knew it wasn't a coincidence, far from a garden variety kidnapping where they held her for ransom. This felt like something more, something premeditated, something sinister.

But what? And why?

Those questions nagged at her as she listened in on their conversation. They discussed rather inane topics, which always baffled Alex. Such casual treatment of an operation was frowned upon by the Magnum Group, any serious operator, really. Instead, these men talked about their lives as if the kidnapping of Alex was just another task on an errand list: go to the grocery store for milk, pick up suit from the cleaners, abduct a woman from a cabin in the woods. The longer they talked, the more annoyed she became. But then she started to notice something she found noteworthy.

Whoever these men were, they all spoke English with the tinge of an accent. Alex deduced that they'd likely been educated in the U.K., probably at a university or prep school. Some of their banter included uniquely western slang. Their faint accent betrayed them, off just enough that she could tell they weren't British-born speakers.

But did that really matter?

Maybe when it came to finding out who the men were and their motive for detaining Alex. But in the grand scheme of things? No, it didn't matter. She wanted to take their manhood from them whether they were Chechen, Saudi, Russian—or even Irish. A wrong had been committed that she intended to make right. Or at least have someone else make right.

As the minutes dripped past, the men seemed uninterested in tending to her, not even asking her if she needed to use the restroom. They seemed resigned to let her wallow in her own pain and discomfort. She yanked again at the handcuffs, more out of frustration than a misplaced belief that she could get free by just pulling hard enough.

While she was doing this, she remembered Dr. Z showing her the trick to getting out of handcuffs. It only worked when they were behind your back and not practically over your head while lying on the ground.

Dr. Z!

She looked at her shoe and smiled. A couple of days earlier, he'd sent her a gift, one of his latest gadgets. It was a simple one, but, at the moment, one she was most grateful for. It was an emergency tracking beacon. According to Dr. Z's instructions, she cut a little slit in the tongue of her shoe and placed the device there. In order to activate it, all she had to do was bang the top of her shoe against something, anything. The bottom of her other shoe would suffice if she could hit it hard enough.

The edge of the beacon dug into the top of her foot as she slammed it against the bed frame. She heard a high-pitched beep, signaling that the device was active.

Come on, Hawk. Now you know where to find me.

Alex dozed off, awakening to the sound of heavy footfalls storming toward her room from down the hall. The door swung open and two men rushed over to her. One of the men freed her from the handcuffs while the other yanked her to her feet.

"Where's Brock Hanson?" one of the men demanded.

"What? Who?" she asked, struggling to regain her bearings.

"Brock Hanson," the man repeated. "We know that your husband helped free him. Where is he?"

"I—I don't know what you're talking about," she stammered.

"Don't play games with us, Missy," one of them said with a growl. "We know you work with your husband, and we've identified him as the one who snuck Brock Hanson out of the country. Now, where's Hanson?"

"I seriously have no idea what you're talking about," she said.

Another backhand to the face.

"Don't make me ask again," he said. "I don't like to beg."

"I wish I could help you, but I can't."

"You can help us," another man with a thick Cockney accent said as he walked into the room. "The question is whether you want to or not."

He worked a toothpick over in his mouth as he drew nearer to Alex, who was now being restrained by two other guards.

"We'd rather not involve little J.D., but we know where he is if it's going to come to this," the man said.

"You leave him out of this," she said.

"Like I said, that's my preference," the man said with a shrug. "But it's up to you whether or not things stay like they are. Now, where's Brock Hanson?"

Alex swallowed hard and closed her eyes, wondering how long she could hold out before Hawk arrived—if he was even coming.

CHAPTER
TWENTY-TWO

WASHINGTON, D.C.

BIG EARV SUCKED his gut in as he stuffed the shirt tail into the pair of pants he grabbed from the employee changing room in the basement of The Hay-Adams. His options were limited, forcing him to wear dress pants that were a little short.

One of the bellboys ambled into the changing area, head down staring at his phone. Then he glanced up briefly to look at Big Earv, stopping to study the gap between his shoes and hem of his pants.

"You shrink, old man?" the teen said, gesturing with his cell phone toward Big Earv's feet.

Big Earv furrowed his brow and then shook his head.

"Actually, I'm just getting ready for a flood," he said, deciding that self-deprecation was a better route than feigning offense.

Big Earv didn't care, except for the fact that he was worried it might make him stand out. After the teen shuffled on to the restroom, Big Earv pulled out his pocket knife and removed the hem, allowing the now ragged bottom of his pants legs to cover his feet. It was still a mess but less noticeable than the three-inch gap that even a disengaged bellboy saw within seconds of entering the room.

As soon as Big Earv looked as good as he was going to get, he entered the lobby and walked over to the front desk. He introduced himself as a new hire and inquired about the man who'd just booked a room a few minutes earlier.

"We're not supposed to ask about the guests," said the clerk, who sported an oval badge with the name Le'Andre etched on it. "If a supervisor hears you doing that—boy, you're gonna be in so much trouble. They're liable to fire your ass right there on the spot."

"Just trying to do my job," Big Earv said.

"And what job is that? Being a little Miss Nosey Pants?"

"That's not it. I just—"

"Look, I don't know where you worked at before, but at The Hay-Adams, we fiercely protect the identities of our customers. That's why we're the only hotel people trust in this city. And why we get so many damn tips. You can't tell me you ain't ever heard that before? Hell, that's why most people want to come work here. That and the five-star service, of course."

"Of course," Big Earv said. "It's also why this hotel can afford to hire the best available workers in the city."

"No, sir," Le'Andre said, wagging his finger. "You get compensated nicely, but the people they hire here understand what it takes to make customers happy."

"That's right. Just like I said, the best of the best."

"Making customers happy doesn't mean you're the best of the best, per se. Making money for your hotel? Now, that's what makes you the best of the best. And that's what I do here all night long. I convince you to upgrade, to pay the extra bucks to indulge the luxury we offer."

"Exactly," Big Earv said. "And part of that luxury is having your gloves delivered to you after they dropped out of your pocket."

He held up a pair of gloves, waving them at Le'Andre. The clerk pursed his lips and then thought for a moment.

"In a situation like this, I always say to myself, 'WWJD'," Le'Andre said.

"What would Jesus do?" Big Earv asked with a puzzled look on his face.

"No, dummy. What would Juan do?"

"Juan?"

"That's right," Le'Andre said. "Juan, the man who trained me. Come on, man, didn't you learn anything in orientation?"

He sighed and shook his head.

"Rookies."

"Can you just give me his room number so I can give him these gloves?" Big Earv asked.

"Only if you promise to split the tip with me."

Big Earv squinted, pretending to think about the offer for a moment.

"What about sixty-forty?" he asked.

"Deal," Le'Andre said with a smile. "It's room 314."

Big Earv decided to take the stairs, avoiding the security cameras as much as possible. A couple of minutes later, he stood outside the room and waited to knock. He heard muted voices coming from inside the room. Leaning closer, he tried to make out some of the conversation.

"You know we're playing with fire," Singletary said.

"You think so?" O'Donnell asked.

"Let me ask you this," he said. "Do you think anyone is on to what we're doing?"

"Other than that investigator guy—or whoever he is—I don't think anybody knows what's going on."

"All it takes is one to blow something like this wide open. I mean, we're just a few blocks away from where Watergate happened, all thanks to a single informant named Deep Throat."

"Don't you think you're being paranoid?" she said. "I mean,

we've taken extreme steps to avoid detection, way more so than President Nixon ever did."

"When you start getting too comfortable, that's when you make a mistake and they catch you."

"Nobody's going to catch us," she said.

Big Earv took a deep breath, contemplating if he wanted to listen in some more or not. Then he wondered if he should knock or simply wave his all-access key card in front of the pad next to the door handle and surprise them. He fingered the card in his pocket for a few seconds before deciding to knock.

After banging on the door three times, he held his breath and listened to their conversation again.

"See," Singletary said in a hushed tone. "I told you. They're probably standing outside the door right now, just waiting to bust in and expose us."

O'Donnell chuckled. "Don't be so ridiculous. Just ignore the knocking and they'll go away."

"What if it's housekeeping?" he asked.

"Then they'll tell you it's housekeeping and you can tell them to get lost," she said.

"And if it's not?"

"Just go see who it is so we can end this little game of speculation."

Big Earv heard footsteps thumping across the floor. He put his head down to avoid being identified by Singletary.

"Who is it?" he asked.

"It's Larry, one of the bellboys," Big Earv said. "Your gloves fell out of your pocket in the lobby."

"I doubt that," Singletary said. "I didn't even wear gloves here."

"I know," Big Earv said. "They were in your pocket. And then they fell out. I mean, if you don't want them, I'll be more than happy to keep them and sell them online. I bet I could get some nice coin for these."

Big Earv heard Singletary whispering something, but it was

unintelligible.

"Just leave them in the hallway and I'll get them later," Singletary said.

"Okay," Big Earv said.

He dropped them in front of the door and then took a few steps down the hallway before plastering himself against the wall and waiting. After a beat, the deadbolt clicked and the door swung open. Singletary eased into the hallway, first looking left and then looking right. By the time he turned to the right side, Big Earv put a shoulder into the State Department employee, pushing into the room.

Big Earv didn't initially see the knife in Singletary's hand but saw in time to avoid a swipe from him. Instinctively, Big Earv grabbed Singletary's wrist and squeezed until he yelped in pain and dropped the blade. Big Earv kicked the weapon aside.

"It's you," Singletary growled.

Big Earv shoved Singletary against the wall and then collected the weapon.

"You got any more of these?" Big Earv asked, pointing toward the knife.

"I'm all out," Singletary said with a sardonic smile. "But you're gonna be hearing from my lawyer."

"If I let you live," Big Earv said.

He grabbed a fistful of Singletary's shirt and forced him across the room. But when he saw O'Donnell on the floor in silky red lingerie, Big Earv released Singletary and sighed.

"So, you two are just having an affair?" Big Earv asked.

Singletary and O'Donnell looked at one another knowingly and then back at Big Earv.

"Yes," Singletary said. "Guilty as charged. Now can you get out of here so two consenting adults can resume this evening's activities?"

"Does your husband consent to this, Catherine?" Big Earv asked.

"Please don't say anything," she pleaded. "What he doesn't

know won't hurt him."

"I'm thinking that's a terrible philosophy for anyone who's working at the agency to have, let alone someone who has access to all of the organization's personnel files. And right now, they're leakier than the hull of the Titanic."

"Please," O'Donnell begged again, "we're not hurting anyone."

Big Earv held up his phone.

"No one's being hurt?" he asked. "I'll bet your husband would beg to differ."

He feigned like he was taking a picture.

"You don't have to do this," she said. "What do you want? I'll give you anything. I swear, there's nothing else going on here."

"Nothing but a little hanky-panky," Big Earv said with the shake of his head. "That's not how this works. You two will have plenty to answer for. But of course, if there's anything else that's going on, this would be tame in comparison. We might be able to handle things discreetly."

"I swear, nothing else is going on," she said.

"She's telling the truth, man," Singletary said.

Big Earv emptied the contents of O'Donnell's briefcase on the desk in the corner. From what he could see, she appeared to be telling the truth.

"It's just an affair," O'Donnell said.

Big Earv eyed her cautiously for a moment.

"It's never *just* an affair," he said.

Big Earv was convinced more than ever that it was *just* an affair. But he didn't want them to think that. They'd be scared to make a move now. And if someone did under the current circumstances, it'd be easy to tell who it was—and confirm that Singletary and O'Donnell were merely engaged in some questionable practices but not an illegal one.

More than anything, it meant that neither one of them were sharing state secrets.

But if they weren't, then who was?

CHAPTER
TWENTY-THREE

RED LODGE, MONTANA

AN HOUR before touching down in Montana on the Magnum Group's private jet, Hawk received a notification on his phone alerting him to Alex's precise location. He quickly instructed the pilot to change their course and land at the Red Lodge airport. It was only a thirty-minute drive from Bridger, but Hawk understood how every minute was precious in his race to retrieve his wife.

He sat back down in his seat, his hands clutching the armrests as the plane banked south.

"You all right?" Ryder asked as he stared at Hawk's hands.

"I will be once I take care of the bastards who took Alex," Hawk said.

Ryder paused, acting as if he was unsure of how to respond.

"Are you sure this is a good idea? I mean, a good idea for you to be on this mission?"

Hawk glared at Ryder, whose lips formed a tight line.

"Would you want to sit out a mission to get your wife back from some random assholes?"

"Well," Ryder said, cocking his head to one side. "They might not be so random. I'm just—"

"Keeping your mouth shut?" Hawk said, interrupting and attempting to keep Ryder from finishing his sentence. "I've got no qualms with rearranging your teeth if you want to lecture me on protocol and procedure."

Ryder put both hands in the air.

"Okay, okay," he said. "You were the one who told me a few days ago to never get emotionally involved in a mission and how that could jeopardize everything."

"Mentoring is a delicate task," Hawk said, speaking through a clenched jaw. "And part of being experienced is understanding when to shirk protocol and when to use instinct. When you're as green as you are, getting a solid grasp of protocol is important so you don't kill yourself. But as you become a more—how should I put this—vintaged operative, trusting your gut is also vital to avoid getting killed. And right now, protocol suggests you should shut your mouth. Got it?"

Ryder nodded and sank back in his seat. Hawk was glad to have the young agent's help, but he had a way of testing his patience.

Once Ryder settled down, Hawk dialed his number for his neighbor, Jack Lacey, and asked for a favor.

"I need you to bring me my truck to the Red Lodge air field—and fill up the back seat with all the rifles and ammo you can find," Hawk said.

"Want to tell me what this is about?" Lacey asked.

"I'd rather not if it's all the same to you," Hawk said.

"Fair enough."

Hawk sent the man instructions for how to get all his weapons and then let out a long breath through puffed cheeks. He was antsy about getting on the ground and rescuing Alex. He often wondered if it wasn't safer for her to be in the thick of the action than holed up on the ranch. Despite all the high-tech security they'd installed, they were always dealing with skilled professionals, not some band of porch pirates. But then there was little J.D.—and Alex had refused to compromise on that point, something he agreed with. He just wished there was another solution. That was a topic for another day. At the moment, he needed to figure out a way to retrieve her safely.

Once the plane landed, Hawk stepped off and immediately spotted Jack Lacey leaning against his truck at the end of the runway. Hawk motioned for Ryder to join him as the two hustled over to the vehicle.

"I think I found every last gun in your barn," Lacey said as he offered his hand.

Hawk and Lacey shook.

"You're the best, Jack," Hawk said.

"Are you sure you're all right?" Lacey asked. "I mean, where's Alex? Is she all right?"

"I hate to do this to you, Jack, but, honestly, the less you know, the better. I've just got a personal matter I need to deal with. Now, can I trust you to keep this between us?"

Lacey glanced at Ryder and studied him for a few seconds before turning his attention back to Hawk.

"I guess so," Lacey said. "You just be safe out there, okay?"

"Always," Hawk said as Lacey dropped the truck keys into Hawk's hand.

Ryder waited until they were in the truck before saying anything.

"You trust that guy?" he asked.

"When you live out here, you have to trust one another," Hawk said. "Small towns and small communities might be the only place you still get that in this country. And as it relates specifically to Lacey, I don't have much of a choice. I've helped him round up his cattle a few times and he seems trustworthy enough, but for all I know, he could've been the one who kidnapped Alex."

"Well, let's go find out," Ryder said. "Is the beacon still transmitting?"

Hawk held out his phone and nodded. Then he pasted the coordinates into his map app as it plotted a course for Alex's location.

Hawk left the airport parking lot and navigated onto a dirt road that wound up a mountain and led them near Cole Creek, a run-off that meandered along the ravine. Tall pines dotted the landscape along with rugged ridges and jagged peaks. Hawk rolled his window down and inhaled the fresh air.

"You don't get that in the city, do you?" Hawk asked.

"What?" Ryder said.

"That fresh air smell," Hawk said, waving it toward his nose. "Go ahead. Drink it in."

"Nothing says home to me like the lingering diesel exhaust on a city bus."

Hawk shook his head and stared out his window.

"You're weird, you know that?" he said.

Ryder chuckled and shook his head.

"Says the man who wants to get lost in the woods and wouldn't care about seeing another human for the rest of his life."

Hawk held up a finger.

"That's not true. Alex and little J.D.—I've got to see them. Everyone else ..."

He paused and turned his attention to the road ahead.

"And you think I'm weird," Ryder said.

Hawk smiled and eased down the hill until killing the engine about five hundred meters before they reached the house, choosing to coast as close as he felt comfortable doing.

Coming to a stop about two hundred meters from the house, Hawk and Ryder got out and organized all their equipment. Then they trekked down a small ridge and followed Cole Creek until they neared the site of the beacon.

Searching for a blind, they found a pair of thickets, one on each side of the creek that faced the house, and bunkered down in them. After they devised a plan for attack, they discussed when to go in.

"I think we should go now," Ryder said.

Hawk chuckled.

"Man, you remind me of myself years ago, throwing caution to the wind."

"And it's obviously worked out for you."

"Not without some good fortune," Hawk said. "You live on the edge and all it takes is one mistake before everything's gone."

"Then what's the voice of experience say?"

"Wait," Hawk said. "Count the number of hostiles so we know what we're facing before we approach."

"I thought you were a good shot," Ryder said.

"I am, but what's that got to do with the price of tea in China?"

"If you're a good shot, you can end this quickly. You start taking people out, and it's over before it started. Look, you're a good shot. And I'm a good shot. We don't need to over think this."

"What you're suggesting is what I consider mindless warfare," Hawk said. "Maybe you played too many video games growing up, but you don't get multiple lives in the real version. Just one bullet and you're dead. Now, I'd prefer to hang back and have a better idea of what we're up against before we advance. Understand?"

"Yeah," Ryder said, his voice suggesting that he didn't necessarily agree with Hawk.

Ten minutes passed before Hawk saw any movement at the house. An armed man marched onto the porch and lit a cigarette, straddling the railing and leaning against one of the support pillars. He tilted his head back and launched a swirling plume of smoke. He stared at the treetops before breaking into a hacking crouch.

"This is gonna be a piece of cake," Ryder said.

"Why? Because he coughed? Because he doesn't think anyone is watching him?"

"I have a hundred reasons I could give you, but it's obvious this guy isn't some elite military commando."

"He could be the tech guy," Hawk said. "There might be three elite guards inside right now."

"Or not. You don't know that."

"Which is why we're waiting until we're sure. Can you see the back of the house from your position?"

"Yeah," Ryder said. "Just another pot-bellied scumbag sucking on a cancer stick, signaling his position to the world. Seriously, this is a joke. We're just wasting our time waiting on them."

"We can't be sure how many people are in the cabin," Hawk said. "Gathering intel is never a waste of time, especially when your life depends on it."

Hawk glared over at Ryder, who was rustling behind the blind. They'd agreed to modify their plan, if necessary, after determining how many hostiles were in the cabin. Hawk was going to approach from the front and Ryder from the back. They estimated four people were sent for the job. They would be able to provide round-the-clock coverage of the prisoner without tiring themselves—at least, that's what Hawk would do in an ideal world. Four six-hour shifts each day. The math was easy, as was the assignment of watching a single prisoner likely bound up in a room.

But Hawk wasn't sure that was the case. Were there more? Maybe less? He needed to know before he charged in like a tornado. What if there were other hostages? All the variables needed to be accounted for. Yet at the center of everything was the possibility that Hawk was maybe being too cautious. Alex was in there and he couldn't chance a mistake.

The man on the porch went inside, the door rattling shut behind him.

"You seen enough?" Ryder asked.

"Not yet," Hawk said. "We need to sit tight."

"Well, I have, damnit."

"Ryder, wait."

But it was too late. Ryder darted out of his blind and headed straight for the cabin, staying low as he ran with his weapon trained in front of him. He slowed as he neared the porch.

Then the door opened and a burly man wearing military fatigues with hiking boots ambled onto the front porch. He worked a small blade against the side of a block of wood as he smiled. Then he heard Ryder. The man stopped his carving and scanned the woods. Before he had a chance to react, Ryder dropped the man with two center mass shots.

The thump of the man's lifeless body hitting the porch drew out another guard. But this time, Ryder missed before the man ducked back inside upon seeing the dead man.

"Damnit, Ryder. What are you doing?" Hawk squawked over the radio.

"I'm saving Alex."

The sound of breaking glass arrested Hawk's attention. Moments later, a rifle muzzle poked through the opening and started firing into the woods.

Hawk cursed under his breath and realized he didn't have the luxury of sitting back any longer. Not if he wanted Alex to survive. Not if he wanted to keep Ryder from succumbing to a similar fate as the carver on the porch.

Hawk crept around toward the back of the cabin, while Ryder took aim at the spot where the gunman was. However, neither of them seemed to have any success, continuing to exchange fire.

By not firing a shot, Hawk had concealed his presence. But he wasn't going to stay in the woods much longer, at least not if he could help it. He figured Alex was in the back of the cabin, likely in one of the back bedrooms.

Seconds later, the screen door on the back porch clattered shut as a man exited the house, struggling to carry Alex with him. With her hands bound in front of her, she fought the man, dragging her feet and then stiffening only to jab him in the ribs with her elbow. In most cases, Hawk would be proud to see Alex giving her captor hell, but now he just wanted her to stay still so he could get off a shot.

After another brief struggle, Alex stood upright, almost as if she heard him. She didn't move for a few seconds, despite violent prodding by the man. He stopped and sighed, shaking his head and muttering something in a foreign language.

This is it.

Hawk took aim at the man and fired a shot, dropping him. He fell face-first into dirt.

Pick up the gun.

Alex looked into the woods and offered a relieved smile. Then, as if she heard him, she knelt to pick up the weapon. But before she could get her hand on it, another man barreled out of the back door and bowled her over, sending her skidding across the ground. She spun on her back and swiped at his legs, but he jumped, avoiding contact. Then he stomped on her ribs.

Hawk saw red and charged, shouting at the man as he flew out of the woods and into the clearing. Caught off guard by the noise, the man stared at Hawk for a second. He didn't hesitate, emptying a magazine into the man before he even collapsed in a heap.

Hawk knelt next to Alex and brushed aside the hair matted to her face, now stained with blood, sweat, and dirt.

"Oh, my God, I thought I lost you," Hawk said. "Are you all right?"

"I've been better," she said with a grimace. "I think he did a number on my ribs."

She winced as she raised the side of her sweater to reveal a bruise that was already turning a shade of purple.

"Bastards," Hawk said as he spat in the direction of Alex's dead captor.

He jammed another magazine into his gun and scanned the woods.

"How many were there?" Hawk asked.

"I don't know," she said. "They all kind of looked the same to me. Meatheads with buzzcuts. Four, maybe five."

The back screen door creaked as it opened. Hawk wheeled around with his weapon in front of him to see Ryder.

"You son of a bitch," Hawk said with a glare. "You almost got Alex killed."

"Sometimes you have to force the action," Ryder said with a shrug. "We could've sat around all day and done nothing."

Hawk set his jaw.

"That's *not* how we do things. Understand?"

Ryder nodded, casually walking down the porch steps to join Hawk and Alex.

"The house is clear," Ryder said. "I got three of them. Looks like you took care of the other guy."

"If you ever try anything like that again—" Hawk said before stopping short as Ryder trained his weapon toward him.

Hawk's eyes widened.

"What are you—"

Before he could finish his sentence, Ryder fired two shots right past Hawk. He spun around to see another man stumbling face-first into the dirt clutching a gun.

"Guess there were five of these assholes," Ryder said.

Hawk thanked Ryder for saving his life, though all he really wanted to do was slug his little protégé. Ryder was proving to be either a slow learner or a stubborn one. Either way, Hawk wasn't looking forward to training him.

They discussed the best way to dispose of the hostage takers, which they decided was to pile their dead bodies into their SUV and shove it off a nearby cliff.

"The wolves will tear them apart before anybody finds them," Hawk said. "I doubt any of our local law enforcement is going to launch a serious investigation into what happened. Just chalk it up as an accident and move on."

"What about your neighbor?" Ryder asked.

"He won't say anything," Hawk said. "If I didn't trust him, I wouldn't have called him in the first place."

After they loaded the bodies into the SUV and rolled it off the cliff, the trio turned their attention back to the bigger issue at hand: Why did these men target Alex?

"They were looking for Brock Hanson," Alex said as they bumped along the washboard dirt road. "Kept saying he was a *tajný špión.*"

"Czechs," Ryder said, leaning forward from the middle of the backseat.

Hawk nodded in agreement and then glanced at Alex.

"They found out Hanson was a spy from the leak. But why kidnap *you?*"

"They knew you took him?" Alex offered. "They must've figured out you extracted Hanson and were trying to figure out a way to lure you to them so they could find out where Hanson was. They probably wanted to kill him, so he must know something pretty damning at this point."

"Hanson said he hadn't really penetrated the highest level of leadership in the crime syndicate he was embedded with," Ryder said. "What could he have possibly known?"

Hawk drove their vehicle through a big puddle that stretched across the road.

"Probably still plenty," he said. "Or it could just be the principle of it. They want to send a message that no one will be allowed to get away with such betrayal."

"We need to talk with him, find out what he knows," Alex said.

"There's only one problem with that," Ryder said. "We won't be able to reach him. He said he was going dark for a while."

Hawk chuckled and shook his head.

"Rookie," he mumbled under his breath. "There are other ways to reach someone, like visiting them in person."

"You know where he's staying?" Alex asked.

"He's in the Florida Keys," Hawk said. "I'll be able to get his address from the agency. But that'll have to wait."

"What could be more pressing than tracking down Hanson and finding out what the hell was going on here?" Alex asked.

"It's Mayhem," Hawk said. "We found him—and we need to pay him a little visit."

CHAPTER
TWENTY-FOUR

WASHINGTON, D.C.

ROBERT BESSERMAN SAT in a small meeting room in the West Wing of the White House and inspected his tie. He noticed a spot tinged with teriyaki sauce from lunch and licked his thumb before trying to rub out the stain. It faded slightly, but it was still there. He doubted anyone would notice, but he did—and it was bothering him.

Is this how it happens?

Besserman drummed his fingers on the table and considered what his life had become. Meeting the president had become so mundane that instead of feeling excited about the prospect, Besserman was mulling over his options for cleaning his tie after returning home later that evening. And he wasn't sure if he was looking forward to that more than meeting with President Bullock and dealing with his imminent tantrum. The thrill of running with the world's most powerful person had devolved into drudgery.

This job isn't about you, Besserman reminded himself.

He refocused, turning over in his mind all the questions he was sure to be asked. And as annoyed as President Bullock was sure to be with the answers he would be given, Besserman was more so. He was frustrated, irritated, and angry all at once. Uncovering the source of a breach in the agency's server was one thing. That kind of attack was expected, especially when it came from an outside source. But this was betrayal, an affront to the thousands of people who worked tirelessly to secure the nation. And any progress he'd made had merely been ruling out suspects. No hunch had been confirmed, simply elevated to a level that required a closer look. Even Singletary, their most promising suspect, appeared to be a dead end.

A few minutes later, a Secret Service agent opened the door and escorted President Bullock inside. He dismissed the agent and then greeted Besserman with a terse handshake before they sat down.

"Coffee?" Bullock said as he nodded toward the small table in the corner with a steaming pot sitting on a hot pad.

"Got anything stiffer?" Besserman said.

"So I take it that you don't have any good news for me?" the president said.

"Unless you consider no news to be good news."

"In this case, absolutely not," Bullock said before he stood and paced the floor. "Do you know what kind of pressure I'm under? What kind of pressure I was dealing with before this breach? I'd like to win a second term and push through some of the ideas I have that will not only make this country safer but make it better. But that's hard to do when the guys in the other party can sling around the accusation that I'm not doing enough to secure our country. Above all else, Americans crave safety. And if I can't give them that, they're going to look elsewhere for leadership."

"I understand, sir."

Besserman proceeded to update Bullock on what had happened, including the disappointment with the promising lead of Singletary, who was doing nothing more than having an affair with the head of the agency's HR department. Bullock growled, continuing to pace. Then a few awkward moments of silence before Bullock slapped his hands against the back of his chair.

"Look, Bobby, you know I like you, right?"

Besserman nodded slowly.

"But this job demands that I put the best in the most critical positions," Bullock said. "I can't have weaknesses or else I look weak. Now, I empathize with your situation on some levels because this wasn't a problem of your own making. You didn't screw up an assignment or miss some major piece of intelligence that cost thousands of innocent Americans their lives. So, please realize I understand what's happened here. But also understand, I'm in the same position. I didn't do anything, yet I'm the one who will get all the blowback if the traitor in our midst isn't caught sooner. I'm the one who will ultimately shoulder the blame for allowing such an intelligence disaster to occur. It's my watch and I will be held accountable. And the people have the power to do so at the ballot box. You, on the other hand, serve at my pleasure."

"Of course, sir," Besserman said. "And know that we're working diligently around the clock to find the person responsible and bring them to justice."

"I know you are, but you must do so with the understanding that my patience is running thin. I'm a man of action—and I'm going to take action if this isn't resolved quickly, the kind of action that will have you packing your things into a box and taking a long walk of shame out of Langley. Can I be any clearer?"

Besserman shook his head.

"I wouldn't expect anything else," he said.

And while Besserman fully understood the nature of serving in such a high-level position, that didn't lessen the sting of Bullock's words. He resumed ranting before telling Besserman that he had three days to produce some actionable results or else a change would be made.

Besserman thanked the president and promised another update soon before marching out of the room.

On the drive back to Langley, Besserman reviewed the facts the Magnum Group team had gathered. And none of them buoyed his hope that they would find the traitor by the deadline Bullock established. He considered announcing internally that an investigation would be conducted and every agency employee was expected to comply. But he concluded that it would only send the traitor underground or into the shadows, ruining their chances of uncovering the person's identity. Man? Woman? Inside the agency? Or a liaison to the agency? Young? Old? Nearly everyone was still a suspect.

It could be the janitor for all we know.

Given the time crunch, Besserman decided that he would go to the Florida Keys to visit Brock Hanson. For as much help as the Magnum Group had given him, he needed them to do the tasks he couldn't. And visiting the mysterious Mayhem was something Brady Hawk was far more equipped to do. But a conversation with Hanson was in his wheelhouse. And he figured sinking his toes in the sand, even if only for a few hours, might be refreshing and ultimately revive the creative juices necessary to come up with more suspects—or ways to catch the ones they had.

Ten minutes out from arriving at the office, Besserman's phone rang with a call from Mia Becker at the Magnum Group.

"Director May asked me to call you directly," Mia said. "She would've passed this along to you herself, but she's busy working on this situation as well."

"Of course," Besserman said. "Now, what do you have for me?"

"While my expertise is more in the hacking, I started reviewing some of the agency's security footage in an effort to speed up the investigation," Mia began. "And I found something a little curious."

"Go on."

"We've been looking for patterns, anything that matches up with the release of the officers' names by Mayhem. And I found something. Almost a week to the day before the names were announced, I found footage of a consistent visitor. I double checked with the visitor logs to make sure I wasn't making something out of nothing."

"And?" Besserman said, his patience growing. "What did you find?"

"There's an NSA analyst who had never once visited Langley," she said. "But she has four times now, and it coincided with the leaks."

"So you think this analyst could be our traitor?" Besserman asked. "Because I'd like to know how an NSA analyst is getting this information."

"We're still working on that," Mia said. "After I told Director May about this, she's decided to move on this, deeming it actionable."

"And who is this analyst?"

"A young woman by the name of Payton Quick."

"Keep me posted," Besserman said before ending the call.

It wasn't much, but it was something. And it was something that might buy him more time with the president, at least until he could learn more about what this breach was really all about.

Besserman had a hunch there was far more to it than he understood at the moment. But he wasn't going to stop until he did—or Bullock relieved him of his duty. And that wasn't an option for Besserman.

CHAPTER
TWENTY-FIVE

BLÖNDUÓS, ICELAND

THE STEERING WHEEL rattled in Hawk's hands as he navigated along the Icelandic Highway 1, a two-lane blacktop ravaged by the effects of frost heaves. Ripples and dips in the asphalt made for an intense drive as the two Magnum Group agents discussed how they were going to capture Mayhem. But after a while, Hawk turned the conversation toward their last mission in Montana.

"Am I gonna have any trouble out of you on this one?" Hawk asked. "Because what you did with Alex—"

He let his words hang in the air while shaking his head subtly. Ryder shifted in his seat, sitting upright as he stared out the window.

"I didn't realize how much danger I'd be putting her in," Ryder admitted. "I just got a little impatient and—"

"Being impatient will kill you out here. You got lucky. We all did, truth be told. You didn't know how many men were in that house. There could've been another half-dozen hiding in the basement or hiding in the woods or at the store. You absolutely cannot do that again—and I'm not just saying this because my wife was caught in the middle of it all. What you did would've pissed me off under any circumstances in any operation."

Ryder nodded slowly.

"I'm sorry, okay? I get it. I won't do it again."

"I mean it," Hawk said, his eyes widening. "You won't get a second chance with me if you try to pull something like that again. Director May thinks you can learn a thing or two from working with me. And it's evident you've got a lot to learn. It's also evident that you've got a knack for this. I just don't want to see you waste it all or—even worse—get killed because you lack the discipline this job demands."

"You sound like my old man," Ryder said.

"I'll take that as a compliment," Hawk said.

"You don't know my old man."

Hawk grunted and shrugged.

"I don't know mine either."

According to the briefing Mia gave them, Mayhem lived on the top of a ridge, giving him a sweeping view of the ocean about two miles away as well as a three-hundred-and-sixty-degree view of the surrounding countryside. Nobody lived within two miles on either side of him and his driveway wound up the ridge, three-quarters of a mile off the highway. Mayhem had found an isolated location, but it was the kind of isolation that made it difficult to surprise him. He had established a fortress that appeared impenetrable for any modest group of hostiles. Hawk turned off Icelandic Highway 1 and onto a smaller highway, this one nothing more than a well-maintained and densely-packed dirt road, according to Mia's description of the area. But at the moment, it was coated in snow. Mayhem held all the advantages and undoubtedly had an escape route. And Hawk sought to identify every single one of them as he neared the long driveway leading to Mayhem's house.

Just five years earlier when Mayhem purchased the single-story home just outside of Blönduós, it didn't meet all of his required living conditions. While the isolation was satisfactory, the infrastructure was not. The small city and surrounding area didn't have the blazing-fast internet speed he needed to launch all his cyberattacks and conduct his covert hacks. However, a generous donation from an anonymous benefactor provided fiber cable for the area. Two years later once it was installed throughout the entire region, Mayhem moved into the house and made it the base of his operations. At least, that's what Mia had concluded based on all the information she'd gathered.

Hawk skidded to a stop near the transformer box located at the corner of Mayhem's property. Hidden by a clump of snow-covered bushes, Hawk almost missed it. But he and Ryder climbed out and wasted no time in killing the power to Mayhem's house. Then Ryder pulled out a battery-powered saw and affixed a pair of goggles to his face. Moments later, he was slicing through the fiber, cutting off Mayhem's ability to connect with the outside world. They'd hoped he might believe the issue with his computer was simply a power outage, at least for a few minutes. That'd give them the opportunity to rush up to the house and capture him. Hawk finished the first stage of their operation by launching a device Dr. Z had created that jammed all cell phone signals for a two-mile radius. Then the agents prepared for their next step.

Driving their SUV rental up the driveway was sure to alarm Mayhem, something Hawk didn't want. A sneak attack would eliminate all of Mayhem's advantages, increasing Hawk and Ryder's odds.

The two agents crouched low as they moved across the snow field, navigating over a handful of small creeks as the property rose to the ridge line. Hawk continued to check the house, stopping every couple hundred meters and using his binoculars to scan for any activity. He didn't see anything except the smoke puffing out of the chimney.

After a twenty-minute slog through the snow, Hawk and Ryder approached the tight perimeter around the house.

"We won't be able to communicate with our coms this time," Hawk reminded Ryder. "That cell tower jammer works on all radio signals too, meaning we'll only be able to talk via gestures. Understand?"

Ryder nodded.

"Ten-four, good buddy."

Before they had a chance to review their plan, a two-cycle engine roared to life. Seconds later, the doors to a barn swung open and a snowmobile exploded into a clearing, sending up a rooster tail of snow in its wake.

Hawk didn't have a chance to say anything to Ryder, who had already turned and was four steps into a sprint toward the barn.

Another snowmobile lurched forward, flying through the air and nearly bowling over Ryder. Based off Mia's briefing, Mayhem famously worked alone. Hawk hadn't considered for even a second that there might be multiple hackers in the house. However, he pushed the thought aside and raced toward the snowmobile, taking an angle to intercept it on foot.

As Hawk drew closer, he dove toward the man on the snowmobile, driving him into the snow. The snowmobile sputtered and scooted down an embankment before coming to a stop a few meters away. Hawk pushed himself off the man before punching him in the face several times until he fell unconscious. Then Hawk pulled the ski mask off the driver's face to make sure it wasn't Mayhem. Hawk didn't recognize him.

"Come on, let's go," said Ryder, who'd already straddled the snowmobile seat and was revving the engine.

Hawk marched through the snow before stopping just short of the vehicle.

"Let me drive," Hawk said.

"I was a go-kart champion when I was fourteen," Ryder said, refusing to budge.

Hawk glared at him.

"This isn't a go-kart. Now move."

Ryder sighed and reluctantly slid back, while Hawk moved to the front. He put the snowmobile in gear and took off after Mayhem.

Mayhem had a decent head start, but Hawk sought to take another angle to close the distance. Mayhem wasn't streaking straight across the ridge, but instead heading slightly northeast. As Hawk surveyed the land below, he drove straight east along the ridge, engine at full throttle.

"What are you doing?" Ryder shouted. "He's over there."

Ryder pointed in the direction of Mayhem.

"We'll never catch him if we go straight after him," Hawk said. "We need to take a different approach."

Hawk looked to the horizon and saw the ridge was set to vanish in a couple hundred meters. That's when Hawk set a course in a northeasterly direction, one wide enough that he'd be able to intercept Mayhem around the edge of the property—if Hawk's rough calculations were correct.

As they drew closer to Mayhem, Hawk wasn't sure they'd be able to overtake him. Once they left Mayhem's property, Hawk would be at a severe disadvantage, unfamiliar with the area. About another mile down the road, a thick patch of trees began and seemed to extend for miles up to the next major ridge.

"If you don't catch him, he's going to get away," Ryder shouted from behind.

"You think I don't already know that?" Hawk fired back.

Forty meters ... thirty meters ... twenty meters. Hawk bore down on Mayhem, his engine sputtering as Hawk edged closer.

Hawk hunched over the handlebars and leaned forward, his eyes focused on Mayhem. But Hawk was so focused on him that he didn't see the ditch fast approaching. And when Mayhem slammed on the brakes, Hawk flew past.

But not Ryder.

Hawk felt the snowmobile lighten and slammed on the brakes. Out of the corner of his eye, Hawk noticed Ryder flying through the air, arms stretched wide. He torpedoed Mayhem, knocking him off his snowmobile and into the powder. Mayhem struggled to get to his feet, his blue and orange stocking cap covered in snow. As he stood upright, he drew a pistol and trained it on Ryder.

However, Hawk had dismounted and was running over to Ryder's aid, standing far enough apart that Mayhem would never have enough time to shoot both of them, no matter how good of a shot he was.

"I think you need to put that down," Hawk said, gesturing for Mayhem to surrender the weapon.

But Mayhem remained defiant.

"I've got you over a barrel right now, and you hate it," Mayhem said. "I've got another suggestion. You walk away and never come back—and I promise not to destroy your lives."

Hawk fired a shot at Mayhem, nicking the orange tassel on the top of his cap.

"The next one is going to be a few inches lower," Hawk said. "I doubt you want that."

Mayhem eased his gun onto the ground.

"Smart move," Hawk said. "Now, come with us. We've got lots to talk about."

CHAPTER
TWENTY-SIX

STIRRUP KEY, FLORIDA

ROBERT Besserman drank in the sunshine as he adjusted his sunglasses, fending off the relentless sunshine reflecting off the turquoise Gulf Coast water. It was hard not to smile and enjoy the nice respite after being stuffed into President Bullock's pressure cooker. Despite all the political wrangling and endless threats from a city notoriously navigated by stepping on necks of others, Besserman still appreciated the opportunity to do what he did. He just had to remind himself of his purpose as the director of the CIA—to keep the country safe from foreign enemies. Though at that moment, Besserman realized that the biggest enemy was likely someone lurking from within.

The captain of the boat eased back on the throttle as they entered the no-wake zone inside the canal of Stirrup Key, a tiny key sitting off the northwest tip of Marathon. After a couple of minutes, the engine fell silent, the boat drifting slowly toward a dock tucked away behind a house hidden in a cove. A Cuban Mahogany swayed in the gentle breeze, which picked up and carried with it the tree's rich scent. Besserman also detected the aroma of a cigar wafting toward him. He looked around the property before glancing up at a man leaning on the stone balustrading, a cigar firmly wedged between his index and middle fingers.

"Director," the man said as he slightly lowered his sunglasses and peered over the top of them.

Besserman gave a lazy wave before climbing out of the boat and onto the dock. He plodded up the steps around the side of the house leading to the veranda and gave a weak smile to Brock Hanson. The two men shook hands before turning and looking back across the water.

"Hell of a view," Hanson said. "I've been to plenty of safe houses, and I haven't found any quite like this one."

"Well, don't get too comfortable. We need all hands on deck back at Langley, but I think you've deserved a little time to decompress after all you've been through."

"Those bastards who did this," Hanson said, clenching his fist and then his jaw, "I swear, I just want five minutes alone with them. It won't make up for the last two years of my life that's just been wasted, but it'll be the consolation I need."

Besserman gestured toward the two lounge chairs facing the water, suggesting they sit down. Both men eased into their seats before Besserman continued the conversation.

"I wouldn't say it's wasted," he said. "Even if an operation doesn't meet its stated goal, the overall objective of intelligence is for us to gather information about our enemies and help us predict their next move and stop it before anyone gets hurt. And based on what I've read about some of your initial debriefings since returning from Prague, I think you might be able to help us in some very significant ways."

"I wouldn't count on that," Hanson said. "I was just starting to learn about the inner workings of the Kúdela crime family, Tomáš Kúdela in particular."

"You were working your way in with the head man?"

Hanson nodded.

"I had been in a handful of meetings with him and he was

about to assign me to my first solo job. In a way, I'm glad I got pulled out before I had to do it."

"What did it involve?"

Hanson slid his feet across the concrete deck and looked off.

"I don't really want to talk about it," he said. "Just know that those people were monsters."

"You're going to have to talk about it at some point."

"I know. I will. It's just—well, it's just difficult to talk about it. Even as long as I've been doing this, there are just some parts of this job that are difficult to stomach."

The two men sat in silence for nearly a minute, both staring out across the water.

"I get why you came down to see me in person," Hanson finally said as he indicated toward the water. "This place is beautiful. But I know you're busy. Couldn't you have just called?"

Besserman propped his sunglasses on top of his head and winced.

"It'd be nice if it were that simple," he said. "And while I do enjoy this, you're right. I'm super slammed right now. However, the reality I'm facing at the agency is that I don't trust anyone. I couldn't be sure that someone wouldn't overhear our conversation and further delay or misdirect this investigation. As it stands, no one even knows that we've opened an investigation. I want everyone to think we're just going about our business so everyone doesn't become paranoid. The agency won't be able to accomplish its mission goals if we're all suspicious of each other."

"Fair enough," Hanson said. "But why the strong interest in what I was doing? I already underwent an exit interview of sorts. Was there something else you were looking for?"

"You remember Agent Hawk who was in charge of the mission to extract you?" Besserman asked.

"How could I forget him? That dude saved my life."

"Well, his wife was abducted by a group of Czech thugs. We're still trying to find out who they were, which isn't so easy since they're all lying in a heap at the bottom of a ravine in the Montana mountains."

"Wait. They abducted Hawk's wife?"

Besserman nodded.

"Found her at the Hawks' secret hideaway in the woods," he said. "According to her, they were speaking in Czech and demanded to know where you were."

"Me?"

"Apparently they figured out you're CIA—and they targeted Hawk's wife, Alex."

"Thank God she's okay," Hanson said before he took a long drag on his cigar and launched a swirling plume of smoke.

"So, I ask again, Brock, what do you know that's made them so aggressive that they sent a team over here to find one of our men's family and threaten her just so they could find out where you were. What did you do?"

Hanson eased to his feet and put his hands on his hips as he eased toward the edge of the veranda, eyes glued to the horizon.

"It's not really about what I did as what I know," he said.

"What did Tomáš Kúdela tell you?"

"I didn't learn it from him, but I have a feeling I know why they would want to shut me up, though it's just some things I was able to piece together during my time there. But nothing definitive. Understand?"

"So, this is just your theory?"

"More or less," Hanson said with a shrug and the tilt of his head. "At least, it's a theory about why they might go to the lengths they went to in order to get to me."

"Go on," Besserman said.

"The whole reason I was in Prague working with the Kúdela family was to discover if they were selling any illegal weapons on the black market. We would obviously want to put a stop to that, with a list of their buyers being the ultimate goal. If we shut them down, it'd just redirect buyers to other sellers. But if we were able to target the sellers—well, you already know all this."

"Please, continue," Besserman said with the wave of his hand.

"It didn't take me long to figure out that the Kúdela family was working with The Alliance," Hanson said. "They had all kinds of business interests intertwined with Jun Fang and his conglomerates. But what I found out just a few days before you extracted me was that The Alliance had placed an agent inside the federal government known only as The Sleeper. I never heard anyone say his real name, nor did I hear anyone ever say where he worked. It was just an accepted fact that he worked in a high profile position within the U.S. government."

"And what was this Sleeper supposed to do?" Besserman asked.

"I'm not sure," Hanson said. "Like I said, I only learned of his existence just a few days before you guys extracted me."

"Anything else?"

"The Kúdela family was very well connected to Jun Fang, the Chinese billionaire. How familiar are you with him?"

"Oh, I know all about Fang. We've had our eye on him for a while, and we've put him under the microscope."

"Well, let me tell you, it's worse than you could imagine."

Besserman arched an eyebrow.

"How so?"

"Fang has his fingers in plenty of illegal activities, but one of the most heinous is the *shipments* I had to help the Kúdela family with."

"Shipments?"

"Children," Hanson said.

"Street kids?"

"No, kids who'd been abducted."

"Are we talking like teenaged kids?"

"No, young ones. Some as young as two or three, snatched off playgrounds. I don't know how involved the Kúdela family was in rounding up these children, at least I never heard anyone I worked with mention doing this or even talk about it. I just knew they were involved in the transportation of these kids."

"Seems like if kids were being snatched, some reporter would write a story about it."

"These people operate at such a high level above the law—and have law enforcement and judges in their pocket—that it's just about impossible to bust them. Of course, my goal was to learn about their illegal arms business and suss out all their buyers. But the stuff I learned along the way was disturbing to say the least."

"Even if they were just transporting children, that's sick," Besserman said, still hung up over that revelation.

"Yeah—and the real question is what the hell is Fang doing with young children? And, frankly, I don't even really want to think about it."

"That makes two of us," Hanson said. "Though the possibilities are many—organ harvesting, child soldiers, selling kids on the black market in China, and some real unsavory things that shouldn't be discussed in any company, polite or otherwise."

"Agreed," Besserman said with an emphatic nod.

"But I do think we should at least do what we can to either stop it or curtail it, even if it's just intercepting a shipment or two of these kids and returning them to their parents."

"Of course. Give us what you know about how they operated."

"But it's Fang that you have to look deeper into," Hanson said. "He's the one spearheading a lot of the illegal activity that the Kúdela family is involved with, which leads me to believe he might be the one running everything."

"We'll investigate them," Besserman said. "And we'll do what we can to stop those children from being sold. I just find that horrifying."

Hanson nodded and took a long puff on his cigar.

CHAPTER
TWENTY-SEVEN

WASHINGTON, D.C.

BIG EARV DOUBLE-KNOTTED his shoelaces while sitting on a park bench then reached for the top of his shoes, stretching out his calf muscle. He'd long since learned the importance of stretching. He wasn't twenty-five anymore and able to just jump up and run five miles without proper preparation. After scarfing down a protein bar, he checked his watch and looked down the Anacostia Riverwalk. Plenty of people were jogging toward him, all embarking on an early afternoon run. But Payton Quick wasn't among them.

After learning about Payton's odd visits to the agency, he wanted to learn more about her reasons why. Although there was a fair amount of cooperation between the two intelligence behemoths when it came to sharing information, NSA analysts didn't usually make in-person visits to CIA headquarters. Even more unusual was the fact that Payton held high-level security clearance at Langley. To be fair, there were a handful of support staff that had less clearance than she did, let alone the ability to venture almost anywhere in the building.

The question as to *why* needed to be answered if Big Earv was to remove her from the list of suspects. The twenty-seven-year-old analyst was bold, one of the reasons she had a fair amount of experience already despite her age. Most analysts at age twenty-seven had only been operating for a year or two at the most. But Payton was entering her sixth year of service and proving her value to the NSA all the time, if her evaluations were accurate.

Big Earv squinted as he studied the faces of the runners flooding the riverwalk.

Where is she?

After several more minutes, she finally appeared, her wavy golden locks bunched into a ponytail. It swung back and forth as she ran toward Big Earv's position. He stretched again, leaning to his left and then back to his right, hoping that he could at least blend in for a few minutes before approaching her.

Once she passed him, Big Earv broke into a fast-paced jog, faster than he wanted, making him question if he'd be able to ask her the questions without forcing her to stop. His feet pounded the boards that comprised the riverwalk until they were almost in rhythm with Payton's. All he had to do was lengthen his stride.

"You can do it," he mumbled in an attempt to encourage himself.

The way his lungs felt at the moment, the whole venture felt in doubt. But after another minute, he eased up next to her, matching her stride for stride. She shot him a glance and then moved away.

"Miss Quick," Big Earv said. "I'd like to speak with you for a few minutes when you come to a stopping place."

She looked him up and down.

"From the looks of things, I'm not sure you'll be able to survive that long."

"You only know if you give me a chance," he said. "Besides, what could it hurt to speak with me for a few minutes?"

"Depends on what you want to talk about," she said.

"I think you know exactly what I want to talk about," he said as he reached into his pocket and produced his credentials.

"You people from the agency are so lame," she said with a huff. She stopped running and stared across the river. "Why couldn't you just schedule a meeting to come talk with me? It'd be a whole lot easier and much much faster."

"But why do that when I can get my run in for the day and interview you at the same time?" Big Earv said with a shrug. "You see, I'm a busy person, so I'm always looking for ways I can combine two tasks. Helps make me so much more efficient."

"Well, we're only wasting time if you don't get to it," she said. "Because in a couple of minutes, I'm going to leave you in the dust. Better talk fast."

"In that case, I'll get right to the point," he said. "Why are you making regular visits to Langley?"

"I wouldn't call them regular visits, just whenever I'm asked to go."

"Fair enough," he said. "So, what are you doing when you go?"

"I'm afraid I can't give you any specifics. I doubt you have the security clearance level to hear that kind of information."

"So you're going to stonewall me?"

"Not at all," she said, her breathing measured and calm. "I just can't tell you without getting authorization from my superiors."

"You aren't going to tell me anything, are you?"

"I'll tell you whatever I need to tell you to make you go away."

"But here you are," Big Earv said, his mouth forming a tight-lipped smile.

She stopped and walked over to the edge of the riverwalk. After glancing over her shoulder, she looked directly at Big Earv.

"You have to understand that what you're doing is very unconventional and could get both of us in big trouble," she said.

"I fully understand," he said. "There are some shady things going on at Langley, and I've been tasked with sniffing it out. Now, while I will admit there's a level of convenience associated with conducting an interview while we're out running, I also did this to give you the benefit of the doubt. If someone saw me at the NSA, they'd start asking you questions, maybe even harassing you. You wouldn't want that, would you?"

"Of course not."

"So, tell me what you do know, what you can tell me. You do that and I'll be out of your hair. Then you can be back on your solo run lickety-split. Understand?"

Payton sighed and crossed her arms over her chest.

"Yeah, I get it. But like I said, there's not much else I can tell you."

"Then just tell me what you think you could get away with telling me. Because if you keep dodging my questions and acting like I have to have this certain clearance level in order to hear what you have to say, I'm going to visit you at your office and make it very known who I am and why I'm there."

Payton chewed on her bottom lip for a moment, her eyes locked on something floating across the water.

"Would you look at that?" she said, pointing at a piece of driftwood.

"Changing the subject isn't going to help you," he said.

She offered a weak smile.

"Okay, you win. The only thing I can tell you without you having clearance is that I've been making those trips to deposit some transcripts and files into the archives. That's it."

"Current files?" he asked.

"I guess you could say that, though I don't really look at them."

"Now I know you're a liar."

"I swear, I never look at them. Okay, I did once, but it was nothing. And none of it made sense to me anyway. So, it didn't really stick with me."

"I know that's a lie," he said.

She rubbed her nose and looked off.

"No, it's not," her tone emphatic, her voice calm. "I'm not lying."

"What did you see?"

"I can't tell you," she said. "I just told you everything I could —or felt comfortable telling you."

"So, to wrap up, you simply make these deliveries whenever your boss tells you to?"

She nodded.

"Who's your boss?"

"That's a good question," she said. "And one that I'll leave unanswered for now."

"You're not going to make this easy for me, are you?"

"Not a chance," she said, popping her earbuds back into her ears. "Are we done here?"

Big Earv offered his hand. They shook before he gestured back toward the riverwalk.

"Thanks," she said before darting down the path and leaving Big Earv behind.

While the conversation had been a necessary one, he still didn't feel like it yielded much in the way of results. All he'd learned was that she visited Langley on a regular basis whenever the boss told her to so she could drop off this collection of *supposedly* highly classified papers.

Were they transcripts? A paper trail for someone to protect themselves? Or were they designed to incriminate someone else?

The possibilities felt too numerous to boil down into just a few scenarios. And even if he could winnow his list, which one was true? Big Earv needed to know if he was going to be able to move on to the next suspect.

Big Earv called Besserman to let him know how his conversation with Payton Quick had gone. After he finished, Besserman said he had a little news of his own.

"Is this about Brock Hanson?" Big Earv asked.

"Actually, it's about Payton Quick," Besserman said. "At least, it's related to her."

"I'm listening."

"We just got a tip that there's going to be another name

released within the next few days, which means Payton Quick might be making a return visit to Langley."

"But she's only made the visits that coincide with the release of the names," Big Earv said. "And she didn't go last week."

"Says who?"

"I don't know. The data? That's what Mia found anyway."

"Double-check that when you can. But in the meantime, I want you to put surveillance on her. Watch her every move. If she makes another *random* visit, I want to find out exactly what she's doing and what she's taking to our archives."

"Why don't you just ask her—or ask Wicker?" Big Earv asked. "I'm sure you have the clearance level necessary to hear about what she's doing."

"Of course, I could. But I want to keep this investigation as low profile as possible. I only want to get involved when absolutely necessary."

"I understand," Big Earv said.

He ended the call and then let out a long breath through puffed cheeks. Navigating this investigation was akin to finding one's way through a minefield where the mines are mere inches apart. One slight misstep and it's all over.

At least, that's how Big Earv felt.

But he put his feelings aside. He could deal with them later—after he found out what Payton Quick was really up to.

CHAPTER
TWENTY-EIGHT

BLÖNDUÓS, ICELAND

Hawk secured Mayhem's hands behind his back and then prodded him forward back toward the house. The wind whistled across the field fronting the hacker's property, pelting their face with shards of frozen snow and ice. Ryder stayed behind both men, his weapon discreetly trained on the prisoner in order to avoid attracting attention from the occasional car that crawled along the ribbon of white highway in the distance. It gave Hawk a moment to think, a chance to ponder how exactly to leverage the information he held that guaranteed Mayhem would talk. At least, he thought it would.

Just before they reached Mayhem's house, Ryder secured the hacker's colleague, who was just starting to come to as they approached him. But Ryder yanked him to his feet and added him to the procession of prisoners. Once inside the house, Ryder tied the accomplice to a pole in the basement, while Hawk tied Mayhem to a chair in the center of the room. For the first time, Hawk had a chance to study the face of Elias Korhonen, also known as Mayhem.

He drew back when Hawk eased his chin up, averting his eyes.

He'd made it clear he wasn't interested in playing along. But Hawk hadn't tracked down one of the world's most infamous hackers just to be stonewalled.

"You can make this easy or you can make this difficult," Hawk said. "It's totally up to you."

"You will regret this," Mayhem said with a sneer.

If Hawk hadn't known who Elias Korhonen was and simply passed him by on the street, there would've been compassion for him. The half-inch thick scar that ran diagonally from his left temple to his right cheek marred his face but also sparked intrigue. At least, it would have if Hawk didn't already know the story.

According to intel gathered on Mayhem, he grew up in Finland but spent significant time in his late teen years and early twenties as part of an anarchist movement. During a protest gone wrong in Amsterdam, he was part of a group that attacked local police. Mayhem and the crowd broke through a metal barrier as it rushed toward the law enforcement clad in riot gear. Mayhem and another fellow anarchist cornered one cop and pinned him to the ground, beating him mercilessly. However, in their rage-induced attack, they didn't see the officer pull a knife from the sheath on his belt. He slashed at them, ripping across Mayhem's face before slicing the other rioter's jugular vein. Mayhem scrambled off the officer and was left to hold his fellow rioter until he bled out on the sidewalk. The scar on Mayhem's face was as much physical as it was mental, leading him to walk away from the violence—but not the cause.

The incident made Mayhem more determined than ever to wreak havoc on governments and other institutions his fellow anarchists deemed oppressive. And ultimately, it had given rise to one of the most destructive hackers in the world. Mayhem relished every opportunity to strike back at those he considered tyrants, ruining people's lives by often manufacturing damning information about them if there wasn't anything in their closets that would create an outcry.

When Hawk looked at Elias Korhonen, he saw the faint

echoes of a young man standing on his principles. But any tenderness was gone, long since traded for a bitter callousness that drove him to embody his online handle.

Mayhem fought against the bindings, struggling to get free in the presence of Hawk and Ryder. The exercise proved futile, but it signaled to Hawk what a challenge Mayhem presented. Hawk could only hope there was a little compassion in the scarred man.

Hawk paced the floor, studying the bank of computer monitors on one side of the room, while the other was packed with servers.

"You don't get many visitors, do you?" Hawk asked.

Mayhem looked down and shook his head.

"Who are you and what do you want?"

"We were hoping you could help us solve a big mystery right now," Hawk said.

"And you think tying me up and dragging me into my basement is going to make me want to help?"

"Give us what we want and we'll go easy on you, it's just that simple."

"Why would I help you?"

Hawk glanced to his left and then his right.

"At the moment, it looks like you need all the help you can get. Your friend is tied up and we're the only ones who can do anything to change the direction of where this is headed if you don't cooperate."

Mayhem grunted and then chuckled.

"So, what are you going to do? Beat it out of me?"

Hawk swallowed hard, disgusted with what he was about to say.

He's the one making me do this.

"Elias, we know why you're here—in Iceland. And it's not just because it's a remote place. You're here because of your mother Anneli."

Fear flickered in Mayhem's eyes.

"What do you know about anything?"

"I know that Anneli has cancer and that you and your sister both moved here to take care of her and help her," Hawk said. "Thought a naturopathic approach might heal her after chemotherapy failed, right? You and your sister Sophia are taking turns driving her to geothermal hot springs, hoping to soak away all the toxins that are killing her."

Mayhem narrowed his eyes.

"You know nothing," he hissed.

"It doesn't take much to get her flagged as an illegal immigrant," Hawk said. "She'd be on a plane by the end of the week, returned to Finland with nothing."

"I swear if you—"

Hawk wagged a finger at him and clucked his tongue.

"Let's not make any promises that you can't keep," he said. "You've ruined plenty of people's lives. And personally, I'd rather you didn't force my hand. Your mother doesn't deserve to die a slow painful death because of her anarchist son. But if you insist on exposing CIA officers around the world who are doing their jobs, leading to their murders, we'll just have to start playing by the same ruthless rules."

Mayhem sighed and dropped his head, a tear trickling down his face and across his scar. He squeezed his eyes shut and clenched his fists.

Hawk decided to let Mayhem take his time. He needed to sit with the reality for a moment, consider the consequences of not cooperating. Hawk stepped back and glanced at Ryder, who watched Mayhem intently.

"Don't do it," the other man from the basement yelled. "You're going to ruin everything."

Ryder kicked the man in the face, slamming his head against the pole and knocking him unconscious.

After a few more uncomfortable moments of silence, Mayhem spoke.

"What do you want?"

"We want the name of the person who is sending you all of

the information about the embedded CIA officers you've outed on the dark web," Hawk said.

"The moment I give you that name, I lose all leverage."

"Any leverage you think you have right now is merely an illusion," Hawk said. "We will take this place apart and send it all back to our cyber forensics team to unpack. Then we'll let it be known that you traded information for safety and turn you loose. Everyone you've ever done business with will want their pound of flesh. We'll be the last thing you'll be worried about."

Mayhem shrugged.

"Maybe I'll just take my chances."

Hawk swiped on his phone to a video, his last bullet. He started playing an AI generated video that Mia created for him with Mayhem's mother and sister, begging and pleading for him to do whatever they asked. The video was close enough that he could see and hear them but not so near that he could tell it was faked. Hawk could only hope it would change Mayhem's mind.

"So, what do you say?" Hawk asked once it ended. "Want to help out your mother and sister or let them twist in the wind?"

"If only I could help you," Mayhem said. "But I don't know the name of the person who's been sending me the information. They just send me a package every week with the information—and I post it."

"I'm sure you know more than that. And I'm counting on you to tell me before we have to take further action to eventually get what we both know I'm going to get."

"I'll take my chances," Mayhem said.

"Bold choice, but I can respect that," Hawk said. "A man of principle taking a stand. The problem is you don't know how to stand with integrity."

"And you do, threatening to harm my innocent mother?" Mayhem scoffed. "We're the same, me and you, warriors fighting for a cause in whatever way we see fit. But there's one difference— you've enslaved yourselves to these people, engorging your bank accounts while blood drips from your hands."

Hawk bristled at the comment, knowing that he'd merely *appeared* to play by the anarchist's rules. If there was one thing Hawk would never do, it was make an innocent person suffer to get what he wanted. Once he ventured down that path, he knew he was fast on his way to becoming just like the people he opposed.

"I'm not going to beg," Hawk said, ignoring Mayhem's barbs. "You either agree to help or not. I don't have much time and we're ready to move on."

"Do whatever you see fit," Mayhem said.

Hawk walked over to Ryder, pulling him away from the two men so they could speak privately.

"So, what now?" Ryder asked. "He's calling your bluff."

"We're going to turn this place upside down," Hawk said.

"Looking for what?"

"We'll let the forensics team search for what they can find on these hard drives," Hawk said. "But if everything is analog, we need to look for papers, anything that gives us a clue as to who might be involved at the agency or within the federal government. Got it?"

They split up and began searching filing cabinets, carefully going through them one by one. Meanwhile, Mayhem hurled insults, mocking them as they rifled through his papers.

Fifteen minutes into their search, the doorbell rang.

"If you don't let me get that, everyone is going to know something's up," Mayhem said.

"No," Hawk said, "the local authorities know what we're up to. They're just waiting for the call to come in and arrest you. I'll get the door."

Hawk hustled up the basement steps and glanced at the monitor displaying the front porch. A delivery man clutching an envelope stood outside whistling.

Hawk opened the door.

"Oh, sorry, is Gordon not here today?" the delivery man said. "I usually practice my English with him. It's getting betterer."

"Much better," Hawk said.

"How do you know—oh," the man said, breaking into a laugh. "You're telling me the correct way to say it, no?"

Hawk smiled and nodded.

"Gordon is running an errand at the moment," Hawk said, holding out his hand to receive the package.

"Okay," the man said as he handed it over and then held out a tablet. "Would you mind signing right here?"

"Sure," Hawk said before thanking the delivery man and closing the front door.

Hawk returned downstairs to find Ryder still engrossed in his search.

"What was that all about?" Ryder asked.

Hawk glanced at the return address, a post office box in New York. He doubted it was even real, depending on which direction this transaction was going. If it was correspondence, it could be authentic. But he thought it was more likely to be a random address, someone filling in a box to complete the sender's address.

Hawk pulled the tab and spilled the contents out onto a small table. It was a manila folder, chock full of documents formatted in a way very familiar to Hawk. He used a pencil to open the folder and found the picture of a CIA officer staring back at him.

Ryder snatched it up and studied it more closely.

"What are you doing?" Hawk snapped. "We could pull prints off this thing. Put it down right now."

"Sorry," Ryder said as he dropped it. "Rookie mistake, I guess."

Hawk furrowed his brow while carefully easing all the papers into an evidence bag he'd removed from his ruck sack.

"Looks like we didn't need you or your mother after all," Hawk said. "You're going to regret not helping."

Hawk dialed a number on his phone and told the Icelandic authorities that Elias Korhonen was all theirs now and that they'd find him in the basement.

Hawk sighed in relief as they exited the house, nodding to the authorities as they rushed toward the house. He was excited that they'd manage to get the information, but irked at Ryder.

What was he thinking grabbing the documents like that?

Hawk wasn't convinced that Ryder was a suitable agent. He also was beginning to wonder why Ryder kept seemingly sabotaging all their efforts.

CHAPTER
TWENTY-NINE

WASHINGTON, D.C.

ROBERT BESSERMAN SIPPED his coffee while waiting for the traffic light to turn green. He checked his watch and relaxed. The GPS navigational app in his car said he was only five minutes away from the Magnum Group's new office in the capital. He had only seen it once but felt he needed to be present for the discussion about how to proceed given where the investigation was into the leak.

Before the light changed, his phone rang with a call from The White House.

"Please stay on the line for the President of the United States," a woman said.

After some silence followed by a couple of clicks, President Bullock's voice boomed through Besserman's cell.

"Shoot me straight, Bobby. Where are we at with everything?"

"Two operatives just returned from Iceland where they raided the hideout and headquarters for the digital disruptor known as Mayhem."

"And?"

"And we're still evaluating everything they gathered from the raid," Besserman lied.

The truth was he knew the results from what they'd found so far. Sure there were forensics specialists still combing through Mayhem's machines, but they quickly found that Mayhem had smartly mirrored everything from a server offsite that had a seemingly impenetrable firewall. But the early reports weren't promising about being able to pull off any useful information in the future.

Besserman was also reticent about telling anybody anything until it was definitive—and that included the president.

"But we've at least shut down the source of the leak?" Bullock asked.

"For now, yes. We have Mayhem in custody, though I don't suspect he'll talk. But he won't be posting the identities of any more of our CIA officers."

"Good work," Bullock said. "Keep me posted."

"Will do, sir."

Bullock ended the call, leaving Besserman to wonder if he should've been more forthcoming and say the quiet part out loud. While Mayhem wouldn't be sharing any more information, some other hacker eager to make a name for himself could. And if that happened, Bullock would go ballistic.

Besserman could only hope that they discovered the traitor before another CIA officer's name surfaced on the dark web.

MORGAN MAY GREETED Besserman and invited him to sit in her chair at the head of the table. The rest of the Magnum Group team had gathered to discuss their next steps and share what they'd all found in their recent missions. Hawk nursed a cup of coffee, still struggling after being back in the U.S. for just under forty-eight hours. Ryder gulped an energy drink, while Big Earv and Mia sifted through papers they had brought to the meeting.

The monitor where Alex's face appeared as a virtual participant was dark.

Dr. Z pushed away from the table, spinning around as his chair stopped in the far corner of the room. He used a magnifying glass to study a small object about the size of a bug twitching in the palm of his hand.

"Dr. Z, are we going to have any issues with you today?" Morgan asked.

Dr. Z looked up sheepishly, his cheeks flushed.

"I don't think so, at least not after they see this new drone I created," he said.

"Maybe later," she said. "But we're here to discuss how we're going to catch the source of the agency's leak since the raid on Mayhem's place didn't yield any actionable information on that front."

"We didn't find any fingerprints?" Mia asked.

Morgan shook her head.

"Only those of Ryder's and the clerk who originally filed the paperwork. So, that was a dead end," she said.

Big Earv shared that he'd only been able to rule out suspects with the exception of Payton Quick. He admitted he didn't have anything on her yet, but he wasn't ready to dismiss her. Mia shared what she'd found from digging into the CIA's server and still hadn't discovered any breach or cyberattack, confirming that the information was being transmitted from Langley via the old-fashioned mailing system through typed notes.

Besserman detailed his conversation with Brock Hanson, which had sparked a deeper dive by Mia and Morgan into Jun Fang.

"While we know that Fang has strong ties to The Alliance," Morgan began, "we can't help but see how The Alliance could somehow be behind this leak, targeting certain agency officers. We've been able to discern a pattern in the ones that have been chosen, especially when we factor in the latest one who was supposed to be outed, Cindy Collins. She's been embedded with a hacker group that has been hired by one of Fang's close affiliates. And we'd be foolish to believe that this business associate wasn't directed by Fang to hire them."

"So, what are we thinking?" Hawk asked. "Is Fang trying to clean house?"

"Maybe making sure his house is clean," Morgan suggested, "which leads us to believe he might just be one of the people behind The Alliance, if not the one in charge. Either way, shutting him down would be a big blow to the organization. Fang appears to be moving illegal weapons, money, information—anything he wants. Hell, he's even moving people if you want to count his adoption agency."

"This man makes me sick," Mia said. "He'll try to profit off anything."

"As long as it's illegal," Morgan said. "That seems to be the caveat here, all while maintaining a legitimate business as a front for it all."

"So, what are we going to do about Fang?" Besserman asked. "I mean, it's a delicate situation, to say the least. Fang has many allies within the CCP, meaning that we better have some rock solid evidence against him—and proof that it's also a threat to the Chinese government's sovereignty—before we request their help or even bring them into our investigation of him."

Morgan nodded.

"I understand, sir. It's a geopolitical nightmare, no question about it."

"But are there any solutions?"

"Maybe not quite yet," Morgan said. "However, I have a plan for how we can get more intel on Fang, or at least give us a chance to get more intel on him in a discreet way."

Besserman arched an eyebrow and stroked his chin.

"We're listening."

Morgan picked up the remote off the table and clicked on the screen at the far end of the room.

"Two years ago, Fang purchased a major motion picture distribution company in Beijing, the one that handles most of the big U.S. blockbusters. Then three months later, he bought an up-and-coming production company that does films in both English and Chinese, using storylines that bridge Europe and North America with China. To be honest, it's actually a smart idea and one worth investing in. And it's only going to further legitimize him on the world scene."

"So, how's this going to help us?"

"Tomorrow night, Fang is kicking off a press junket for his company's new movie, *The Mandarin Matrix*. It's an action flick about a case of mistaken identity for an American who's there to learn the language but gets accused of robbing a bank. And he must prove his innocence all while on the run and struggling with Mandarin."

"I'm not gonna lie," Big Earv said. "I'd watch that."

"Alex and I would watch it if it was set in India," Hawk said.

Morgan snapped her fingers and pointed at Hawk.

"We're not getting into a Bollywood debate right now," she said. "We need to stay focused, okay?"

"Listen close to what I gotta say," Hawk sang as he shimmied.

"Hawk," Morgan said sharply.

"What? Do you guys not know *Sway Se Swagat*?" he asked.

"What the hell are you talking about?" Ryder asked.

Big Earv sighed and rolled his eyes.

"Hawk's got a thing for Bollywood movies, especially musicals."

"Seriously?" Ryder asked.

Big Earv nodded.

"Don't get him started."

"Exactly," Morgan said. "We're not talking about Bollywood right now. Hawk, stay on topic."

He offered a coy grin.

"Now, Fang is hosting this press junket at his home and I've got you and Ryder credentials, attending under the guise of being two movie critics for Asian movies."

"How did you pull that off?" Hawk asked.

"Mia worked her magic. You both write for a website with a long history of reviewing these types of movies—and you've got a big audience. Read the briefs I've put in front of you, and that should tell you everything you need to prepare for this mission."

"Sounds easy enough," Hawk said. "Just need to brush up on all those reviews I wrote."

"That makes two of us," Ryder said as he reached for his packet.

"Wheels up in two hours," Morgan said with a clap. "Let's stay dialed in on this team and keep communicating about what we find. We need some answers ASAP."

———

HAWK DIALED Alex's number as soon as he left the meeting and drove back to his apartment to pack.

"How are you doing?" he asked once she answered.

"I'm okay," she said. "Back at the house and practicing my marksmanship every day. I miss you—and I know J.D. does too."

"I'm hoping to get back soon and spend some good quality time with both of you, maybe take the horses out on a long backpacking trip into the wilderness."

"What I really want is a weekend at a spa," she said with a laugh. "How are you?"

"Well, I'm sure you saw the message that I'm going to Beijing."

"I read that. But I mean how are you doing after confronting Mayhem? I know you weren't keen on the approach of using his mother against him."

"I'm fine," he said. "I know I have to do some unsavory things from time to time in this business. But there has to be a better way. We got bailed out by the delivery guy. But I'm still not sure what lengths I would've gone to in order to coerce him to talk."

"In this business, we need to do whatever we can to maintain our humanity. It's hard enough when we're just out there living our daily lives. It's so tempting to look for ways to cheat and cajole the system to get what we want without doing it honestly. So if it takes more time and requires a little more creativity, I'll stand with you. We'll do what it takes."

"I appreciate that," Hawk said.

After a few more minutes of catching up, Hawk ended the call. He took a deep breath and smiled. Alex always had a way of buoying his spirits.

But at the moment, nothing would buoy his spirits more than bringing down Fang's empire and The Alliance with it.

CHAPTER
THIRTY

WASHINGTON, D.C.

BIG EARV BALANCED himself on a road bike and looked through his binoculars at Payton Quick as she jogged along the Anacostia Riverwalk again. Her mid-day run was a stark departure for the NSA analyst who worshiped routine. Based on what Big Earv had learned about her, Payton's daily schedule was regimented to the hilt. And for Payton to leave the office for a jog along the river—it was a move that stunned him.

He scanned the area, struggling to understand why she was here. She used a park bench at the edge of the bank to stretch. By all indications, she looked like she was about to tackle a run of at least several miles. She ran in place for a second and then studied her cell phone for a moment, likely starting her exercise playlist. And then with a skip, she began her run.

Trailing her by a good fifty meters on the other side of the bank, Big Earv kept pace with ease. When they ascended hills, he dropped down the gears on his bike but kept moving. Other than the odd time of day, nothing appeared out of the ordinary for Payton. Had she taken the day off, he likely wouldn't have thought much of the early run, even though she still maintained her schedule on the weekend. He couldn't identify it yet, but he couldn't shake the feeling that something was off, something was different.

Ten minutes into the run, Big Earv's suspicions were confirmed. She took a sharp turn off the paved pathway, darting down a connecting dirt path.

Big Earv crossed the river at the next bridge and pedaled hard to catch up to a place where he could still keep an eye on her. The moment he left the paved pathway, he encountered the unforgiving terrain—gnarled roots stretching across the path, deep mud puddles clogging up the sides, large rocks half-buried beneath the surface and waiting to throw a bike rider.

Realizing it was more trouble than it was worth to ride, he hid his bike at the edge of the woods, covering it with several fallen branches. The early spring foliage was enough to conceal it for the short time he intended to be gone from it. He trekked through the woods, hurdling fallen logs and ducking under thick briars, as he continued on in the direction he'd last seen Payton take.

After a couple of minutes—and Big Earv starting to wonder if he'd lost her—he spotted her in a small clearing, no bigger than a quarter of an acre. A man in a black leather jacket with sunglasses and his hat pulled down low across his brow, glanced around the area before handing her an envelope. He wasn't close enough to hear what they were saying, but Payton tilted her head to one side and squinted, if anything to indicate that she didn't understand what he wanted—or didn't agree with it.

They spoke for a couple of minutes before she started down a different path leading out of the woods. Big Earv waited for a moment, trying to get a better look at the man who clearly didn't want to be recognized. But it was pointless. He had no visible markings on the scant amount of skin that was showing and his gait was really indistinguishable. He considered following the man for a moment who left in the opposite direction of Payton but decided to go after her and see where she was headed.

She exited the woods and navigated back to the opposite side of the river she'd been on before heading to her original starting position. Big Earv joined her but stayed a good forty meters behind her to avoid attracting any suspicion. While putting his bike on the rack affixed to his truck, he watched her walk to her car and then peel out of the parking lot.

Big Earv followed her, maintaining a discreet distance. And fifteen minutes into the drive, he figured out where she was going. He shook his head in disbelief.

Maybe I got it all wrong about her.

Ten minutes later, she turned into the CIA headquarters entrance. Three vehicles separated them at the gate. Once he was waved through, he parked and followed her inside the building. He ducked into a janitor's closet and found a pushcart. Pulling a cap low across his brow, he shoved the cleaning cart down the hallway, trailing her.

He noted what floor the elevator stopped on and followed her there. A couple of minutes later, he was half-heartedly mopping the hallway outside the archive room, waiting for her to exit. Once she did, she wound her way around the long corridor and used the stairs.

Big Earv returned to his car ahead of her and was waiting to see where she went next. But that opportunity was cut short when she locked eyes with him and stormed over to him. She slapped the window and gestured for him to roll it down.

"Just what the hell do you think you're doing?" she asked as the window slowly sank.

"Actually, I was about to ask you the same thing."

Payton glowered.

"I'm half inclined to call the police."

"Be my guest," he said. "Maybe you can tell them what you did with that envelope the man in the woods gave you."

"How long have you been following me?"

"Long enough to know that you're up to no good."

She rolled her eyes.

"You don't know anything, do you? Who do you really work for?"

"I already told you."

"No, you didn't. You showed me some bogus credentials. I want to know who you really are and why you're creeping on me."

"I'm not creeping," Big Earv said, waving dismissively at her. "It's called surveillance. And your behavior definitely warrants it."

"Says the creeper," she said.

"I'm just doing my job."

"And who sent you to follow me? Because I sure as hell don't believe that you're a CIA employee."

"Yes, the CIA, where they let just anyone in the building," Big Earv said with a snicker. "You must be delusional. Would you like to see my credentials again?"

"Your forged credentials? I'll pass."

"I'm not going anywhere," he said. "You better watch what you're doing—and be careful about who you do it for."

"Piss off," Payton said before turning on her heels and walking back to her car.

Big Earv waited until she drove away before walking back into CIA headquarters and heading to the security department. After displaying a letter from Director Besserman giving him permission to review security footage, the guard called to verify the letter's authenticity. Once confirmed, he asked Big Earv what he wanted to see.

Big Earv gave the corresponding time and location for when he was in the archives following Payton. The guard cued up the footage according to the time stamp, but nothing appeared. Rather than a bustling hallway around the archive, it was dead. As in no movement whatsoever.

"Are you sure this is right?" Big Earv asked.

The guard pointed to the upper corner of the screen, which showed the same time as he'd requested.

"And you're sure the time stamp is correct?" Big Earv asked.

"It's all right, as far as I can tell," the guard said.

He proceeded to go outside and wave at the camera, demonstrating that it worked in real time.

"This can't be right," Big Earv said. "I was right there."

"The camera doesn't lie," the guard said with a shrug. "I don't know what else to tell you."

Big Earv trudged back to his car, convinced more than ever that Payton Quick was involved somehow. He just wasn't sure to what extent or what she was doing. But he couldn't shake the fact that she looked guilty as hell.

CHAPTER
THIRTY-ONE

BEIJING, CHINA

HAWK TIGHTENED his bolo tie and checked himself in the mirror one final time before turning around and looking at his partner. Ryder was running a comb through his thick golden locks for the one thousandth time, hoping to accomplish some modern feat of greatness by getting his wavy hair to sit exactly as he wanted it to. After watching Ryder grow frustrated after raking his comb through his hair ten more times, Hawk shook his head and broke into a laugh.

"Are you aware of the definition of insanity?" he asked.

"Please enlighten me, sensei," Ryder said as he continued his quest to have his hair lay exactly like he wanted.

"The ancients used this natural resource known as water to help train their hair to lay flat," Hawk said. "But in recent years, the ancient ways have been replaced by a revolutionary new hair product called hair gel, which, when used properly, will make your hair sit exactly as you want it."

"What a novel concept," Ryder said, his voice dripping with sarcasm. "Maybe I can use it on people too. Will it get them to do exactly like I want?"

"Is there any particular purpose you might have for it?"

"Yeah, to make someone shut the hell up and leave me alone."

Hawk chuckled.

"I'm impervious to its power."

Ryder continued, his tongue sticking out the side of his mouth as he concentrated on achieving his goal without the help of hair gel.

"The actors aren't going to be at the party," Hawk said. "You're not going to be able to ask out Scarlett Johansen."

"But if she happens to be there—"

"This is ridiculous," Hawk said, glancing at his watch. "We've gotta go."

Ryder growled and inspected himself once more before sliding his comb into his back pocket.

"I guess that'll do," he announced.

"Finally," Hawk said. "I hope you know that my wife—a full-grown woman—requires less time than you do to primp."

Ryder shrugged.

"We'd make a terrible couple anyway."

Hawk shoved Ryder toward the door.

"Come on," Hawk said. "Enough fun and games. We've got to hustle or we're not going to make the train that will supposedly get us there on time."

Hawk and Ryder rushed out the door and headed straight to the subway station across the street. In a matter of minutes, they were on a train headed north of downtown to a conference center on Yanqi Lake. Hawk and Ryder attended separately not only to avoid suspicion but also to double their intelligence gathering efforts. If Jun Fang really was the mastermind he appeared to be, they needed to gather as much information about him as possible. And they could do a better job if they were apart—at least for the first part of the night.

The red carpet premier was hosted at a large conference center on the lake and open to members of the public who'd entered a drawing and won. But Hawk knew from the list of people who'd supposedly won that it wasn't a fair drawing. Fang had clearly hand-selected the people he wanted to attend, a list of influencers in the realms of music, theater, sports, and social media. Based off Hawk's brief scan of the room, only a few of the people who'd "won" a chance to attend the premier of "*The Mandarin Matrix*" were commoners.

Following the showing of the movie, Hawk and Ryder milled around with some of the other journalists at a mixer in a back room. A few actors and actresses were brought in to conduct less formal interviews.

Hawk watched as Ryder tried to get a one-on-one with Scarlett Johansen, but she was inundated by journalists, a throng of mostly men hovering around her like flies on a carcass. Ryder quickly realized he wasn't going to get a chance to interview her, let alone see her with the swarming media closing in on her from all sides.

Guess that's why they call themselves the press.

After a couple of minutes, Scarlett popped out and found her personal publicity manager and then disappeared through the people, most of them left wondering what had happened to her by the time they realized she was gone.

Ten minutes later, a woman picked up a microphone and announced that all media members who received a golden invitation in their welcome packet would be invited to Jun Fang's private residence on the banks of the lake.

"Would you look at this?" Hawk said, waving his golden ticket.

"I've got one too," Ryder said with a wink.

"In that case, I say we get a head start, maybe get a chance to see the lay of the land. What do you say?"

"Is Scarlett Johansen going to be there?" Ryder asked as he finger combed his hair.

"Who knows?" Hawk said. "The invite promised that there would be several surprise guests as well as an open bar and a cover band playing some of the hit songs from the movie."

Ryder cocked his head to one side, a faint smile leaking across his lips.

"So you're saying there's a chance?" he asked.

"Did you just watch the premier?" Hawk asked. "*The Mandarin Matrix* is supposed to be a serious movie."

"Moments of levity is what will carry the story, mark my words. That's now what all these yahoos are going to write, if they even write any original content anymore."

"So, let's go."

"I wouldn't miss this for the world—plus, isn't this part of the mission?"

Hawk sighed and shook his head.

"It's not just *part* of the mission, it's *the* mission."

Ryder winked and patted Hawk on the back.

"Relax, old man. I was just having a little fun at your expense. Of course I'm coming. I wouldn't miss this for all the tea in—well, China."

They walked outside and caught a shuttle over to Fang's summer home on the opposite side of the lake. And it was as lavish as could be expected from a flashy billionaire, both on the outside and the inside. Sculpted gardens with marble statues greeted them on the way in. Tall ceilings with intricate glass work were a staple in almost every room. Each room contained some measure of exquisite craftsmanship, from inlaid oak panels on some walls to rare rugs knitted by Bedouins. As Hawk strolled from one room to the next, he thought he was in a showroom for an architectural firm catering to billionaires.

The decor contained in each room was also lavish. Expensive art decorated the walls, while ornate artifacts that had clearly been restored decorated the end tables and bookshelves. A crystal chandelier glistened overhead, illuminating the room swirling with busy wait staff bustling through the crowd with trays of drinks and entrees.

Following a tour of the home, Hawk wondered if this press junket was really to show off the movie or show off his home. He meandered over to Ryder, who was caught up in a conversation with another journalist who, judging from the snippet of conversation overheard, also had an affinity for Scarlett Johansen.

Hawk gave Ryder a slight head nod, signaling that he wanted to speak. Ryder excused himself and joined Hawk.

"Quite the place, isn't it?" Ryder said.

"Look, I know this is an incredible environment, but let's not get sidetracked and forget why we're here," Hawk said. "Director May didn't send us over here to ogle mansions and movie stars. We've still got a job to do, right?"

Ryder nodded.

"So, let's stay focused," Hawk said. "Okay?"

"Got it," Ryder said.

The plan was for Ryder to run interference and then serve as a lookout while Hawk found his way into Fang's study. The plan was a rather simple one, but it required Ryder to be on top of his game, which he clearly wasn't at the moment. Hawk had them check their coms units and then they split up, swinging into action.

According to the layout Mia had placed in the briefing, Fang's study was located on the second floor just off the great hall. A husky guard with a buzz cut stood at the foot of the stairs with his arms crossed, a permanent sneer etched on his forehead and nose. The idea was to distract him so he missed Hawk casually stealing away upstairs. And the idea worked better than it sounded when they initially discussed it.

Hawk followed Ryder toward the stairs and bumped into buzz cut from behind, hitting him on the back left shoulder. Ryder tumbled to the ground, spinning around and landing on his rear end. He looked up from his spot on the floor and scowled at the guard.

"Watch where you're going, buddy," Ryder sneered.

The guard glowered, the veins on his neck protruding. Ryder took the man's hand as he eased him to his feet. That provided Hawk with all the time he needed. He scampered up the stairs and found the office, just as Mia's layout detailed. Hawk jimmied open the lock and was inside within a minute.

He pulled out the drawers one by one, looking for anything that could explain the true nature of Fang's business entities. At first, they looked like benign personnel records, contracts, and development ideas. But then there was a section that caught Hawk's eye: "Adoption Placements." Hawk probably wouldn't have thought much of it if there wasn't another folder right next to it that said "Adoptions."

As Hawk explored the difference between the two files, he heard Ryder's conversation come through his earpiece. Hawk's protégé was caught up in a conversation with Scarlett Johansen. And it was clear from what Hawk could hear that she wasn't interested in whatever it was that he was saying. Hawk had learned from experience that the best way to maintain a good cover was to say as little as possible. He'd even reminded Ryder to say as little as possible. But instead, Ryder sounded like he was trying to get Scarlett Johansen to join him for drinks later that night at a Beijing nightclub.

"Knock it off," Hawk said through clenched teeth into the coms.

But it was like Ryder couldn't hear him—or didn't want to hear him. Ryder was living his dream, talking with a beautiful movie star and hoping for a chance to talk further. Either way, his behavior, whether it was reckless or simply hypnotized by starry-eyed puppy love, had endangered Hawk.

"Are you watching the stairs?" Hawk asked.

Ryder continued talking.

Hawk cursed under his breath as he turned his attention back to the folders, knowing that he needed to hurry. Rifling through the pages, it didn't take him long to see an important distinction. In all the documents from the Adoptions folder, the report discussed how the child was merely adopted. But in the Adoption Placements folders, each child was referred to as placed. For a moment, Hawk thought maybe it was because the adoptions occurred years apart and maybe an institutional change in the way they referred to the adoptees could explain the difference. However, that theory was obliterated when Hawk found two forms adopting out children on the same day, one recorded in the regular Adoptions file, while the other was in the Adoption Placements.

After Hawk snapped a few pictures, the sound of Ryder's voice came through his coms again—and this time it was worse than the first. Instead of hearing him practically beg Scarlett Johansen to go out with him, her sultry voice was replaced by the gruff sound of the guard's voice from the bottom of the steps.

The man growled—and Hawk could hear the sound of a physical struggle. Grunts, scuffed feet, and tense voices marked the altercation.

"What's going on, Ryder?"

"Sorry, man," he said. "I pissed off the wrong guy."

Hawk replaced everything as he found it, abandoning his mission earlier than he wanted, and headed for the door. But then something caught his eye. A date on the calendar. In two days, Fang had a meeting—in Bali. Yet even more interesting was the title of the meeting: "The Alliance Gathering."

Hawk made a note of it and scrambled out of the room, only to be met by the hulking guard.

"What are you doing in there?" the guard barked.

"I got lost," Hawk said. "I was looking for the restroom."

"We told you that everything was on the main floor and there was no need to go upstairs."

"Sorry, I must've not been paying that close of attention."

"You think you can just apologize and everything's fine?" the guard asked. "Who are you anyway?"

Hawk wasn't interested in sticking around to placate this beast of a man.

"Would you look at the time," Hawk said as he glanced at his watch.

The man looked down with Hawk for a moment, poised to

respond before Hawk smashed the man in the face. He staggered backward for a moment, teetering as he neared the stairs. Hawk jumped up and rammed his feet into the man's chest, sending him tumbling backward down the stairs.

Hawk flew down the stairs after him, hurdling the man and racing outside. Ryder was on the front steps with a motorcycle, the engine clattering as he sat in neutral. He patted the seat behind him.

"Come on," Ryder said. "Hop on."

Hawk sprinted toward the bike, straddling it and holding on as Ryder popped a wheelie and then sped off.

"Where'd you get this bike?" Hawk asked.

"Desperate times call for desperate measures," Ryder said. "I thought maybe I had a better chance with Scarlett if I had a bike. I heard she liked riding motorcycles."

Hawk knew Ryder was joking, but he wasn't in a laughing mood.

"You almost got me detained back there—or worse," Hawk said sharply.

"Sorry," Ryder said. "I promise to make it up to you."

"If I didn't know any better, I'd think you were trying to ruin this entire mission," Hawk said.

But Hawk wasn't sure if he knew any better. He'd deal with Ryder later. In the meantime, he'd gathered an important piece of evidence—and a potential way to uncover who was part of The Alliance.

And for now, that was all that mattered.

CHAPTER
THIRTY-TWO

WASHINGTON, D.C.

BIG EARV ZIPPED up his jacket and jammed his hands into his pockets. The front charging through the city came with a brisk breeze. Flags snapped in the wind as debris tumbled down the street, disappearing into the corners unlit by street lamps. Big Earv inhaled the smell of cooked oil and grease pumped into the air by a food truck inundated with party goers taking a break from dancing.

A half-block away, the pulsating sounds from the Opera Ultra night club reverberated in the street. And Big Earv could already feel the bass thumping in his chest. He increased his pace as he watched Payton Quick weave through the congestion just outside the club's front doors.

She slipped into the short line and flashed her ID before paying the cover charge and then entering. Big Earv stopped, allowing a few young twenty-somethings to cut in front of him. While he figured she had to know that he was following her by now, she didn't seem to care as she never once glanced over her shoulder, devoid of the paranoia that usually accompanies someone who knows she's being watched.

Is she trying to waste my time? Did she lead me to a club to wear me down?

Big Earv wasn't sure if he was being played. He also wasn't sure if Payton Quick was playing at all.

He marched toward the front of the line with the rest of the revelers until he was asked to present his ID. Then the man laughed and just waved him inside.

"Are you sure you don't want to check my ID?" Big Earv asked.

"If anybody is unsure if you're a grown-ass man, they're probably on something," the bouncer said with a shrug. "Now, enjoy your visit."

Big Earv forked over the cash for the cover charge and walked inside. Bright neon lights illuminated the dance floor, which was packed with people drinking while dancing to the rhythmic beats thumping from the speakers.

He searched the hazy room for Payton and didn't take long to find her. She tucked her hair behind her ears and eased into a booth. If she was looking, she would've seen Big Earv since she sat down on the side of the table facing him. But instead she was looking intently at the man across the table from her. Big Earv couldn't see the man's face, but there was something about him. Maybe just a familiarity in the man's mannerisms. Based on how Big Earv's investigation had been going, he figured the man wouldn't be someone he knew. It'd just be another lead for him to follow up on.

Big Earv meandered over to the bar, keeping an eye on Payton. She relaxed in the booth, signaling to one of the waitresses that she wanted a drink. Upon approaching the bar, Big Earv ordered a rum and Coke. It wasn't his favorite, but he needed something quick and easy for the bartender to make. After paying for the cocktail, he sought out a different position in the club, one where he could see both Payton and the face of the man she was meeting with.

Clutching a drink with arms raised, Big Earv navigated across the dance floor to an empty table directly across the room from Payton and her suitor. Or maybe it was a work colleague. Or maybe it was—

Big Earv stared slack-jawed at the man seated across from Payton. If he didn't have any red flags about her before, he did now. There was no way she could talk her way out of this one. Security footage from the club couldn't cover it up.

The man she was meeting with was Kwon Choi, a notorious North Korean spy who still walked around freely in the U.S. due to his diplomatic standing. Everyone in every intelligence circle knew Kwon Choi—or at least knew who he was.

Choi's hands were neatly clasped in front of him, his eyes sparkling as he stared back at Payton. She smiled and laughed, followed by a gentle brush of his hand.

Payton knows, doesn't she? She has to know.

As Big Earv took a long pull of his drink, he contemplated how to alert her to the fact that she was sharing drinks with a North Korean spy—just in case she didn't. Delivering the message would likely result in her causing a scene, but he didn't care. She needed to know.

After sliding out of his chair and easing to his feet, Big Earv stopped, the alcohol rushing to his head. He paused a moment before beginning the trek.

Big Earv maneuvered closer to her table, mulling over the best way to get Payton alone.

Then Big Earv stopped. He widened his eyes, his mind starting to wonder if he was imagining things. He squeezed his eyes shut and then opened them again.

Nope, the other gentleman was still there.

Big Earv stared as he studied the man to make sure he wasn't hallucinating.

It's him all right.

Big Earv couldn't believe NSA Director John Wicker had joined them. He did another double-take, confirming it was indeed Wicker.

Why not just meet at the office?

Something seemed a little off to Big Earv. But he wasn't sure there was much he could do about it except to document the scene and confront Payton and Wicker about it later. Big Earv snapped a discreet photo and headed toward the door.

CHAPTER
THIRTY-THREE

BALI, INDONESIA

HAWK TURNED on his front-facing camera and offered a toothy grin for Alex, who was watching on the other end. As he climbed behind the wheel of their rental, a black Land Rover, he used the moment to make a last-second adjustment to his bowtie and then checked to see if he had anything in his teeth.

"How do I look?" he finally asked, turning on the cabin lights.

"Lonely," Alex said while adding a pause for dramatic effect. "I wish I could be there with you."

"It sounds like it's going to be a lot more fun than it actually is," he said, trying to persuade her that she wasn't missing anything.

"Bali? A masquerade? Jun Fang?" she asked. "Please sign me up."

"Well, I doubt we'll even get a chance to sink our toes in the sand. And Ryder and I are only going to be parking cars at the event. Plus our mission is to avoid Fang for now. We just want to clone his laptop and see where that leads. I'm not going to be wowing the audience with my deft dancing skills."

Alex chuckled but didn't respond.

"What?" Hawk asked. "You think I'm a good dancer, don't you?"

Mia, who was hammering on her laptop keyboard from the backseat, snickered.

"Seriously?" Hawk said. "Perhaps you guys have forgotten how I dance out of trouble when necessary."

"You do more dancing *into* trouble than out of it," Mia quipped.

"See," Alex said. "Even Mia knows about your dancing."

"It's legendary," he said. "That's how she knows."

"The legend is more about how bad you look," Alex said. "You watched a Bollywood movie and you think you could be an extra in one of those choreographed scenes, but instead you look like you've been stricken with some sort of muscular disease."

"It's not that bad," Hawk said as he turned around and glanced at Mia. "Tell her, Mia. Tell her I'm not that bad."

He kept the phone focused on her face, patiently waiting for her to respond.

"You're not that bad," Mia said. "You're worse."

"And you get to see Hawk's unsynchronized gyrations for yourself," Alex said. "And as much as I don't want to see you dance, I still want to be there with you."

"Mia's staying in the car," Hawk said. "She won't even see the inside of the ballroom. And, coincidentally, I won't be going inside either. Ryder and I are just parking cars as valets."

"I doubt that," she said.

Hawk chuckled.

"You'd probably win a bet for most missions, but not for this one," he said. "We just want to get access to Fang's car so we can clone his laptop. It's not time to approach him yet and lay all our cards out on the table. We just want to find out what he's been up to—and see if we can leverage that information to make him reveal more about The Alliance or shut him down altogether."

"Well, good luck," Alex said. "But before you go, there's someone who wants to tell you good-night."

The phone jostled as a couple of seconds passed. Eventually, Alex's phone found its way into little J.D.'s hands. He puckered up his lips and made a smacking noise.

"I love you, Dad," little J.D. said. "And I miss you. When are you coming home?"

"As soon as I can, buddy. You be good for Mommy, okay?"

"Yes, sir," little J.D. said before he handed the phone back to Alex.

"You get all that?" she asked. "We'll be counting down the minutes until we can meet again."

"Of course," Hawk said before ending the call.

The part about not sticking his toes in the sand was likely true, but everything else Hawk told Alex lined up with what his expectations were for the gathering of The Alliance masterminds. The Alliance conducting the meeting under the guise of a masquerade ball would prevent any of its members from being identified. And Jun Fang was a wildcard, proving to be as slippery as he was powerful. Nevertheless, Hawk wished Alex could've joined them for it all, but she refused to let her thirst for adventure trump her insistence on being there for J.D. And he was fine with her decision.

Hawk adjusted the rearview mirror as he backed out of the parking space at their hotel and took a quick glance at Mia. He hadn't noticed her being in a dress before.

"Did you change, Mia?" Hawk asked as he shifted into drive.

She nodded, her face lit only by the glow of her computer screen.

"You never know," she said. "I might have to go inside."

"I hope not," Hawk said.

"I'm sure it'll work out. Just always better to be prepared."

Ten minutes later, Hawk pulled into a parking spot close to the building. He needed to be close enough to the wireless network so Mia could hack into it and activate the audio for the security cameras. After a brief search, he found a spot near the far end of the conference center close to where the IT hardware was stored.

"Can you connect from here?" Hawk asked.

Mia flashed a thumbs up.

"Go get 'em, cowboy," she said. "I'm already on."

Hawk left Ryder to stay with Mia as she worked her magic. As Hawk walked up to the valet stand, he double-checked his outfit to make sure it matched what everyone else was wearing.

The operation was simple in nature: Determine which one was Fang from his voice after Mia activated the sound function on the security cameras, and then slip a transmitting device into his car that Hawk would do when Fang came out to retrieve it. Ryder would then keep them close enough to Fang's car so Mia could clone Fang's computer. It all came down to execution as the plan itself was nearly flawless.

Hawk made fast friends with the valets, informing them he'd just been hired and it was his first night. They showed him how and where they wanted the vehicles parked. Most of the cars were high-end—Lamborghinis, Bentleys, Rolls Royces, Aston Martins. According to Marcus, the ex-pat from London who oversaw the team of valets at Royal Aces Conference Center, Hawk would need to prove he was proficient in driving certain types of vehicles before they would let him drive them on his own. So, he spent the first hour before the event, parking cars with Marcus.

"Where'd you say you were from?" Marcus asked.

"I didn't," Hawk said. "But I'm from Texas. Drove a lot of famous people's cars while working as a valet in Dallas."

"You certainly know your stuff. I'll let you park anything tonight. Just wait for my signal to take a car. There are still a few guys here who can't drive the custom cars yet, so we want to make tonight run as smoothly as possible for everybody. No matter what, be cordial and stay alert. I know you've done this before, but I want you to be at the top of your game."

"Absolutely," Hawk said, bumping fists with the man.

Once Hawk was finished with his testing, the cars started

flooding the drop-off zone in front of the building. He stayed quiet on the coms until he was given the go-ahead to park his first car. He settled behind the steering wheel of a black McLaren Elva and turned on his mic.

"How's it looking, Mia?" Hawk asked.

"Not good," she said. "This place has recently upgraded their network security."

"So, what's that mean?"

"I'm going inside."

"How the hell are you gonna do that? There are guards swarming this place."

"I didn't just bring a dress, Hawk. I've also got a mask."

"It doesn't work like that," he said. "I found out that the masks were sent to the attendees ahead of time. Each one has a unique barcode that is scanned upon entry. So, you can't just bring your own. This mission will be over before it starts."

"It already is over if we can't get inside and determine which one is Fang. And I don't want to sit here and bang my head against a firewall all night long, trying to hack my way in."

Hawk sighed.

"That sounds like Ryder talking," he said. "Is he the one feeding you these ideas?"

"We were talking about it together, yes."

"Sit tight," Hawk said. "I'll figure out a way inside."

After Hawk parked the Elva, he hustled back to the stand and found a lull in the rush.

"You know what this meeting is all about?" Hawk asked one of the other valets.

"I don't know," the young man said with a shrug. "We're not supposed to ask questions. But you're not getting through those doors without a special mask."

"I heard."

"But, if you're really brave and you don't care about getting fired, I just saw an extra mask lying on the passenger seat of an Aston Martin I parked a few minutes ago."

"Hell, yeah," Hawk said. "I'm willing to risk it."

"Be my guest," the valet said before giving Hawk the number of the car and its approximate location in the nearby lot.

Hawk hustled over to the car and unlocked it. He snatched the extra mask off the seat and slipped back to his group of waiting valets. Five minutes passed before he had a chance to park another vehicle. After he did, he made a pit stop to deliver the mask to Mia.

"Good luck," he said.

Ten minutes later, Mia was inside. She found her way to the IT room and bypassed the firewall to gain access to the security system. After turning on the audio, she slipped out a stairwell in the back and returned to their SUV.

"I'm back," she said. "And ready to listen."

Once the meeting started in earnest, Marcus sent the valets on an hour-long break. Hawk took advantage of that time to join Mia and Ryder to listen in on the proceedings. Other than a few sketchy details mentioned in passing, the meeting was conducted in an esoteric code. They'd have to take time to decipher it, but Hawk could easily see they weren't talking about what they were *really* talking about.

But the participants did enough talking to narrow down which person was Fang. But as the night wore on, it was more and more obvious who he was. With a slight hitch in his gait, Fang could hide his face but not his walk. He wore a gray suit with a blue tie and a pair of brown wingtips. Satisfied they'd identified the right person, Hawk asked for Mia's mask back and then reported back to Marcus.

A half-hour after the meeting concluded, Hawk huddled with the other valets a few meters behind the stand awaiting Marcus to assign them a client. Hawk noticed Fang and made it clear that he wanted to drive the man's Pagani Codalunga sports car. And while Hawk appeared to get himself in line to drive Fang's car, Marcus whistled for him to take the client right in front of Fang in the line.

Hawk forced a smile and nodded, all while cursing under his breath. He couldn't be awkward about it or Fang would know something was up. Instead, Hawk wracked his brain for another solution as he walked to the client's car. Then he had an idea.

After parking in front of the conference center, Hawk got out and kept the door open. The man tossed his cane into the backseat and then pressed a hundred-dollar bill into Hawk's hand. He thanked the man and then turned his attention to the Codalunga easing up to the front of the building. Hawk watched Fang toss his laptop into the backseat before getting in.

Once the driver's side door was shut, Hawk darted over to the passenger side door and tapped on the window before gesturing for Fang to roll it down. As the window was all the way down, Hawk leaned slightly inside and held out the mask he'd borrowed for Mia.

"I'm sorry, sir, but did you drop this?" he asked.

Fang scowled and shook his head without saying a word. Instead, he waved dismissively with the back of his hand, shooing away Hawk. But Hawk didn't care. The mask and the open window provided him with the opportunity he needed to discreetly drop the transmitting device into the passenger side pocket of the car.

He was assigned another car, but once he grabbed the key fob from Marcus, Hawk offered them and the hundred-dollar bill to any takers. One of the youngsters snapped up the opportunity, allowing Hawk to slip away without being noticed. After he was free, he sprinted toward their SUV and urged Ryder to start driving. He pulled onto one of the main streets in pursuit of Fang.

"There he is," Hawk said, pointing up ahead. "Just don't get too close or else he'll think we're following him and get paranoid."

Before Hawk finished talking, the Codalunga lurched forward, the tires leaving fresh marks as it zoomed ahead.

"Come on, Ryder," Hawk said. "Don't lose him."

"How the hell can I not lose him?" Ryder said. "That car will smoke this thing. Why'd you get it anyway?"

"I couldn't find a white van, plus I thought this would be better suited for pursuing another vehicle if it came to that."

Ryder shook his head as he rammed his foot all the way onto the accelerator pedal. Suddenly the ride took on a different feel, seeming more like a video game than a real life chase. They drove through intersections, risking it on red lights. They jumped curbs and struggled to stay on the road as they rounded corners. Meanwhile, Fang remained cool in his Codalunga, only goosing the engine when Ryder got closer.

"How much closer do I need to be?" Ryder asked.

"About twenty more meters, according to the app," Mia said.

A few minutes later, they edged within a safe distance to activate the device—and Mia got to work on cloning the hard drive.

"Stay close," she said. "If we fall away from more than the prescribed distance, I'll have to start over."

"Well, we've got plenty of gas," Ryder said.

"That's not important," Hawk said, slapping Ryder on the back of the head.

"Owww," Ryder said. "Was that really necessary?"

"Yes, yes it was," Hawk said. "Now, stay focused and keep us close enough to pick up the signal."

The cloning commenced with Mia keeping her eyes affixed on the status bar, calling out the progress.

"Five percent ... ten percent ... fifteen percent ..."

Three minutes passed and they still weren't done. Fang continued to drive through the city, doing his best to lose them. But he couldn't shake them, not with all the traffic lights and congestion on the roadways. Fang tried doubling back, going slow then suddenly accelerating, and slamming on brakes. Nothing enabled him to shake the SUV behind hm.

Once they reached eighty-five percent, Mia alerted everyone to just how close they were.

"It's taking about twenty seconds per each five percent," she said. "So, just about a minute more. Think you can do it?"

"Of course," Ryder said.

With thirty seconds remaining, the sunroof slid back and Fang popped out of the opening, weapon in hand. He started firing at the SUV. Ryder whipped the vehicle back and forth, tires barking, nearby motorists honking. He adroitly avoided the spray of bullets from Fang's gun, the shots peppering the pavement behind them. Fang appeared to reload and took aim at Ryder.

"Got it," Mia said.

Ryder immediately spun the SUV around in the opposite direction. He ventured off a side street and found a circuitous route back to their hotel.

"Holy shit, that was close," Ryder said.

Hawk patted Ryder on the back.

"Excellent work," Hawk said. "I can't believe you didn't eat a bullet there."

"Well, I've got something for you to chew on," Mia said, her eyes bright beneath the computer's glow.

"Already?" Hawk asked. "That was fast."

"That's what I'm known for," she said. "How else do you think I could orchestrate all those attacks?"

Hawk shrugged. "I don't know, but I'm looking forward to hearing the spoils earned from this successful op."

She smiled and shook her head.

"You're never gonna believe this."

CHAPTER
THIRTY-FOUR

LANGLEY, VIRGINIA

ROBERT BESSERMAN STARED out across the courtyard from his office perched atop CIA headquarters and twisted his watch on his wrist. His security chief called him to alert him that the president's convoy was pulling up to the front entrance. Besserman watched as members of President Bullock's Secret Service detail poured out of the black SUVs before opening his door. Bullock smoothed down his tie and buttoned his dress coat before striding up the steps and entering the building.

Besserman hustled down to the main floor and arrived in time to greet the president. After exchanging pleasantries, Besserman led Bullock and his entourage up the stairs. Once they reached Besserman's office, he retreated inside with the president, leaving the Secret Service members outside to guard the room.

Besserman shut the double doors behind them and gestured toward a sitting area in the corner of his office.

"Can I get you a drink, sir?" Besserman asked as he sauntered over to the small mini bar in the corner of the room.

"I'll pass," Bullock said. "This meeting is going to be brief."

Besserman swallowed hard.

This is it. He's going to fire me. Impatient bastard.

"You didn't have to come all the way out here," Besserman said as he took a seat. "I know you're busy. You could've just called."

Bullock sat down and shook his head.

"Absolutely not. You know how much I value my people. And I think it's important that we meet face to face when possible."

"Look, I know you're not happy with how long this investigation is taking, but—"

Bullock held up his hand.

"You can stop right there," he said. "I understand that there are things outside of your control and that you're working hard to get to the bottom of this."

"Why do I feel like there's a *but* coming after this sentence?"

"Because there is. As hard as I know you're working, Washington has always been about the bottom line."

Besserman stood up and headed back to the mini bar.

"If you're not going to have a drink, I will. Sounds like I'm going to need one to hear what you're about to say," he said.

"Sit back down," Bullock said with a scowl. "You need to let me finish."

Besserman sighed and returned to his chair.

"Now, in this case, the bottom line is about the results of your investigation into the CIA breach, the one that's exposing our officers embedded around the world and endangering their lives. Aside from the physical danger each one of them is facing, it's also bringing new geopolitical problems for me, presidents and prime ministers wanting to know why we have people in their sovereign soil without prior permission. It's a mess, I swear."

"We're doing our best."

"I know you are, but sometimes a person's best just isn't enough," Bullock said. "You made a decision early on to avoid announcing an open investigation. And while that might have been a good approach initially, it hasn't led to the results we needed. We've already lost two agents who were murdered and two more who had to be extracted from important positions."

"Three," Besserman corrected. "We caught the fifth one before Mayhem could leak it, but we decided to play it safe."

Bullock shook his head.

"And how many more are there going to be before you catch this traitor? How crippled will our intelligence be in these critical criminal theaters? From where I sit, it's going to be in shambles if it isn't already."

"Sir, we have thousands of officers embedded all over the world. It's not going to continue for much longer. We're very close."

"I've heard that before from you—and we're still at ground zero, sticking our heads in every hole in the ground looking for the person or group of people who are doing this. And with no better results. Now, I've been more than patient with you and, for the most part, pretty fair."

"I just need a few more days," Besserman said. "We're very close. I haven't had a chance to tell you that we had a special operation last night that infiltrated a secret gathering of The Alliance. Agent Hawk and his team were able to clone the laptop Jun Fang took into the meeting."

Bullock stood and ambled over to the window. He rubbed his temples, closing his eyes as he prepared to respond.

"Okay," Bullock said with a snap, "I'll tell you what, this is my final ultimatum for you. You've got two days to give me something, anything, that shows me you're close to catching the bastards who are grinding our intelligence efforts to a halt. Two days. Got it?"

"And after that?" Besserman asked.

"I'm going to make a change."

"Who? Do you have someone in mind?"

"That's nothing you should worry about, especially if you're really as close to catching the traitor as you say you are. Good luck, Bobby. You know I'm rooting for you."

The two men shook hands before Bullock walked out. He held up two fingers above his head.

"Two days, Bobby. Two days."

Besserman didn't need the extra reminder, especially within earshot of some of his staff. If anything, the president's personal visit was going to crank up the rumor mill. Besserman imagined that every political blog would be on fire within hours of the news regarding the president's surprise visit—and the speculation would be wild and rampant.

Besserman let out a long breath through puffed cheeks and interlaced his fingers, resting them on top of his head. He knew his time was short and he didn't know if he could slow it down enough to satisfy Bullock.

PRESIDENT BULLOCK RETURNED to his vehicle and immediately took a call from George Hix.

"How's it looking, General?" Bullock asked. "Are you still vetting potential replacements for me?"

"Right now, everything is looking good," Hix said. "If you want to make a change, I think I can whole-heartedly endorse at least one candidate for the position."

"And you're sure there aren't any skeletons in the closet?"

"No, he's damn near perfect, a true American comeback story. An orphan who worked hard to climb the ladder to success in U.S. intelligence."

"Okay," Bullock said. "Run it up the flag with the communications team. I want to make sure they don't see any PR pitfalls. I want this to be smooth, especially because nothing else has been smooth about this whole process."

"I think you'll be happy with the results."

"So, who's our prime candidate?" Bullock asked. "Is it who you've thought it was this whole time?"

"Yes, sir. I think John Wicker is your star hire who'll get things done for you."

"Excellent," Bullock said. "I'll let you know when I'm ready to make the announcement."

CHAPTER
THIRTY-FIVE

WASHINGTON, D.C.

BIG EARV TOOK a brochure from the woman at the help desk at the National Gallery of Art and flipped through it, stopping on one of the pages and briefly scanning it. When he was a member of the Secret Service, he'd spent plenty of time in the building, visiting it often while dating a woman who worked as one of the gallery's curators. Pretending to read the pamphlet was his effort to portray himself as a casual tourist. But he wasn't there for the art. He was there for Payton Quick.

Despite snapping a photo of Payton meeting with John Wicker and a known North Korean spy, it didn't cause near the alarm that he thought it would. Though his expertise consisted of personal security of dignitaries—particularly the president—he considered himself somewhat versed in the world of intelligence. And he wasn't aware of any time when it was okay for the director of the NSA to meet with a foreign spy, especially a spy whose country was among those counted as an enemy of the United States. But Big Earv was told he was wrong.

After showing the photos to CIA Director Robert Besserman, Big Earv was commended for not stepping in.

Besserman warned him that it could've been the end of his career in Washington as Wicker would've surely blacklisted him. According to Besserman, Wicker and Payton Quick were working to bring in Kwon Choi. For the past few months, Choi had hinted he was interested in defecting, reaching out to a handful of U.S. intelligence officers. For safety reasons, Besserman declined to meet with Choi, not trusting that his intentions were pure. But Wicker, who had known Choi's adopted father while studying at UCLA, volunteered to have a conversation with Choi. If Big Earv had confronted them at the Opera Ultra, there's a good chance it would've spooked Choi. And despite the intelligence community's reluctance to embrace Choi, the potential information he had on Pyongyang would've proved invaluable for U.S. efforts to get a better idea about how the North Korean dictator thought and acted.

But Big Earv still had questions, the kind he didn't want explained away. Something felt off to him. And not even Besserman could reasonably explain Payton Quick's visits to the agency. Big Earv needed to find out for himself what was really going on.

The late afternoon patrons at the National Gallery of Art were sparse in comparison to the early morning crowd packed with school trips and tourists. Big Earv clasped his hands behind his back, strolling casually from one room to the next in search of Payton. He'd followed her to the gallery and watched her enter sporting a smart business suit and clutching a briefcase. Though she'd only entered about a minute ahead of him, she had seemingly vanished. Big Earv would've sworn on his Grandma Viv's grave that Payton entered the west wing of the building, but she wasn't in sight.

Big Earv weaved from room to room as he searched for her, sometimes needing only a cursory glance to see she wasn't inside. As he plodded ahead, he finally identified her sitting alone on a bench staring at Homer Winslow's painting "Home, Sweet Home." Instead of immediately approaching her, he stopped in front of a painting, pretending to look at it so he could watch her out of the corner of his eye. She sat still, hands clasped in her lap, head looking straight ahead at the painting. Then Big Earv realized her briefcase was missing.

Where was it?

From his angle, he couldn't see the very front of the bench. The briefcase could be on the floor near her feet, which would seem like the natural place to put it. But then she stood and moved toward the room's exit, hands empty and relaxed by her side. Big Earv turned his back to her, casting only furtive glances at her until she was gone. Then he walked briskly over to the bench and didn't see the briefcase. Big Earv checked an adjoining room and found it tucked neatly against the side of a bench.

He picked up the briefcase and resumed his search for Payton, who'd slipped into another room. After a short search, he found her heading toward the exit. Once she left the building, she put on her sunglasses and pulled a scarf over her head. Big Earv trailed after her, curious to see where she planned to go next. Payton walked with purpose, never once looking behind her for three blocks. Then she ducked into a cocktail bar.

Big Earv sat down next to her at the bar and pushed the briefcase in front of her.

"You forgot something," he said.

Her eyes widened as she turned slowly and glared at him.

"What do you think you're doing?"

"I saw you leave this next to a bench at the art gallery," he said.

"Are you following me?"

"Absolutely. And I'm not going to stop until you tell me what the hell you're doing. Why were you meeting with Choi and Wicker? Why do you keep making visits to Langley? And this time, I don't want your bullshit. I want the truth."

"Please," she said, raising her voice, "would you leave me alone?"

Her comment drew stares from nearby customers, all looking at Big Earv and giving him disapproving looks.

"Now, if you don't mind, I'm going to leave now and you're not going to follow me."

She collected her purse and then spun around and marched out of the bar.

Big Earv hustled toward the door and was about to walk outside when a hulking man put his hand on his chest.

"Leave the little lady alone, buddy," the man said.

Big Earv looked at the man's hand and then slowly turned his gaze toward him.

"If you don't want me to break your hand, I advise you to remove it from my chest."

The man, stocky but a head shorter, slid in front of Big Earv.

"Something tells me your mouth is cashing checks your body can't cash," the man said with a sneer.

Big Earv held the man's gaze for a few seconds before grabbing his wrist with both hands and bringing it down across his knee. The man doubled over and clutched his hand, groaning from the pain. Big Earv grabbed a fistful of hair and forced the man's head downward, driving a knee into his face. A crack preceded and more intense cries of pain from the man. Other patrons began to stand up and stare at him, though no one else approached Big Earv. He said nothing as he put a shoulder into the door and walked outside.

He looked up and down the sidewalk, scanning the area for Payton. But she was gone again.

Big Earv cursed under his breath and went back inside to get the briefcase. As he reached for it, the bartender put a hand on it.

"I think this belongs to that woman who ran off," he said. "I'll be keeping it for her."

Big Earv narrowed his eyes.

"Unless you want to end up like that guy," he said, jerking a thumb over his shoulder, "I suggest you take your hands off this."

The bartender didn't move for a moment before conceding and easing away.

Big Earv snatched the handle and grabbed it. He left the bar and returned to his car, casting the briefcase onto the passenger seat. Putting his thumbs on the two latches, he pushed down and they released. He opened the case and let out a low whistle as he stared wide-eyed at stacks of cash.

What exactly are you hiding, Miss Quick?

CHAPTER
THIRTY-SIX

ONCE THE MAGNUM Group jet soared over the Indian Ocean and reached its cruising altitude, Hawk, Ryder, and Mia huddled around a table with a big pot of coffee in the center. Hawk poured himself a cup, wrapped his hands around it, and closed his eyes as he inhaled the rich aroma of Colombian beans swirling upward. After drawing in a long breath, he exhaled slowly and leaned back in his chair.

"It's the little things, you know," Hawk said.

"I agree," Mia said, pecking away on her laptop. "And it's the little things that we miss that allows these monsters to fester in the shadows."

Hawk studied her for a moment, her eyes flitting back and forth while looking intently at her screen. Gone was her easy-going demeanor, trading it out for one that was hyper serious, maybe even angry. The lines creasing her forehead had been there for a several minutes and had only deepened the longer she typed.

Meanwhile, Hawk noticed Ryder seemed a little discon-nected, studying his fingernails and not engaging with either of them.

"You all right?" Hawk asked, punching Ryder playfully on the shoulder. "Some girl do you wrong?"

"I look that pathetic, huh?" Ryder asked.

"Your words, not mine."

Ryder furrowed his brow, thinking for a moment before responding.

"How long have you been doing this?" he asked.

"Well over a decade and counting."

"And you're still here?"

Hawk smiled.

"I see a lot of myself in you when I first started," he said. "I didn't just throw caution to the wind—I chucked it into a hurricane. There wasn't a situation where I didn't think I could navigate my way out of. And I still don't. But how I approach them has changed."

"Well, you're reading me wrong," Ryder said. "I didn't ask if you're still here to suggest that you've survived after being in the business. I asked it because I can't believe you're *still* doing this."

"I'm afraid I don't understand what you're getting at."

"This is too easy. Not enough danger."

"To be honest, you're lucky to be alive," Hawk said. "And based off some of the positions you've put me in, I'm lucky to be alive too. If you think this job isn't exciting enough for you, I don't know that you'll ever find anything that will give you the thrill you're seeking. But this job isn't about thrills—it's about putting everything on the line to complete a mission, to finish a task. Sometimes it puts us a hair's breadth away from death. Other times it simply requires creativity. But it's certainly not boring, and it's more often than not dangerous as hell."

"Maybe I'm just built differently."

"Have you considered tightrope walking?" Hawk suggested. "Maybe you can string a wire between two skyscrapers and see if that fills the need you're seeking. Because I can tell you that this job's ultimate mission is about others, doing things to keep others safe. The only thing you're going to get out of it is a lot of broken bones, bloodied noses, and a bruised ego to go along with the simple satisfaction of knowing you're doing something to protect innocent civilians from terrorists and tyrants."

"There wasn't exactly a brochure to read when they recruited me."

"Maybe you'll feel differently once this mission is over with," Hawk said. "Just hang in there until we've completed the job. This team needs you."

Mia cleared her throat and then adjusted her glasses.

"I hate to break up this little career counseling moment," she said, "but we need to talk about what I've uncovered on Jun Fang's laptop."

"What've you got?" Hawk asked, turning his attention to Mia.

"So, I think we already knew that Fang oversees a conglomerate with businesses involved in a wide range of industries," she said. "And many of them seem somewhat innocuous, right? A company that builds high-powered solar panels that are being used in remote areas of Africa. Another one that manufactures ball-bearings. And then there's his service-oriented business, including one that serves as a recruiter for the tech industry. He also has several others that appear to be more charitable than anything else. According to his records, he loses money every year on his adoption agency. But that's always been the one that stuck out to me, the odd duck in this pond of high-profit ventures. Why keep losing money like he has for years?"

Hawk took a sip of his coffee and scooted to the edge of his seat.

"Did you find anything related to adoption from the files I found in Fang's office?" he asked.

"That adoption agency is a legitimate business, placing older children all around the world, many of whom have aged out of orphanages," she said. "But Fang's agency takes them in and more often than not finds a home for them. Yet, it's not what it seems."

She spun the computer around to show spreadsheets for the adoptions versus the adoption placements.

"What are we looking at?" Hawk asked.

"Based off of what you found, I suspected this was something worth looking into," she said, becoming more animated as she continued. "I mean, why make such a distinction between adoptions and adoption placements? Seems like merely a lack of continuity in labeling them. But you could tell that wasn't the case. And now we know that hunch is true."

Hawk squinted as he peered closer at the screen.

"Please explain all these numbers."

"From what I can tell, this spreadsheet was how Fang's team evaluated the potential for certain adoptees," she said. "There's a column for their IQ, reflexes, strength, problem-solving skills, foreign language aptitude."

"If I didn't know any better, I'd say he was searching for operatives," Ryder said, suddenly becoming engaged in the conversation.

"Then you don't know better," Mia said, "because that's exactly what he's doing. Now most of what I found was coded, at least the names were. The adoptees were assigned a number, so we don't have the identity of any of them. Their placement locations were also coded by numbers. There's a list of those who were dropped from the program and entered into the general adoption pool, too. So, it's easy to see what we're looking at. What's even more frightening is how long this program has been going on. According to this document, there are people listed here with birthdates more than fifty years ago. From what I can tell, the program was started forty years ago. And he's still tracking these people. It's impressive as it is concerning."

"So Fang could have agents positioned around the world trained and ready to carry out his bidding?" Ryder asked.

Mia nodded.

"If this program is designed to insert sleeper agents around the globe, all he would have to do is activate them," she said. "And then who knows what they would do. Assassins? Agitators? Ring leaders?"

"And who's to say they haven't recruited others?" Hawk said.

"Or maybe even they're connected, working together," Mia said. "What he's doing with them and how he intends to use them is nothing more than a guessing game. Until we know the identities of these adoptees and where they are in the world, we have no idea about any of these. At this point, all we know is that this program exists."

"This might have been Fang's way into The Alliance, if he didn't found the organization himself," Hawk said.

"It'd be foolish to think he's not one of the biggest players in the group," Mia said. "And he's got a great cover as the leader of JF Dynamics, which is always making news for its innovative products and its subsidiaries. Nobody would see him as some dark criminal mastermind."

"Why would he be one, right?" Hawk asked. "Most people would look at all the money he has and dismiss such an allegation out of hand, unable to see the motive."

"But money doesn't motivate everyone," Ryder said.

"You're right—but the vast majority of people in our society, at least in the West, don't believe that," Hawk said. "They think every decision is driven by the quest to acquire more wealth. Yet for some people, money is a gateway to holding more power. And based off what we've seen about Fang, he seems like the kind of guy fueled by a desire to obtain more power. But we're going to need to pay him a visit."

Mia cracked her knuckles and pushed back from the table, reclining in her chair.

"Good thing I already tracked his private jet, which took off about an hour before we were able to get out of Bali," she said.

"See," Hawk said, "it's good to be rich *and* powerful. So, where's he headed?"

"From the flight tracker I have, it appears as if he's going to London, JF Dynamics' European headquarters, which makes sense because Fang's scheduled to present at the London Tech Expo in a few days."

"I'll let the pilot know," Hawk said, transitioning into an English accent, "we have a new bloody destination."

CHAPTER
THIRTY-SEVEN

WASHINGTON, D.C.

THE NEXT MORNING, Big Earv leaned against a lamp post outside Payton Quick's apartment complex, cap pulled low across his brow as he stared at his phone. An overnight thunderstorm had drenched the area and a heavy morning fog had socked in Washington. Even with daylight breaking, he struggled to make out the faces of the people working the operation.

Payton's resistance to speak with Big Earv made him realize he needed to take a more aggressive approach with her. He was monitoring all her known phone numbers, including her two cells and office phones. Most of her text messages were encrypted and also delivered in some sort of code. It's why he resorted to tailing her. He needed to confront her in the presence of others to see if anyone else could determine if she was lying—and maybe help him uncover what she was really doing.

After devising an op designed to coerce her to be more forthcoming, he cobbled together a team from friends within the CIA and FBI while also securing the cooperation of the closest Metro Police Department precinct. He raised his sleeve to his mouth, activating his mic.

"Operation Quick Time is a go," he said.

A woman walking a Yorkie approached Payton. But before the two crossed paths, another man sprinted near them and ripped the dog walker's purse off her shoulder and kept moving. The woman tumbled to the ground right in front of Payton.

"Oh, my god, are you all right?" Payton asked, kneeling next to the woman to see if she was okay.

The woman, who was lying face down on the concrete, slowly turned around and sat up, her face a bloody mess.

"Did you see that?" she asked, dabbing her forehead with the back of her hand. "He just snatched my purse and took off."

"I know," Payton said. "I saw it all. Do you want me to call the police?"

"Call them and any other law enforcement organization you can get out here," she said. "I won't stand for that. He needs to pay. What has this city become?"

"Of course," Payton said dialing 9-1-1.

"This place used to be such a nice place to live," the woman said. "But now I can't even go outside to walk my dog without endangering my very life."

Big Earv moved to a position further away, but was able to maintain visual of the situation. Payton remained next to the woman, bandaging her up while they waited on the police to arrive. And a few minutes later, a police car rolled up to the scene, lights flashing, siren blaring.

Two officers got out and went straight to the woman.

"Are you the one who called about the mugging?" one of the officers asked.

The woman nodded and then pointed at Payton.

"She saw it all, too," the woman said. "She will confirm everything I tell you."

"Ma'am," the officer said, "would you like to come down to the precinct and give us a statement? We're just around the corner."

"Of course," the dog walker said. "I want you to catch the bastard who did this to me."

The other officer looked at Payton.

"Did you see the altercation occur that this woman is referencing?" he asked.

Payton nodded.

"I was only a few feet away from it all."

"Then would you mind coming down to the precinct and give us a statement?"

Payton hesitated and looked at her watch.

"I really need to go," she said. "I'll be more than happy to give you my number and can talk after I get home from work."

The dog walker narrowed her eyes at Payton.

"You think they'll be able to catch him after you describe what he looks like nine or ten hours after it happened?" the woman said. "He'll probably have spent all my money and maxed out all my credit cards before that happens."

Payton sighed.

"Okay, fine. I'll do it, but I've gotta make this quick."

"Great," the officer said. "Just follow us."

Big Earv pocketed his phone and strolled over to the bike rack. He climbed onto his bike and pedaled over to the precinct.

A few minutes later when he arrived, Payton was already seated in an interview room with a bottle of water in front of her. He stopped into the room next to it and glanced at the monitor. Payton rubbed her hands together and checked her watch twice in the brief time he watched it.

"How's she looking?" Big Earv asked Joe Vance, the FBI agent who pretended to be one of the cops.

"Madder than a wet hen."

"That means nothing to me, Joe. I didn't grow up on a farm."

Joe shrugged.

"She's pissed," he said. "She's already shouted for someone several times, demanding why no one has taken her statement so she can get to work."

Big Earv smiled.

"Care to join me? I have a feeling this is going to be a lot of fun."

"Maybe in a few minutes, but your other guy is on his way down here," Joe said. "Special agent Carlotti is across the hall and said he's ready whenever you get here."

Big Earv introduced himself to Agent Carlotti and discussed how to handle the interrogation before joining Payton. As soon as her gaze met Big Earv's, she rolled her eyes. Then she slammed the table, her lips forming a thin line to go along with her sharp scowl.

"I should've known this was one of your stunts," she said, her index finger pointed at Big Earv and jabbing at him. "I swear, you're going to end up in a basement somewhere filing papers for the rest of your miserable career."

"It's good to see you, too, Miss Quick," Big Earv said.

"You think this is fun and games, don't you?" she said with a sneer.

Carlotti intervened.

"Miss Quick, my name is Special Agent Carlotti, and we're hearing some reports about you that we'd like for you to clear up for us. Would you mind doing that for us right now?"

"That whole purse snatching thing was all a charade just to get me down here, wasn't it?" she said.

"Of course," Big Earv said. "I can't get you to shoot me straight, so I decided I needed some help."

"That's because you kept accosting me while I was trying to do my damn job," she said, slapping the table for emphasis. "I already told you that you didn't know what you were meddling in and to back off. But I see that message hasn't sunk into that thick skull of yours. I'm only following orders, though you're making it rather difficult for me."

Carlotti put his hand on Big Earv's wrist, signaling for him to be quiet.

"Miss Quick, I understand you work for the NSA. Is that correct?"

"What? You need a background on me? Like Sherlock over here hasn't already told you everything about me. It's not like I'm trying to hide anything—except maybe who I am from people who might want me dead."

"Someone wants you dead?" Carlotti asked.

"They might if they see me chatting it up with a fed."

Big Earv folded his arms across his chest.

"I wanted another witness here so they could be present for the lies you spew every single time I simply ask you what you're doing. Now, are you ready to start telling the truth?"

"I've been telling you the truth, the whole truth, and nothing but the damn truth, so help me God," she said, the volume of her voice escalating with each spoken word. "But you can't seem to grasp the concept that an employee of the NSA might be doing some things that she doesn't want the entire world to know about. I've kept a discreet profile, like the well-trained officer that I am, but you just keep pushing, like some wacko activist journalist with an axe to grind."

Big Earv shrugged.

"You're just doing your job. I'm just doing mine. And unfortunately for you, my job requires that I turn over every rock and look in every dark corner for the person who's trying to destroy years and years of agency work by exposing some of our country's best and most skilled officers. So, now's the time to start talking about what you've been doing, like why you're meeting with Choi at night clubs, making visits to the agency archives, and leaving a briefcase packed with money in an art gallery."

Payton closed her eyes and took a deep breath. She licked her lips and then opened her eyes again, this time staring directly at Big Earv.

"This is the last time I'm going to tell you anything without the presence of my lawyer," she said. "Do you understand?"

"I'm listening," Big Earv said, nodding.

"We have our own mole at the NSA, someone we believe is leaking intel to bad actors in the Middle East," she said. "My visits to Langley were strictly designed to get certain files and doctor them for our potential mole. We were sending him bad info and looking to see if it would show up in certain sections of the dark web. I was simply following orders, like I told you earlier."

"And Choi and the briefcase?" Big Earv asked.

"I met with Choi because he wanted to defect and he has a connection with Wicker," she said. "I went with Wicker to ensure he wasn't accused of doing anything illegal. And the briefcase was a payment I was asked to leave for an informant, which he didn't get and is upset about. And now I have to meet with my boss—a meeting I'm now late to, thanks to you—who's going to rant at me for a half-hour because I screwed up a simple dead drop."

"Since when did the NSA get involved in cloak and dagger stuff?" Big Earv asked.

"Does the CIA stick to gathering intel abroad?" she asked, arching an eyebrow.

"Point taken," Big Earv said.

"Satisfied, asshole?" she hissed.

"Okay, okay," he said, raising his hands in the air. "We've asked Director Wicker to vouch for you, and if everything checks out, you'll never hear from me again."

"So am I free to go?"

Big Earv gestured toward the door.

"Be my guest. Just don't leave the country."

Payton flipped him off as she stormed out of the room and disappeared down the hall.

"She's pleasant," Carlotti said.

"If I were her, I'd be upset too," Big Earv said. "But I just couldn't let it go until I had all my questions answered."

"And are you satisfied that she's not leaking the names of agency officers?"

Big Earv pursed his lips.

"Probably not, but I still want to hear Wicker's side of things, just to make sure it all matches up. If she's a double agent, she's a damn good one and I'm not going to concede that she's clean that easily."

"Fair enough," Carlotti said as he glanced at his phone. "And it looks like Wicker just arrived."

"Good," Big Earv said. "Let's get this over with."

Big Earv walked across the hall with Carlotti to find Wicker in another interview room. He was sipping on a water bottle and scrolling through messages on his phone when he looked up to see the two men.

"Director," Big Earv said as he offered his hand, "I'm sorry to bring you down here like this, but I'm sure you understand."

"Of course," Wicker said as the two men shook hands. "As I told Besserman, I'm happy to help however I can."

"Excellent," Big Earv said before introducing Carlotti.

They joined Wicker at the table, sitting opposite him.

"So," he said as he put away his phone, "what's this all about with Payton Quick?"

Big Earv recounted his run-ins with her, including seeing her out with Choi at Opera Ultra. When he finished, he gestured for Wicker to respond.

"This is disconcerting, to say the least," Wicker said. "I've brought Payton under my wing, so to speak, training her in the art of spy craft. While most of our work in intelligence gathering is cyber centric, we have need from time to time for officers to do some field work for us. Payton was trained at Quantico, but I've been assigning her various tasks."

Wicker pushed away from the table, folding his arms across his paunch. He palmed the top of his bald head and scratched it, wincing as he did before continuing.

"The deal with Choi is something I asked her to help me with because I wanted her to learn how to vet someone who wants to defect and spill state secrets about a foreign intelligence agency. As you both well know, the bureau usually handles things like that here, while the CIA takes the lead in those cases overseas by working with our embassies there. But in this instance, I had prior contact with Choi so we all agreed it made sense for the NSA to handle it, or, more precisely, it made sense for *me* to handle it."

"And what about the other issues I mentioned?" Big Earv said.

"I can confirm that Payton was making a dead drop payment to an informant from a black hat hacker organization. He required cash payment because, well, he knows how easy it is to track money once it's transmitted."

"That leaves the issue of the visits to Langley," Big Earv said. "Did you send her there?"

"That's the one that leaves me shaking my head a little bit," Wicker said. "I'm not aware of any assignment she would've been given from me or any of her other superiors that would've required her to go to the agency with any frequency."

"Are you aware that all of her visits there coincided with the release of CIA officers' names?" Big Earv said.

"Are you shittin' me?"

"I wish I was," Big Earv said. "All of the releases from Mayhem happened exactly one week after her visits. And according to Mayhem, who's now in our custody, they were all sent via express mail, not digitally. So, they needed time to get there. And that timeline checks out."

"Damn," Wicker said, shaking his head slowly. "Right under my own nose."

"I'm sorry to have to be the one to tell you this, sir," Big Earv said.

"It's not your fault," Wicker said. "So, how do you want to handle this? Is the bureau going to bring her in?"

"That's what we were planning on doing, unless you object," Carlotti said.

"Not at all," Wicker said, putting his hands in the air. "You just let me know what you need from us and we'll get it for you. Files, records, logs—anything."

Wicker stood and put his hands on the table, leaned forward and took a deep breath.

"I can't believe she did this to us," Wicker said, "especially after all I did for her."

"It happens to the best of us, sir," Carlotti said. "Even Jesus couldn't pick twelve committed disciples. We've all been betrayed."

"But not like this, you haven't," Wicker said.

"I'm sorry," Big Earv said. "We'll be in touch."

Big Earv and Carlotti ironed out the details for how they would proceed. Once they finished, Big Earv called Morgan May.

"Well, I've got some good news for you," he said. "Eh, maybe it's more kind of good news-bad news."

"I'll take anything after the way things have been going. Lay it on me."

"We found the mole," he said. "And it looks like it *was* Payton Quick."

"I'll be damned," she said, shaking her head. "Just after we ruled her out."

"I know," Big Earv said. "But I never did. Something just felt off about her and what she was doing."

"Glad you stayed on it. Besserman will be happy to hear that news. I'll call him right after I end this call. And thanks for your good work."

Big Earv wasn't ready to celebrate quite yet. He wanted someone to gather all the details necessary to prosecute her, but he felt like a big weight had been lifted off of him.

CHAPTER
THIRTY-EIGHT

CAMP DAVID | MARYLAND

As the sun set over the wooded property of Camp David, President Bullock swirled the rum inside his tumbler, watching it for a moment before picking up a dart off the table. The oak and pine trees surrounding the veranda swayed in the wind, the fresh green leaves rustling softly. After waiting for the wind to die down, Bullock eyed the line, slid his foot just behind it, then took aim at the bullseye. His throw barely landed on the board, drawing a snicker from his guest, John Wicker.

"You think you can do better?" asked Bullock, who'd invited Wicker to Camp David for a few days to relax and get to know one another better, especially if the president intended to hire him as the new director of the CIA.

"Are we talking darts or national security?" Wicker asked with a wry grin.

"Dealer's choice."

"How about I take them in order?" Wicker said as he set his drink down and eased out of his chair. He grabbed a handful of the darts off the table and dabbed his tongue on the tip of one.

"Is that your secret? Just lick the end? Does it make it more aerodynamic?"

"It's probably just the operator," Wicker said with a wink.

He pinched the dart's shaft, drew it back near his ear, and then let it fly. The dart stuck inside the bullseye.

"Impressive," Bullock said. "Now, can you do the same thing when it comes to national security?"

Wicker shrugged before launching another dart, which also hit the center of the target.

"You're the one who appointed me to head up the NSA," he said. "How do you feel like that's going?"

"It was one of your people who was caught sending the identities to Mayhem, at least allegedly," Bullock said.

"I wouldn't say allegedly. We found out she had an account in the Caymans that was amassing quite the nest egg. Well over five million and counting."

"Okay, so, it was definitely Payton Quick then. You're not exactly instilling a lot of confidence in me that you can do better, especially since it was one of your people doing the leaking."

"If that was my building, it would've never happened in the first place," Wicker said. "I know we often exchange information, especially when we're looking at older files, maybe some older intel we've gathered that hasn't been digitized yet or we want to limit access to on-site officers and analysts. But the fact that she was able to get in so easily, gather that intel, and take it out is unfathomable."

"So, what would you do?"

"For starters, I'd prohibit any digital devices from entering the archives. Hell, the National Archives have stricter rules than the CIA for what's allowed in and out of their research rooms. It's not that difficult."

"What else?"

"Cameras would provide full coverage of the archives. No blind spots. The number of entrants at a time would be limited. A dedicated security team would monitor all activity in the archives as it was happening in real time."

"I can see you've thought about this."

"Those are just a handful of the things I've implemented at the NSA if they weren't already in place," Wicker said.

He picked up his final dart and whistled it toward the target, hitting it dead center of the bullseye.

"I can have my assistant send over my paper on this if you'd like to read it," Wicker said. "Now, how'd I do?"

"I'd say two-for-two on darts and security. Now, do you have any answers for vetting officer and analyst candidates?"

Wicker smiled as he pulled his darts out of the board.

"I've got plenty of thoughts on that too, but I think I'll definitely need another drink if we want to delve into that this evening."

Bullock eased to his feet and chuckled.

"This is one helluva way to spend a Thursday night and get a jump on a long weekend up here," Bullock said. "But why don't we take this inside and continue over a game of pool? I can see that a game of darts wouldn't be very much fun for either of us."

"I guess you've never seen me play pool," Wicker said.

"Trust me," the president said, gesturing toward the door. "It'll be much more competitive than this. Plus, I want to hear all about how you're going to change things here as the new director of the CIA."

Wicker paused, his brow creased.

"You are talking hypothetically, sir, right?" he asked.

Bullock shook his head.

"No, I'm talking about introducing you as the new CIA director as early as Monday afternoon. What do you say?"

Wicker took a deep breath then bowed.

"I serve at the pleasure of my president."

Bullock rolled his eyes and waved dismissively.

"Enough of your ass kissing. Let's get inside so I can kick yours in a game of pool."

Bullock waited for his guest to enter the house first, pausing for a moment once Wicker passed him. Bullock drew in a deep breath and took a quick look around the backwoods of Camp David. He couldn't resist a slight smile.

I've definitely found my new director.

CHAPTER
THIRTY-NINE

LONDON

HAWK SECURED his cuff links and the costume goatee before taking quick inventory of Mia. She wore a tight-fitting scoop-neck blouse, her hair curled and glossy. After pulling down the visor mirror, she studied it closely while applying her lipstick.

"Are you sure Fang never saw you when you entered that conference center in Bali?" Hawk asked.

"I didn't see anyone," she said. "I mean, I saw people. But I kept my head down and stayed focused on getting to the IT room. Did my job and got out of there."

"If you're confident, I'm rolling with it," he said. "This seems like the best way to approach him and have a shot at getting him alone."

She grabbed a microphone and held it close to her mouth. Hawk nudged it away about a foot to a more normal distance.

"You don't want to look like you're about to eat it," Hawk said. "That would be a dead giveaway that you weren't the TV personality you claim to be."

"Then he'll lure you up to his lair and slice you up with his martial arts skills," Ryder said, chuckling from the backseat.

"That kind of knowledge is good, but maybe you could try sharing it in a much more positive way," Mia said.

"Why?" Ryder said. "It's more fun to deliver information like that."

"Well, thirty seconds ago, I wasn't worried about the billionaire narcissist killing me, but now I'm worried he's going to feed me to the piranhas lurking in the giant koi pond in his office."

"Wait," Ryder said, his eyes bulging. "Fang has a koi pond in his office?"

"Guess you'll never know," Hawk said, "because you're going to stay *in the van*—emphasis on *in the van*—understand?"

Ryder sighed.

"I still don't understand why I couldn't put on a disguise and join you."

"To begin with, these are natural consequences for burning your own cover with a target," Hawk said. "If you hadn't tried to start a 'WrestleMania: Beijing Edition' while we were there, I'd figure out a way to get you in. But as it stands, we can't afford to risk being exposed or, even worse, Fang allowing us all into his office."

"You looked him in the eye in Bali," Ryder said. "Why wouldn't he remember you?"

"It was dark and a brief interaction—and I'm not wearing a disguise," Hawk said. "Now, stay in the van."

Hawk turned around and put the van into drive. Twenty minutes later, they scooted under the JF Dynamics barrier gate arm by following closely with the car in front of it. The practice, while frowned upon given the glare they received from the guard in the security hut, was a common one, and the guard didn't seem interested in really stopping any violators.

They parked in the company's underground garage and grabbed all their gear. Hawk hid his gun in his camera bag's false bottom. He hoped their gear would get a pass at the security checkpoint. But if his plan worked, one that sought to leverage Fang's massive ego, it likely wouldn't matter.

Hawk shouldered a camera bag laden with gear on his left side while his right hand clutched a professional production quality video camera. He looked at Mia, who held nothing but a reporter's notepad and a mic.

"This is exactly what it felt like when we went on a trip with little J.D.," Hawk said. "I lugged every piece of equipment known to the world that would care for and entertain a baby everywhere we went."

"As it should be," Mia said with a wry smile. "Now, trusty cameraman, where to next?"

"Fang's parking spot is on the bottom, right next to the elevators," he said. "If our intel is accurate, he should be here within five minutes."

Hawk opened the door and gave one last reminder to Ryder before trudging closer to Fang's expected arrival point. They stayed out of sight, taking cover by a concrete pillar as they waited. Five minutes later without a second to spare, Fang skidded to a stop in his Aston Martin mere inches from the post with his last name emblazoned on a placard. He collected his briefcase and a cup of coffee before climbing out.

"Go," Hawk whispered.

He trailed Mia, who strode confidently up to him.

"Mr. Fang, Mr. Fang," she said, tucking her notebook under her arm and offering her right hand. "Olivia Drake with Cinema News. I was wondering if I could get an interview with you this morning about the buzz coming out of Hollywood regarding *The Mandarin Matrix*."

Fang shook her hand and then cocked his head to one side, his curiosity obviously piqued.

"What buzz?" he asked.

"That it's already being discussed as a possible Oscar nominee for best foreign film."

"I haven't heard anything about that, though it doesn't surprise me."

Hawk hoisted his camera up onto his shoulder as he slid into a better position to capture their conversation.

"I'm really busy this morning. I'm preparing to speak at a conference later today and—"

He paused and looked at his watch.

"Oh, what the hell. I'm sure I can spare fifteen minutes for something like this," he said with a smile. "What'd you say your name was again?"

"Olivia Drake."

"Well, Miss Drake, you do look familiar," he said.

"Perhaps you've seen my show on HBO. I'm always doing fun interviews with the stars—and you're the star I'm talking with today."

Fang eyed her closely as a thin smile formed across his lips.

"You know they say flattery won't get you anywhere," he said. "But *they* are wrong. Let me just clear my schedule for the first half-hour this morning and I'll be happy to answer any questions you have about *The Mandarin Matrix*."

Fang thumbed a short message on his phone and then slid it into his pocket.

"Do we need to go through security?" she asked, her eyes big and head slightly tilted.

Hawk couldn't believe that Mia didn't have any theater training. The subtle yet sultry look. The tuck of her hair behind one ear. A playful touch of his arm and a laugh at Fang's lame attempt at humor.

She's a natural.

"If you got into my facility, I'm sure you've already been vetted by security," Fang said. "So let's take my private elevator. It'll get you in and out as quickly as possible since I'm sure you're busy too."

Fang had hardly looked at Hawk, who hid behind the camera and the bill of his hat pulled low over his brow. And that was exactly how he wanted it.

They rode up to the top floor of JF Dynamics and trailed after

Fang, who walked with purpose, ignoring every single person who stopped to smile at him and let him pass. As he marched into his office, his executive assistant looked up from her keyboard, a smile quickly giving way to a furrowed brow.

"Good morning, sir," she said as she stood. "I didn't have any media interviews on your schedule today. Did I make a mistake?"

"Not at all," Fang said. "But that's why I texted you to clear my schedule, which I trust you've already done."

"Of course, I just—"

Fang opened the door to his office and gestured for Mia and Hawk to go inside.

"See you in thirty minutes," he said to his assistant before following his two guests inside and shutting the door, locking it behind him.

Hawk scanned the room, which appeared to be more of a small waiting area than an office, a deduction proven right as Fang walked over to a bookshelf lined with encyclopedias. He hoisted his camera on his shoulder, capturing everything on video.

"Most people don't even use these things anymore," Fang said. "But I've found they're great at concealing entrances."

He tilted back one of the books near the end of its shelf and stepped back. The wall next to the bookshelf rotated ninety degrees, creating a passageway for them to enter. Fang smiled and walked inside, coaxing them to join him.

"Isn't this the coolest?" Fang asked. "Keeps us well out of earshot of my employees so we can discuss anything in peace and quiet."

Mia nodded and then turned to Hawk.

"Are you getting all this, Tyler?" she asked.

"Of course," he said. "It'll be great for B-roll footage."

Once they were inside, the door spun back into place, revealing a lavish office, decorated with plush leather chairs and sofas, while all the dark wood in the room was trimmed with leather. Behind the desk was a large floor-to-ceiling bookshelf, stacked with old leather books, some well preserved, others laboring to stay together. On the wall to the left of Fang's desk was a pair of crossed samurai swords. Hawk thought it looked like the lair of a villain from a Chinese steampunk novel rather than a billionaire executive's office.

"Now, what do you want to know?" Fang asked as he settled behind his desk. "Or would you rather sit over there in the corner on those two couches? Now that I think about it, that might make a much better setting visually."

"Whatever you prefer," Mia said. "This is all about you today. Just give us a second to get all our equipment set up."

As Fang ambled to the other side of the room, Hawk dropped his equipment. He opened a small case and removed his gun. Then he stood and trained it on Fang, whose face fell as he stared at the weapon.

"What's this about?" Fang asked, his forehead creased by deep lines. "What do you want?"

"I'm going to keep this simple," Hawk said. "You give us the names and locations of all the sleeper agents you've placed through your adoption agency and we'll let you live."

Hawk directed Fang toward the couch, away from any objects in the room.

"Get his phone," Hawk said.

Mia snatched it out of Fang's pocket and then backed away.

"So, you gonna cooperate or do I need to use some proven methods I employ when someone is being less than cooperative?" Hawk asked.

Fang studied them both, eyes bouncing between them.

"If it's money you want, I can—"

"If we wanted money, we would've asked for it," Hawk said. "I told you what I want. And I fully expect you to give it to me, that is if you're interested in avoiding any consequences."

Hawk kept his gun trained on Fang while easing over to his desk. One by one, Hawk pulled open the drawers and examined them.

"I don't have anything like that here," he said.

"We'll see about that," Hawk said.

"You're wasting your time. I keep all my sensitive files in Beijing."

Hawk wagged a finger.

"I think you keep a copy of all your sensitive files in Beijing. But let's not make this any more difficult than it needs to be."

"For you, maybe. I plan to make this as difficult as possible for you."

"How?" Hawk asked. "By lying to me for the next twenty-five minutes? You think you can run out the clock on me?"

"It won't be hard to do since I already told you that I don't have the files here."

Hawk chewed on his lip as he continued checking all the drawers, their contents seemingly benign. Contracts with businesses. A list of other business magnates, some of them recognizable names, a few of them Hawk even knew, including the name Thomas Colton. Pens, staplers, paperclips, and notepads filled another drawer.

When Hawk finished, he sighed and scanned the bookshelf behind him.

"If you're not going to talk, I'm going to rip this place apart until I find it, unless—"

He paused as an idea came to him. The bookshelf behind the desk looked more like a decoration than a functioning library—just like the bookshelf outside in the waiting area.

"Unless," Hawk repeated, holding a finger in the air.

"Unless what?" Mia asked.

"Let's suppose for a moment that Mr. Fang is telling the truth, that he doesn't have any of those documents *in this office.* Where do you think it would be? Beijing? Brussels? Or London?"

Mia shrugged.

"Probably wherever he goes the most," she said.

"Exactly," Hawk said, "which is London. But a man like Fang doesn't get to where he is without being careful with his words. He's like a magician, showing you everything you need to figure out the trick but distracting you with misdirection and showmanship. It's the kind of deceit that's allowed, accepted even. But it's still deceit, isn't it, Mr. Fang?"

Fang scowled.

"I take great pride in my honesty and integrity," he said.

"I'm sure you do, convincing yourself that you're still being truthful while you deceive everyone else, and then eventually deceiving yourself."

Hawk stroked his chin and studied Fang.

"What do you say? Why don't we go for a little walk in your library and see what we can find."

Hawk walked his fingers across the top of the books as he watched Fang's face. At first, Fang didn't give even the faintest hint that he cared. But as Hawk neared the end of the shelf, he watched for the slightest sign from Fang. The billionaire's eyes flickered as Hawk fingered a leather-bound edition of *Pride and Prejudice*. Hawk gave it a little tug, but the book didn't move. Then Hawk pulled back on the top of the spine. A mechanism began to whirr as the bookshelf opened inwardly, revealing another secret room.

"How long do you think it would take for the authorities to find your dead body in here?" Hawk asked. "Would it be before or after we left here with the names and locations of all your agents? Or perhaps you can just save us all a great deal of time and pain by simply telling me which one of these filing cabinets it is."

Fang stood and walked over toward the opening, his eyes narrowing.

"You don't know what you're doing," he said.

"Oh, I think I do, and you're going to show us where those documents are."

Fang closed his eyes and sighed, almost resigned to the fact that he didn't have a choice. He slowly entered the secret archive room and pointed toward a filing cabinet against the far wall.

"Everything you want is in there," he said.

Hawk nodded knowingly at Mia, who started rifling through

the files. It didn't take her long until she found a key attached to the copy of the same files they'd retrieved from Fang's study in Beijing. She pulled out some other documents and snapped pictures of them before stuffing the folder into Hawk's equipment bag.

"See," Hawk said, directing Fang back to his office, "that wasn't so hard after all, was it?"

As they moved through the bookshelves that lined the passageway between the two rooms, Fang darted toward the wall just to the left of his desk and ripped down one of the swords.

Stunned by the development, Hawk moved the barrel of his gun toward Fang while stepping in front of the desk. But the billionaire was one step ahead, spinning into a roundhouse kick that dislodged the gun from Hawk's hand.

Hawk dove for the gun, which had landed in an open space in the room between the desk and the sitting area. But Fang flicked it beneath the couch with the tip of his weapon. Realizing he couldn't reach it without getting run through, Hawk rolled aside and scrambled to his feet. Mia, who'd been trailing behind them, snatched the other sword off the wall and tossed it to Hawk.

Before Hawk had even wrapped his hand around the cold steel, Fang charged him. Metal clanged, the two fighters breathed hard. Grunting, twisting, turning. They traded blows, each one blocked, each time more creatively. Around the room they danced. Hawk drove straight at his opponent, forcing Fang to defend before they swapped roles. The businessman jabbed his rapier at Hawk, who slid aside, avoiding the sharp point. Hawk spun and came down hard on Fang's forearm, slicing into it and drawing a yelp.

Fang gritted his teeth and growled as he exploded toward Hawk, who jumped, pulling his knees up to evade another swipe. Then another and another. Fang worked over Hawk and kept him on the defensive. Slowly, Fang worked Hawk toward the corner of the room, hemming him in. A nick along the side of Hawk's face slowed down the fight.

But as Fang took control of the sword fight, he took his eyes off Mia, who had slinked her way across the room to where the weapon had landed.

Meanwhile, Fang and Hawk locked swords. But Fang seized the upper hand, pushing Hawk against the wall, his blade serving as the only barrier between his throat and Fang's blade. Hawk swallowed hard and kicked at Fang. The attempt was a weak one, an effort hampered by Hawk's inability to generate any leverage. He hit Fang's shin, but he didn't move.

Sweat rolled down Hawk's face, blurring his vision for a moment.

"I told you that you didn't know what you were doing," Fang said. "Now you're going to pay."

Mia cocked the gun, a sound that made both men pause.

"It's over, Mr. Fang," she said. "Drop the sword or you're going to die right here, right now."

Fang pushed off from Hawk and spun to realize he was looking down the barrel of her weapon. He knelt slowly and placed his sword on the ground.

"Kick it to me," she said.

Fang complied while Hawk joined Mia. She handed Hawk the gun.

"Would you like to do the honors?" she asked.

"Our business with Mr. Fang is done," Hawk said.

"But he tried to kill you," she protested.

"We didn't come here to kill anyone," he said. "We got what we came for. Killing him in his London office will only complicate matters for us. I'm going to teach you the art of quitting while you're ahead, something I'm sure Mr. Fang will appreciate."

Fang sneered at them.

"I'm going to find you one day and kill you myself."

"If you try," Hawk said, "I can promise you that I won't be so gracious next time."

Without warning, Hawk drew back and smashed his fist into

the side of Fang's face. The billionaire collapsed and dropped to the floor.

"Let's get out of here before he wakes up," Hawk said as he gathered his equipment.

They walked past Fang's assistant, smiling and waving.

"He told us to tell you that he won't be available for another ten minutes," Mia said.

"Wait—what—" the woman said.

Hawk and Mia didn't stop, hustling to the elevators and heading straight to the parking deck where Ryder was sitting patiently in the backseat. Five minutes later, they left the JF Dynamics campus and merged into London traffic.

"So, how close were you to ending up in Fang's koi pond?" Ryder asked.

"There was no koi pond," Hawk said. "It's all a big myth, but he does have an interesting office with a couple of hidden doors."

"How'd you find them if they were hidden?" Ryder asked.

"Intuition," Hawk said. "But most importantly, we got the key for all the sleeper agents that Fang has placed around the world."

"Checking them as we speak," Mia said.

Then her breath hitched and she reached for Hawk's arm and grabbed it, her fingernails digging into him.

"Are you all right?" he asked as he glanced at her staring at the document.

"I have to send this to Morgan right now so she can alert every agency in Washington," she said.

"What is it?" Hawk asked.

"It's President Bullock," she said. "We have to warn him—and we need to do it right now. He's in danger."

Hawk looked at his watch.

"It's two-thirty in the morning in Washington," he said. "You're not going to get anyone."

"I have to try," she said. "I just hope it's not too late."

CHAPTER
FORTY

JOHN WICKER GROANED as he rolled over in bed, his head still feeling the effects of three-too-many drinks over several games of pool with President Bullock. However, Wicker wasn't sure if his head was hurting because of the alcohol or the bright light emanating from the nightstand. He closed his eyes and opened them again, this time to hear the vibrating buzz that accompanied the screen displaying the caller's number.

"What the—" he said as he looked at the number. "Am I getting spammed in the middle of the night?"

Wicker had only a handful of numbers approved for calling him after he placed his phone on silent each night. He almost declined the call, but was confused over how it was actually ringing. Then he remembered that if a caller dials his number four straight times, the phone would eventually start ringing. He scrolled to the call log and sat up when he saw that the unknown number had called him seven straight times. It wasn't one of his usual suspects, but someone apparently wasn't going to give up until they'd spoken with him.

"Hello," he said, his voice gravelly. "This is Wicker."

"John, this is Jun Fang," the other voice said. "I need you to listen to me right now and do exactly as I say."

"Wait," Wicker said. "Who is this again?"

"Jun Fang," he said.

"Oh, Mr. Fang," Wicker said. "You'll have to forgive me. It's not often that I have all my wits about me at three-thirty in the morning. This better be important."

"Trust me. I wouldn't be calling you if it wasn't. In fact, your future depends on your ability to do exactly as I say. Otherwise, you're going to spend the rest of your life in prison. They're going to find out."

"Find out what?"

"Look, I know this isn't a secure line, so you're trying to pretend like you don't know what I'm talking about, but I know you do. Now, here's what I need you to do. I need you to grab your emergency duffle bag and enough cash for a week—and then I need you to—"

"Whoa, let me stop you right there," Wicker said. "I'm at Camp David with President Bullock. I can't just walk out of here, never mind that I don't have a car."

Fang cursed.

"You're in grave danger. And if you don't leave right now, you're going to prison forever."

"I thought you said this plan was infallible," Wicker said. "In fact, that was the exact word you used—*infallible.*"

"Well, there's been a little kink I wasn't expecting."

"The kind of kink that requires me to run and leave everything?"

"It's unfortunate, yes, but I have something else you can do, something else to contribute to our overall goals."

"Does it end with me being set up financially?"

"Of course," Fang said. "I have the means to provide a very comfortable life for you. But it's going to take some creativity on your part to disappear without getting caught. You get out of

there and meet me at the coordinates I'm about to send you and
I'll make it happen."

Wicker's phone buzzed with a text. He tapped on the coordinates, which took him to a map and showed where he was
supposed to meet Fang.

"Are you out of your mind?" Wicker asked.

"Do you not find the terms agreeable?"

"I'm supposed to escape to a place in the Everglades?"

"It's a great place to get lost in," Fang said. "No fear of dogs
catching your scent and tracking you. Plus, nobody wants to
venture into—what do the people of Florida call it—gator
country?"

"There's a reason for that," Wicker said. "And it's the same
reason why I don't want to meet you there."

"That's where I have someone who can pick you up," Fang
said. "Otherwise, you're on your own, which is something I
would advise strongly against."

"Fine," Wicker said. "I'll figure something out."

"Good luck," Fang said before ending the call.

Wicker sat up and rubbed his eyes and thought for a minute.
He grabbed a water bottle from the nightstand and chugged it,
anything to clear the haze of booze and cigars.

Now, think, John. You can do this.

He formulated a plan and tried to poke holes in it. There were
several of them, but far less than other ideas that had popped into
his head. After contemplating the plan for a moment, he decided
to forge ahead.

*I think it just might work. After all, you were trained for this
moment.*

Wicker dug into his bag and found his emergency supplies.
When he was an orphan at The Society in Beijing, he was equipped
with a bag of supplies that could assist him whenever he was in a jam.
He'd been trained to never leave without it, one of the many skills he
picked up and applied liberally to his life. And he couldn't argue

with the results. He'd climbed the federal government ladder, scaling it two steps at a time as a sleeper agent right beneath their noses. And no one ever noticed. They still hadn't, though he was certain if Fang had called him and ordered him to take action, he'd either already been identified or it was imminent. Either way, he needed to leave Camp David immediately—and as discreetly as possible.

Wicker waited until just before sunrise to approach Bullock's room, which was guarded by a pair of Secret Service agents.

"Good morning, gentlemen," Wicker said, patting both men on the shoulder. "Is President Bullock awake yet?"

"We haven't heard him stirring," one of the agent said.

"Well, I really need to speak with him," Wicker said.

"I'm sure whatever it is, it can wait."

"Actually, it can't," Wicker pressed. "This is a matter of national security. And in case you've forgotten, I'm the director of the NSA."

"I know who you are, sir, but we have protocol to follow. Perhaps if you called him."

Wicker sighed.

"Okay, I guess I can call him."

He wasn't halfway down the hall before he heard two loud thumps on the floor. Wicker smiled as he turned around and saw both men slumped on the floor. A few seconds later, Bullock poked his head outside.

"What the hell," he said before looking at Wicker. "Did you see what happened here?"

Wicker shook his head as he walked back toward Bullock.

"Get inside," Wicker said. "We need to talk."

Bullock furrowed his brow.

"What's going on, John?"

Wicker knelt next to one of the men and grabbed his gun before gesturing with it for Bullock to go inside his room.

"What'd you do?" Bullock asked.

Wicker put his index finger to his lips and shut the door.

"Charlie, I know this might come as a little surprise to you, but I'm not who you think I am."

"Well, no shit, Sherlock. Now, would you point that thing somewhere else?"

"Depends," Wicker said with a shrug.

"On what?"

"If you can do exactly as I say. Think you can follow my instructions?"

"I guess that's dependent upon what they are. I'm not killing anyone, if that's what you want me to do."

Wicker chuckled.

"Nothing like that. In fact, I like you, Charlie. It's why I let you win one game of pool last night instead of embarrassing you in every game."

"Why you *sonofabitch*. Who do you think you are?"

"The real question is this: Who do *you* think I am?"

"I'm gonna have you strung up," Bullock said. "The whole world is gonna know what kind of a traitor you were."

"I don't doubt that, but I don't really care. All I want is for you to do exactly as I say so I can get out of here in one piece and leave you alone forever."

"Fine," Bullock said. "Let's just get this over with."

Wicker explained what he wanted done and how he wanted it done. When he finished, he used Bullock's phone to call someone. A man answered the phone and Wicker told him he wanted all power to Camp David shut off. After a few minutes, the entire compound went dark.

"You're up," Wicker said as he nodded toward the phone in the corner of the room. "Just make the call and tell them what I told you to say."

Bullock sighed and shook his head as he dialed the number.

"You're insane, you know that?"

"That might be one of the tamest things anyone has ever said about me," Wicker said. "In fact, that borders on a compliment, given every insult that's been hurled at me."

A small pause followed before Bullock spoke to the person on the other end.

"I want you to get the plane ready," Bullock said. "We need to leave immediately."

Another moment of silence.

"I'll tell you where we're going when I get there. Just gas it up as if we're flying around the world, okay? Thank you."

Bullock ended the call and then eyed Wicker closely.

"If you're going to kill me, why don't you do it right now and get it over with," Bullock said. "I don't want this thing to be dragged out for much longer."

"I already told you that I'm not going to kill you, okay? That's not my end game here. I just want to disappear, okay? Can you deal with that?"

"I guess so," Bullock said. "It doesn't lessen the sting, no matter what you say. You betrayed not only your country, but also me."

"This was never *my* country," Wicker said. "Like I told you, there's so much you don't know about me. But don't worry. I'll explain everything once we're in the air."

CHAPTER
FORTY-ONE

PRESIDENT BULLOCK DRUMMED his fingers on his lap as Marine One soared across Washington and headed toward Joint Base Andrews where Air Force One awaited. A pink hue covered the clouds in the eastern horizon and signaled the arrival of a new day. In the past when he'd been active at such an early time in the morning, he would've reveled in the moment. But not today. He didn't know what was going to happen. He just knew it was a nightmare with no end in sight.

Even if Bullock survived the ordeal, he foresaw days, weeks, months, years—no, decades—of his life where this was going to be his enduring legacy. The president who appointed a sleeper agent to run the NSA. The president who not only invited a Trojan horse into the U.S. intelligence community but went and sought it out. The president who jeopardized an entire nation because of what? His impatience?

The truth was Robert Besserman had done a world class job leading one of the world's foremost intelligence agencies. He'd even resolved the issue at hand, a traitor who was revealing the identities of undercover agents around the world embedded in terrorist groups and criminal enterprises alike. And Besserman had done it the way it was supposed to be done. The assignment necessitated careful detective work and a resistance to rushing to judgment. And Besserman had coordinated with the Magnum Group team that had handled their assignment like the professionals that they were.

Yet here I am, held hostage by someone I trusted completely, not twelve hours ago.

The fall had come hard and fast for Bullock, a man who'd been hoodwinked by various advisors time and time again, all while he ignored the warnings from those closest to him. His phone rang and he picked it up to look at the name on the screen.

Wicker, who was seated across from Bullock, gave him a knowing look, one with echoes of warning and promise. The warning was evident as Bullock could see the bulge in Wicker's pants pockets, the promise likewise. If Bullock so much as gave a secret code word to any of the Secret Service agents, Wicker promised to kill them all.

Bullock pushed a button, sending the call to voicemail.

Almost immediately, his phone rang again with another call from his chief of staff, Emma Washburn.

He held up his phone so Wicker could see her name and number.

"She's not going away," Bullock said. "She's my chief of staff, and it's her job to know where I am and what I'm doing all times. And the fact that I've told a few members of my staff that we're going on a surprise trip has raised the anxiety level of a few, particularly those who hate being left in the dark, like my chief of staff."

Wicker didn't say anything, offering a half-hearted shrug.

Bullock answered the call.

"You mind telling me what the hell is going on, *sir*?" Emma said.

Bullock appreciated the fact that she said "sir," even though it was said about as caustically as Emma ever said anything. She always tried to be respectful, even when it was apparent she wanted to punch him in the face.

"It's a lot to get into right now," he said. "But the long and the short of it is that I have somewhat of a family emergency in South Florida."

"A family emergency? Is everything okay?"

"Of course not," Bullock said. "Like I mentioned, it's an emergency."

"So, that's your polite way of telling me to butt out of your personal life?"

"More or less."

"Well, this is going to result in rampant speculation. You realize that, don't you?"

"I can't ride my bike without it resulting in some sort of speculation about me," Bullock said. "Why did he take that particular route? Was he trying to send a message to developers? Was he trying to stand up for the little people? Or was he showing how he's in the pocket of big business and corporate America? We've got so many damn factions in this country that are looking for reasons to be offended that the best way to handle them is to ignore them and do whatever the hell you please. Because at the end of the day, nothing will stop them from finding fault with you."

"Is that your way of telling me that you're not going to share what's happening?" she asked.

"I thought I already did that."

She sighed.

"Can you at least give me an idea of when you're going to be back?"

"I'll be back in the office bright and early on Monday morning," he said. "Enjoy your weekend."

But Bullock knew she wouldn't. Emma's stomach would be in knots, worried about him until she saw him sitting behind his desk in his West Wing office. However, if he told her the truth, he was afraid she'd storm Air Force One and attempt an extraction.

"You get her all squared away?" Wicker asked.

"She'll be fine," the president said.

Once they touched down at Andrews, the Secret Service

agents left Bullock alone so he could have a private conversation with Wicker.

"As messed up as this is," Bullock began, "I don't want you to end up dead. Are you sure you know what you're doing? I mean, you can come clean now, and we can figure out a way to have you avoid spending the rest of your life behind bars."

Wicker chuckled.

"I'm not living just to avoid the worst case scenario here," he said. "I'm aiming for best case scenario, which means we won't see each other again after this. And while I've appreciated your friendship and all the opportunities you've given me, there's more to my life than simply avoiding a lifetime jail sentence. My chance is right there—and I need to take it."

"I don't even know what you really did."

"You will soon enough," Wicker said. "I'm sure there are people already trying to get the truth to you, but I'll let that wait. For now, just continue to do exactly as I tell you and everything will work out fine for you."

Wicker proceeded to tell Bullock the heading he wanted the pilots to fly. And the soon-to-be former NSA director also directed Bullock to inform the Air Force One staff no one else was going to be on the manifest.

"In that case, how do you expect to be let on?" Bullock asked, his brow furrowed.

"Don't you worry about that."

"I swear, John, if you're going to blow us out of the sky, I—"

"I told you nobody's going to get hurt as long as you do what I tell you to do. Are we clear on that point?"

"I guess so," Bullock said with a shrug. "But I'm struggling with it at the moment. I'm struggling with this whole damn thing, to be honest."

"And that's where character is forged—in the fire," Wicker said.

"Spare me your platitudes," Bullock said.

"Whatever you say, sir," Wicker said as he patted Bullock on the shoulder. "Wheels up by noon, understand?"

Bullock offered a weak thumbs-up signal to Wicker before he darted off across the airfield, enveloped within a hive of activity as crew members prepared for the flight. He sat down on a pallet of supplies and slung his coat over his shoulder.

Then he received a text message from Emma Washburn.

> I know what's happening. Help is on the way.

He wondered how she could know. He also wondered if her meddling would make it worse. He hammered out a short reply.

> Stay away

He didn't like being too curt with Emma, who was a fantastic chief of staff. But he also didn't want her getting involved. She didn't deserve to get caught up in the crossfire.

But outside of warning her to back off, there wasn't much he could do at this point except hope this whole situation resolved itself as quickly as possible so he could start cleaning up what was already shaping up to be one hell of a mess.

CHAPTER
FORTY-TWO

JOINT BASE ANDREWS | MARYLAND

HAWK HADN'T BEEN on the ground for more than fifteen minutes before he was ushered across the tarmac to join the crew preparing Air Force One for a surprise flight. He tried to sleep as much as he could on the Magnum Group jet's blazing fast red-eye flight back to the U.S. But it was an exercise in futility. The few times he entered into dream state, he woke up within minutes, his mind whirring over how to handle President Bullock being abducted by one of Jun Fang's sleeper agents, a sleeper agent that had ascended the halls of power and was under The Alliance's control.

Hawk guzzled an energy drink in an effort to stay as sharp as possible and then donned a pair of coveralls worn by the base's flight operations crew. Once he was ready to go, he jumped onto the back of the fuel truck, clinging to a ladder on the back before the vehicle sped across the tarmac toward the plane.

As they went, Hawk scanned the scene in front of him and tried to read the situation. From what he could tell, the activity appeared normal with usual plane prep occurring by the base's specialized staff. The only thing that looked different was the lack of staffers milling around the plane. After a brief search, Hawk spotted Bullock, who stood at the top of the stairs leading to the main cabin, a cup of coffee in his hand. As they drew closer, Hawk noticed how the president seemed distant, almost as if he wasn't present mentally. Based on his slumped shoulders and dour expression, Bullock didn't look like he wanted to be there physically either.

Where is John Wicker taking you?

Hawk searched all around for Wicker, but couldn't find him, causing Hawk to wonder what really was going on. Was this the president's way of striking back against Wicker? Or was he doing Wicker's bidding? Was Bullock going on his own volition? Hawk had so many questions, none of which could be answered without a brief conversation with the president. But Hawk doubted that would happen. While Wicker wasn't able to be seen, he was surely watching, ready to carry out one of his promises if he saw Bullock break one of his. And for the moment, Hawk could only assume that the president agreed to go along in exchange for not getting hurt or someone he knew getting hurt. Or maybe it was to keep skeletons stuffed far back into the recesses of his virtual closet. Whatever the reason, Hawk recognized the need to extricate Bullock from Wicker.

The fuel truck slowed to a stop near the back of Air Force One. Hawk worked with another crew member to begin the process of fueling the plane. After determining that no one was watching him, Hawk spoke into his coms.

"I'm about to enter Air Force One," Hawk said. "Wish me luck."

"Copy that," Alex said. "Good luck."

Then Hawk flashed his badge and told the Secret Service agent guarding the entrance that he needed to check something mechanically from the inside. The man picked up Hawk's badge to check his clearance level before waving him into the plane.

Hawk retreated to the press room, which was vacant due to the circumstances. He removed his coveralls, sporting a suit underneath. Satisfied that he was wearing the proper attire, he hid beneath a table and waited for takeoff.

The minutes ticked past like hours, taking so long that Hawk began to wonder if something had happened to Wicker or President Bullock—or both. But before he had a chance to consider the idea any longer, the engines spooled up, their high-pitched sound drawing a smile from Hawk.

A Secret Service agent opened the door and gave a cursory glance inside. It was far from thorough, but understandable given the circumstances and controlled nature of who could even get on the base, let alone inside the perimeter to anywhere near the plane. But Hawk was thrilled to take advantage of the lackadaisical approach, something he knew to be atypical among most agents.

Two hours into the flight, Hawk felt anxious and jumpy, concerned for Bullock's future. Hawk consulted with his phone to see where on the map they were.

We're making good time.

Though Hawk couldn't see outside since the press room he was in contained no windows, he could tell from his GPS app they were over Tampa and roaring toward the tip of Florida. Everyone had been tight-lipped about the final destination, making Hawk wonder if the reason for that was because nobody really knew where they were going.

Then he started hearing thumping throughout the plane and noticed the trace of some strange odor in the air.

Hawk cursed, realizing it was a gas. Unsure if it was poisonous or not, Hawk looked in the corner of the room and found a locker with big red letters emblazoned on it: "For emergency use only." He ripped open the chest and dug out some supplies. He found a gas mask and pulled it over his face.

Then he eased open the door to confirm his hunch. Before he was fully in the cramped corridor, he could see the body of what appeared to be a Secret Service agent. The man lay collapsed in a heap, his weapon easily accessible. Hawk jammed it into the back of his pants, adding it to the gun he'd brought with him.

Two weapons are better than one.

But Hawk had three, if he counted his K-bar knife.

After checking to see if the man had a pulse—which he did—Hawk made his way toward the front of the plane on the top level. He felt the plane enter a descent, which made him question if they were about to land.

As he continued down the hall, he saw no more than a dozen Secret Service agents all lying on the ground passed out. There were a couple of chefs as well who succumbed to the gas. Hawk turned off one of the burners that was warming a pan with sizzling bacon.

Hawk eased up to the flight deck and saw both pilots with gas masks on but still flying the plane without any issues.

Someone must've warned them. Or were they in on it, too?

Hawk stole downstairs and slinked his way along the wall toward President Bullock's private quarters, which was directly below the flight deck.

"Everybody's unconscious except for the two pilots and Bullock and Wicker," Hawk said into his coms.

"Copy that," Alex said. "I'm relaying this information back to Morgan and the rest of the team."

"I'll let you know when I can tell you anything else," he said.

"Just be careful, okay?"

"Always."

Hawk ended the transmission and edged closer. He could hear two men talking, one more loudly than the other, both sounding somewhat muffled. Then he recognized Wicker's voice—and it was the more aggressive one.

"D.B. Cooper hijacked a plane and tried to escape with two hundred thousand dollars," Bullock said. "He disappeared with most of the money, too. And nobody ever found out who he was, aside from the random man who makes a deathbed confession every few years. I know it's possible, but those were low odds even with plenty of things in his favor. But you just kidnapped the president and did it in Air Force One. I doubt anyone at the bureau is ever going to stop looking for me. You'll be haunted and hunted—or both—until the day you die."

"Get up," barked Wicker. "I know what you're doing. You're stalling. I don't have time for this. Let's go."

Hawk felt the plane level off. He moved closer to a nearby window and figured they were no more than ten thousand feet off the ground.

The door knob twitched and then flew open, Wicker nudging Bullock forward with his gun, both men masked.

"I said *move it*," Wicker said with a growl.

"I don't know what you're so worried about," Bullock said, gesturing toward one of the agents on the ground. "Everyone's out cold except the pilots."

"You never learn, do you?" Wicker asked. "You never know if someone is lurking in the shadows, someone who might have been impervious to the effects of the gas."

"You're exercising extreme caution, especially for someone who hijacked this plane on a whim."

Wicker stopped and cocked his head to one side.

"But did I really hijack the plane? I mean, you're the one calling all the shots here."

Bullock glared at Wicker.

"In that case, I'm going to march up to the flight deck and have them turn this plane around."

Wicker cocked his gun.

"I wouldn't advise that if I were you."

"So you *are* hijacking the plane?"

"Keep moving."

Hawk kept a safe distance as he followed them down the hall and to the back of the plane. Wicker pushed an override button and then activated the stairs leading to the rear exit. It was the way the president and his staff were trained to exit the plane in an emergency. But this was no emergency. Then Hawk understood the final destination was meaningless because Wicker planned on disappearing into the Everglades.

With the door open, the wind roared through the plane. Papers stacked on a desk nearby swirled around the room. Hawk struggled to hear what Wicker had to say.

The NSA director repositioned his backpack to his front and pulled on a parachute. He cinched the straps and put on a pair of goggles.

"So this is it?" Bullock asked. "You're really gonna do it? You're just gonna jump and try to vanish in what's sure to be the world's most intense manhunt? Well, maybe not the most intense. As long as I'm alive, it won't be that—"

Bullock froze as he locked eyes with Wicker, who had his gun trained on the president.

"There's just one more thing I need to do before I leave," Wicker said.

The plane started to shimmy, hitting a patch of rough air. Wicker put two hands on his gun in an attempt to steady it.

Hawk, his gun drawn and waving wildly in Wicker's direction, shouted in an attempt to get the NSA director's attention. But he obviously couldn't hear it as he didn't even glance in Hawk's direction.

Wicker gave a disingenuous smile, accompanied by a subtle head shake.

Hawk realized what was coming. Wicker wasn't just training a gun on the president to keep him at bay and escape. No, Wicker was about to shoot Bullock.

Gunfire filled the cabin. Wicker staggered backward before turning and leaping out of the back. Hawk rushed over to check on the president.

"What are you doing, Agent Hawk?" Bullock said. "I'll be fine, but John Wicker is trying to disappear."

Hawk noticed Bullock's shirt torn from the entry wound of a bullet, blood staining the area all around it. Scanning the area, Hawk snatched a hand towel off a nearby table and applied pressure to the wound.

"Go! Go!" Bullock shouted.

Hawk didn't move.

"Damn it," Bullock growled. "That's an order from the president."

Hawk opened an overhead bin and located a parachute. He strapped it on and rushed down the steps and into the muggy air over the Everglades.

CHAPTER
FORTY-THREE

EVERGLADES NATIONAL PARK | FLORIDA

THE WIND BEAT against Hawk's face as he sped toward the ground. The minute head start that Wicker had on Hawk was significant but not insurmountable, depending on what happened after he reached the ground. As he scanned the area below during his descent, Hawk immediately spotted Wicker, who was hard to miss with his chute already open and drifting toward the ground. Hawk figured he could make up some time by waiting until he was closer to the ground to open his chute, but not much closer. As Hawk descended, he continued watching Wicker closely, trying to determine exactly where he was trying to land.

Hawk briefly wondered if he'd done the right thing in leaving Bullock, who seemed stable and coherent despite the bullet wound. If Hawk had stayed, Wicker would've had a good chance to disappear before any search party could've been organized. But Bullock wanted Wicker captured—or dead, depending on how the confrontation played out. For the moment, that was all a big unknown as Hawk pulled his cord and began the slow portion of his descent into some of the country's most unforgiving terrain,

terrain that he wasn't all that familiar with. Tracking down Wicker in the raw swamp was going to be a difficult task—*if* Hawk was lucky.

Hawk surveyed the land below as he drifted toward the ground. Mangrove forests provided dense coverage for anyone trying to disappear. Then there was the maze of canals and rivers that wove and twisted their way for miles around the far south-west tip of Florida's peninsula. Either option would be as challenging to find a route of escape as it would be to track someone. Add that to the predatory wildlife of bears and alligators and snakes, and the Everglades was a hellish natural habitat to attempt to survive in. There was good reason this part of Florida had been left alone.

As Wicker grew closer to touching down, Hawk realized where the lunatic was headed—a dock located near a clearing appeared to be home to an Everglades expedition company. Airboats lined one side of the dock, while customers appeared to form a line that snaked back toward a shed on the shore. Wicker splashed into the water near the dock and scrambled ashore. He trained his gun in front of him as the people scattered. Then he looked skyward and fired a couple of shots at Hawk, who was about two hundred meters off the ground. Hawk noticed Wicker acting awkwardly, grabbing his shoulder with one arm. He jumped into one of the airboats and took off, leaving a confused group of tourists who slowly turned their attention skyward.

Hawk watched Wicker speed away into one of the channels in an attempt to escape. The Magnum Group agent could feel the air thickening as he neared the ground, the humidity slamming him with the force of a concrete block. Next, the sulfurous stench overwhelmed him, making him want to gag.

Once he got closer to the water, he activated his coms unit.

"I can't get into everything right now because there's not enough time," Hawk said, "but I want to make sure the pilots know that President Bullock has been shot."

"What?" Alex said.

"You heard me. Bullock's been shot. He needs medical attention—and I've got no idea if the pilots were even aware of what was going on other than the fact that they had gas masks on. I don't know if they were just following orders from Bullock or if they knew from Wicker. But no matter what, someone needs to administer first aid to the president."

"Copy that," Alex said. "I'll have the White House notify the pilots. What else is going on?"

"I don't have time right now," he said. "But I'll tell you when I get a chance."

Then a few seconds later, Hawk hit the water a few feet from the dock, enveloping himself in both the humidity and the funk. He kept moving before unlatching his parachute and hustling toward one of the airboats.

"Sir, I can't let you take that airboat," one of the employees said.

Hawk glowered at the young man, who was a decade younger and eighty pounds lighter than the covert operator standing just a few feet away.

"I'm not in the mood, nor do I have the time to explain," Hawk said. "But I'll bring this boat back—and the other one, too."

The employee didn't protest again, instead gesturing toward the boat.

Hawk climbed onto the captain's chair perched high above the empty passenger seats and revved the engine. He gave a knowing nod to the young man and took off across the water after Wicker.

The boat skipped across the water, bouncing so hard that it jarred Hawk's teeth. He worked the levers that steered the boat, while keeping his foot on the accelerator pedal, all while straining to see up ahead. Although Hawk had hoped to fire a few shots at Wicker, the use of both hands to control the watercraft meant he'd either have to stop to shoot or wait until they were on land.

Hawk estimated that Wicker was about three hundred meters

ahead, running his engine wide open as well. Then he darted left, looking more like a spur-of-the-moment decision rather than a pre-meditated route. Wicker's boat leaned hard left, the boat looking as if it might topple into the water. But before Hawk could see if the boat righted herself out of the turn, it disappeared down the waterway.

Thirty seconds later, Hawk darted down the same tributary Wicker had gone.

Hawk's engine reverberated off the scant banks on either side, amplifying its high-pitched whine. Mangrove branches reached across the water and formed a shaded archway, some of the lower-hanging ones slapping against the hull. While Wicker would've been challenging to track in the swamp, he couldn't escape the wake his boat left behind him. And that made it easy for Hawk to follow him, so long as Wicker didn't get too far away. Based on his erratic behavior, Hawk knew there wasn't much danger of that happening.

After racing down the waterway for a couple of minutes, Hawk noticed the wake had turned down another nearby channel. As Hawk veered down it, he noted that this one was much tighter than the last one, which had barely enough room for one airboat. Two would've made the canal impassable.

Hawk zipped down the canal, which bent to the right. As Hawk began to make his turn, an airboat came right toward him before whipping to the right at the last moment and using the thin bank to skim past. Wicker glared at him as he sped past.

Even as Hawk spun his airboat around in the opposite direction, he felt his heart thundering in his chest. Wicker was acting like a wounded animal. No regard for anyone else, intent on creating as much death and mayhem on his way out. At least, that's how Hawk perceived the NSA director. But it wasn't that surprising to Hawk. Wicker's career was over. His life was over, too, the minute he was apprehended. Even if he could get the best lawyers money could buy—though no self-respecting lawyer would've taken the case due to the stigma that would follow him for the rest of his career—no amount of slick talking would earn an acquittal. Wicker was going to prison sooner or later. And it was Hawk's job—one that was a direct order from the Commander-in-Chief—to see to it that Wicker was captured. Bullock wanted to avenge Wicker's deep betrayal, evident by the decision to send Hawk after him.

Hawk spun his airboat around and resumed his pursuit of Wicker, who'd retraced his steps. As Hawk raced down the canal, he tried to put himself in Wicker's shoes.

What would I do if I were trying to disappear?

Hawk concluded he would've tried to get away on land. But doing so required knowledge of the terrain—and he knew nothing about it. There were a few hiking trails through the Everglades, but they were short, almost all of them of the out-and-back variety. Paths just didn't connect in the Everglades, at least not like waterways did. Then Hawk realized if he was going to stay on the water, he would need to do his best to avoid being in the open. Navigating a maze of canals and streams would increase the level of difficulty for anyone trying to pursue him.

Unless—

Hawk knew what he had to do.

Down another canal they went, this time the gap between them shrinking. As they approached another junction, Wicker drifted right for a second before jerking the boat to the left. The sudden turn created a big wake that came back on Hawk as he followed. His airboat rocked violently for a moment, so much so that Hawk feared he might tip over. But as he increased his speed, the boat leveled out and he sped after Wicker.

For the next minute, Wicker seemed to re-establish a large space between them. Hawk grew frustrated by this fact, jamming the accelerator wide open without getting any results. As they drew closer to a T-intersection, Wicker went right, Hawk following after him. But the direction was the wrong one to choose—for Wicker.

The NSA director found himself barreling down a canal with

no way out except to beach his boat and make a run for it on the shore.

But something made Wicker try to change course quickly. His boat dug into the water, like a mule digging its heels into the dirt. Hawk cut his engine and drew his weapon as Wicker spun his boat around. He stopped and studied the situation for a moment, trying to determine what to do. He also killed his engine and raised his hands in a gesture of surrender. Then Wicker glanced over his shoulder before turning his attention back to Hawk.

For a moment, Hawk wasn't sure what Wicker was doing. Had he worked this hard to escape only to give himself up? Had he just grown tired of running?

Then Hawk saw the reason for Wicker's sudden reversal—two alligators sunning on the shore, while another swam around the boat.

"It's over," Hawk said. "I'm gonna need you to come with me."

Wicker didn't move.

"You don't understand, do you?" he said.

"Understand what?"

"What's happening. Or at least, what's going to happen. You just think you've caught the man who was going to kill the president, but you're sorely mistaken. I didn't kill anyone—at least, not yet."

Hawk steadied his weapon as the boats swayed with the gentle waves.

"You can justify your actions however you wish, but that's not going to change the fact that you shot the president."

"I wasn't trying to kill him. You know that. If I had, he would be dead—and I doubt you would've allowed me to have this conversation."

"I'm not interested in a conversation," Hawk said. "I'm here for justice."

"And you left Bullock to die?"

"I would've stayed, but he's the one who ordered me to go after you. And here we are."

"Yes, here we are."

Hawk dug a pair of handcuffs out of his pocket with one hand, while keeping Wicker in his gun's sights with the other. He tossed the handcuffs into Wicker's boat as they clanked on the fiberglass bottom.

"I want you to handcuff yourself, hands in front of you," Hawk said. "That is, unless you want to take your chances with those hungry reptiles there."

Wicker didn't move.

"I'm not putting those on."

"It's not a suggestion."

Wicker pursed his lips and shook his head slowly, the blood from a gunshot wound staining his white oxford shirt.

"Before I met Mr. Fang, I spent most of my days in chains, my hands and feet bound together. I was enslaved as a small boy, captured in Ukraine and treated like an animal."

"Everyone has stories about their past, the ugly ones they don't broadcast," Hawk said. "You're not all that special."

"I was an orphan, abandoned by my father after my mother died. And I was going to spend the rest of my life living in sheer squalor."

"Put on the handcuffs."

Wicker didn't move, resuming his story.

"But Mr. Fang saved me; at least someone from his organization saved me. And it wasn't long before I was plucked out of the general population of potential adoptees and moved to the special group. For the next year, I was treated like a king and trained to be a killer. After that, I was inserted into a home in the United States, an agent tasked with carrying out a mission within a week of being notified. So, I worked my way up the government ladder, spending years doing what I needed to do to put myself in the perfect position to carry out my mission. And then a few months ago, it arrived: dismantle America's most covert spies embedded around the world. Only, that's not what it was really about."

"I know exactly what you were up to," Hawk said. "But regardless if you were trained for this operation or not, you're still going to pay for your actions."

"It doesn't matter," Wicker said. "There are thousands more people just like me, people who can be reactivated on a moment's notice and be carrying out secret missions within days. You're only going to provoke Fang."

"So, he's the one who's in charge?" Hawk asked.

"He's more of a pawn, controlled by a consortium of people running an organization called The Alliance. Maybe you've heard of them."

"And they're behind all this?"

"They're the ones behind Fang, but it won't matter if they activate all their operatives," Wicker said. "You and many others like you will be dead before you know it. And The Alliance will win."

"You say that as if you don't think they should," Hawk said. "What else do I need to know?"

Wicker smiled wryly.

"You just need to know that all I have to do is activate the contact protocol in my rucksack and you'll be overrun with agents before the week's out."

"Put on the cuffs," Hawk said in a firm but measured tone.

"And now I'm going to go activate a few others."

By this point, the airboats had drifted around and were now facing each other.

Wicker dove onto the hull of his boat and activated the engine. The boat started to move forward before Wicker climbed into the captain's chair and charged forward.

Hawk cursed as Wicker opened up the airboat full throttle.

You're leaving me no choice.

Hawk pumped several rounds into Wicker, the first one hitting him in the center of the forehead. The second one smashed Wicker's center mass, pitching him forward and into the water.

When Wicker fell, he leaned hard on one side, sending the airboat heading to the right. It ran aground, the engine sputtering for a moment before conking out.

Hawk scrambled to fish Wicker out of the water before the alligator made its way over to the body. But Hawk won the race, using a paddle to collect Wicker first and then dragging him into the boat.

Hawk rolled Wicker over and opened up his rucksack. It was virtually empty aside from a gun and some ammunition and a first-aid kit.

"Damn," Hawk said as he realized there was never anything in the pack.

Lying bastard. He was baiting me into shooting him. Death by cop—or death by special ops. It was nothing more than an assisted suicide.

Hawk wasn't sure if the news was welcomed or not as he raised Alex on the coms and filled her in.

"How are you?" she asked.

"I'll live," he said.

"Sounds like Bullock is going to make it too, if the pilots are to be believed. They'll be on the ground within fifteen minutes and we can get a better assessment then."

"That's the best news I've heard all day," Hawk said.

He ended the call and then fired up his engine. He attached a tow rope to the front of Wicker's airboat and proceeded to tow it back to the tour company's dock. When Hawk climbed out, he saw the young man staring slack-jawed at him.

"You brought them both back," the man said.

"I never meant to hurt anyone," Hawk said. "But him—"

He glanced at the dead body.

"He's got a different story," Hawk said. "A sad one, but a true one. And it doesn't have a happy ending either."

"But it looks like his story is over," the young man said. "Thanks for bringing back the airboats."

Hawk smiled as he strode off the dock. He placed a call to Alex and asked her to arrange someone to pick him up. They'd shut down Wicker, but Hawk started to wonder if there really were thousands of agents out there just waiting to be activated.

If that was true, the Magnum Group couldn't do it alone. Every intelligence agency in the U.S. and her allies would need to be involved in shutting down the threat.

And the thought terrified him.

CHAPTER
FORTY-FOUR

WASHINGTON, D.C.

ROBERT BESSERMAN LED Magnum Group director Morgan May and the rest of her team into a conference room in the basement beneath the West Wing. Once they were all seated, Besserman signaled to the Secret Service agent near the door that they were ready. After a couple of minutes, President Bullock entered the room, his arm in a sling.

"Mr. President," Besserman said, signaling that they were ready to begin.

Bullock remained standing. He stroked his chin and grimaced.

"I wish all of you could understand what it's like to wear these shoes and shoulder the burden of responsibility that goes along with this job," he began. "It's not easy trying to discern people's motives and weigh it against what you know and what you think you know. And then throw in a deep betrayal for good measure and you might find just how difficult it is to navigate the leadership necessary to be a good president. I must admit that from the outside, I thought it was easy. Maintain your principles. Do what's right no matter what. Ignore outside pressure. They all sound good in theory, but trying to do all that while faced with the ever-changing face of geopolitics as well as domestic politics isn't nearly as easy as I thought it would be."

He paused and placed his free hand on the back of his chair as he stood behind it.

"Every one of you in this room did what I couldn't do, working tirelessly to see a threat that was literally in the same house as me at one point, even running one of our most critical agencies when it came to thwarting foreign threats. I felt the pressure, even cracking beneath it when it came to stopping a leak that was wrecking years of work from agency officers who'd dedicated their lives to stopping entities bent on destroying this country. I even exerted pressure on some of you, believing that you weren't capable of doing exactly what you did. Meanwhile, my impatience caused me to act unwisely and I nearly paid for it with my life. So, I wanted to both thank you for your work in solving the source of the leak and apologize for how I treated you. Everyone in this room deserves my deepest gratitude and our country's as well. What you've done won't soon be forgotten, even if it's a story I can't tell the American people."

Bullock offered a weak smile and sat down before indicating toward Besserman.

"I also wanted to personally thank every one of you from the Magnum Group," Besserman said as he stood. "This leak was one of the most dangerous we've ever encountered in the history of our agency. And because of you, it's been sealed permanently."

Besserman looked at the monitor on the wall and nodded toward Alex, who was participating on video conference.

"I wanted to let you know that Payton Quick was cleared from all wrongdoing," he said. "Through careful review of the footage from the archive room, we found that Wicker was setting her up, timing her trips to coincide exactly one week before Mayhem exposed each new agent. She was simply doing her job, though it was clear to us through an internal investigation that

Wicker had already obtained all the information on more than a dozen agents about a year ago and was using her as a scapegoat."

"What about Fang?" Hawk asked.

"We alerted authorities in London that he needed to be detained and questioned," Besserman said. "But Fang cancelled his scheduled speech at the expo and has vanished. Finding him will be a priority as it will help us determine more about The Alliance and what his true role is with the group. However, all is not lost thanks to Mia's bravery at The Alliance's masquerade meeting."

Morgan May started clapping and was promptly joined by the rest of the team.

"She's more than just a hacker," she said with a wink.

Mia put her head down, shielding her face with her hand.

"I know you don't like the attention," Besserman said, "but Morgan's right. The sign of a good operative is the ability to solve problems in the field on the fly. And that's exactly what you did."

Mia smiled thinly and nodded.

"Perhaps Morgan will use you out in the field more often," Besserman said.

Morgan nodded enthusiastically.

"But no matter what your future holds with the Magnum Group, your ability to capture all that audio from the event is being analyzed right now by a team at the NSA under the direction of its new director, Emma Washburn. Emma has made that a priority as her team of analysts are trying to determine if they can determine the identities of any more attendees through voice recognition software. It's likely going to be a long process, but it will prove critical in advancing our ability to topple The Alliance."

After the meeting concluded, President Bullock asked Hawk to stay behind, catching him right before he left.

"Have a seat," Bullock said, gesturing toward a chair with one hand while resting his injured arm on the table.

Hawk sat down at the conference table across from the president.

"I know we've had our differences," Bullock said. "Well, I know I've had my differences with you, but I want you to know that you're one of our most valuable assets—you and your wife."

Hawk held out his hand.

"With all due respect, Mr. President, it doesn't feel right for me and Alex to receive some special praise from you. We're a team. And everyone that was around this table today—and even a few who weren't around it—are why we've experienced the kind of success that we have. Without Alex, I can't do my job that well. Without Mia, we don't have the high-level tech support we need. Without Dr. Z, we don't have the gadgets that make our jobs easier and, sometimes, even possible at all. Without Big Earv, we don't have someone investigating various leads to determine who's really behind it all. And without Morgan, we don't have a competent conductor who can orchestrate all the moving parts."

"A man who understands how everything works," Bullock said with a grin. "You're going to make a great director one day."

"Well, that day is in the distant future, if it's up to me," Hawk said with a shrug.

"Of course. That will always be up to you. I'm so grateful for what you did for me as I'm almost certain I would've been dead if you hadn't intervened. And that's also why I'm appropriating some funds to upgrading the security around your ranch. I want you and Alex to feel safe raising little J.D. in Montana. I've also asked Emma as one of her first tasks as the new NSA director to do a complete wipe of your information online, both on the internet and the dark web."

"You're going to turn us into ghosts?"

"That's the plan."

"I appreciate that, sir. About the only thing that will cut my career short—other than the obvious—is me not feeling like we're safe anymore when we're out in the field."

"I promise you that I will do what I can to ensure that happens."

Hawk put his hands on the table, palms down as he prepared to stand.

"Anything else, sir?"

"Keep doing what you're doing."

Hawk shook Bullock's hand before exiting the room. He waited until he was back in his car to call Alex.

"What'd Bullock want?" she asked. "I heard him ask you to stay behind before the video feed was cut."

"He wanted to let me know he's going to improve our security at the ranch. And he wanted to thank us both for what we just did to save his life."

Alex chuckled.

"You're the one who did all the heavy lifting," she said.

"But he knows we couldn't have done it without each other. You were the one who made sure Bullock got medical attention. One bullet grazed his side, but another one tore up his arm. If I would've known what kind of shape he was truly in, I think I would've defied his command to go after Wicker."

"I'm glad it worked out the way that it did because now we can focus on Fang and unraveling what we can about The Alliance."

"It's not going to be easy," Hawk said. "But there's nobody I'd rather be doing it with than you—even if you're not out here with me. And speaking of, are you still dead set on staying home?"

"For the time being," she said. "But maybe I can be persuaded to get in the field again for a short mission or two, preferably for one in Paris or along the coast of Greece."

"Sounds like you want to go on vacation with me."

She laughed.

"How ever did you guess?"

THE END

To continue reading in The Phoenix Chronicles, order THE DRAGON KING now. Or to read more novels from the Firestorm world, check out the Brady Hawk series also available on Kindle Unlimited.

NEWSLETTER SIGNUP

If you would like to stay up to date on R.J. Patterson's latest writing projects with his periodic newsletter, visit the website www.rjpbooks.com to sign up.

ACKNOWLEDGMENTS

I am grateful to so many people who have helped with the creation of this project and the entire Phoenix Chronicles series.

Brooke Turbyfill was a big help in editing this book and this series.

I would also like to thank my advance reader team for all their input in improving this book along with all the other readers who have enthusiastically embraced the story of Brady Hawk and The Phoenix Chronicles.

ABOUT THE AUTHOR

R.J. PATTERSON is an award-winning writer living in southeastern Idaho. He first began his illustrious writing career as a sports journalist, recording his exploits on the soccer fields in England as a young boy. Then when his father told him that people would pay him to watch sports if he would write about what he saw, he went all in. He landed his first writing job at age 15 as a sports writer for a daily newspaper in Orangeburg, S.C. He later attended earned a degree in newspaper journalism from the University of Georgia, where he took a job covering high school sports for the award-winning *Athens Banner-Herald* and *Daily News*.

He later became the sports editor of *The Valdosta Daily Times* before working in the magazine world as an editor and freelance journalist. He has won numerous writing awards, including a national award for his investigative reporting on a sordid tale surrounding an NCAA investigation over the University of Georgia football program.

R.J. enjoys the great outdoors of the Northwest while living there with his wife and four children. He still follows sports closely.

He also loves connecting with readers and would love to hear from you. To stay updated about future projects, connect with him over Facebook or on the interwebs at www.RJPbooks.com and sign up here for his newsletter to get deals and updates.

Made in the USA
Middletown, DE
28 January 2024

48668105R00182